"You wante head off?"

"Of course." Patrick shrugged. "I thought he was trying to hurt you."

Helen sucked in her breath. Had anyone else, ever, wanted to protect her? "Thank you."

"It's my job."

"Is that all?" As soon as the words were out, she wanted to snatch them back.

His silver eyes met hers with an almost audible clash. "No," he said, his voice rasping. "It's not. And you know it."

Slowly he lifted one hand and stretched it toward her.

She wanted to take his hand. To let him pull her into his arms. She wanted it with an ache as frightening as it was powerful. Stepping away was one of the hardest things she'd ever done. "We'd better go or we'll be late."

Patrick turned away. "Sure," he said, and the flat tone of his voice speared her heart. "We wouldn't want that."

Dear Reader,

It's autumn. There's a nip in the air, the light has a special quality it only takes on at this time of year, and soon witches and warlocks (most of them under three feet tall!) will be walking the streets of towns everywhere. And along with them will come vampires, perhaps the most dangerously alluring of all romantic heroes. (The six-foot-tall variety, anyway!) So in honor of the season, this month we're bringing you *Brides of the Night,* a two-in-one collection featuring vampire heroes who are (dare I say it?) to die for. Maggie Shayne continues her wonderful WINGS IN THE NIGHT miniseries with *Twilight Vows,* while Marilyn Tracy lures you in with *Married by Dawn.* Let them wrap you in magic.

We've got more great miniseries going on this month, too. With *Harvard's Education,* Suzanne Brockmann continues her top-selling TALL, DARK AND DANGEROUS miniseries. Readers have been asking for Harvard's story, and now this quintessential tough guy is rewarded with a romance of his own. Then follow our writers out west, as Carla Cassidy begins the saga of MUSTANG, MONTANA, with *Her Counterfeit Husband,* and Margaret Watson returns to CAMERON, UTAH, in *For the Children.* Jill Shalvis, an experienced author making her first appearance here, also knows how great a cowboy hero can be, as she demonstrates in our WAY OUT WEST title, *Hiding Out at the Circle C.* Finally, welcome Hilary Byrnes. This brand-new author is Intimate Moments' WOMAN TO WATCH. And after you read her powerful debut, *Motive, Means...and Marriage?* you *will* be watching—for her next book!

Enjoy! And come back again next month, when we bring you six more of the best and most exciting romance novels around—right here in Silhouette Intimate Moments.

Leslie J. Wainger

Leslie J. Wainger
Executive Senior Editor

Please address questions and book requests to:
Silhouette Reader Service
U.S.: 3010 Walden Ave., P.O. Box 1325, Buffalo, NY 14269
Canadian: P.O. Box 609, Fort Erie, Ont. L2A 5X3

MOTIVE, MEANS... AND MARRIAGE?

HILARY BYRNES

Silhouette®

INTIMATE™MOMENTS®

Published by Silhouette Books

America's Publisher of Contemporary Romance

For Brian—best of husbands, best of friends.

And with many thanks to Nancy Drew, for patient critiquing and generous moral support.

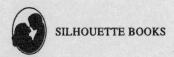 SILHOUETTE BOOKS

ISBN 0-373-07888-9

MOTIVE, MEANS...AND MARRIAGE?

Copyright © 1998 by Hilary Schmidt

Printed in U.S.A.

HILARY BYRNES

has loved books all her life. As a child, she spent whole days curled up with her favorite stories, and she went on to earn a degree in English literature. After working in academic and corporate libraries, she finally fulfilled a lifelong dream by turning from cataloguing books to writing them.

Hilary grew up on Vancouver Island, off the west coast of British Columbia. True love brought her to the city of Vancouver, where she now lives with her husband. When she's not busy reading or writing, she enjoys hiking, sewing and, of course, prowling around in bookstores.

The Silhouette Spotlight
"Where Passion Lives"

MEET WOMAN TO WATCH *Hilary Byrnes*

What was your inspiration for MOTIVE, MEANS...AND MARRIAGE?

HB: I've always been fascinated by criminal law. During college, I planned to be a prosecutor—and even won scholarships to law school—but at the last moment, I realized what I really wanted was to write. So instead of becoming a prosecutor, I wrote about one: cool, ambitious Helen Stewart, whose world is about to be turned upside down by one very sexy cop.

What about the Intimate Moments line appeals to you as a reader and as a writer?

HB: I love the excitement. Mystery. Adventure. And romance, of course! Intimate Moments stories are a unique blend of all those things. As a writer and a reader, they keep me coming back for more.

Why is this book special to you?

HB: Writing MOTIVE, MEANS...AND MARRIAGE? gave me the best of both worlds; it allowed me to blend my passion for writing with my longtime interest in crime and the law.

voice as a siren began to wail in the distance. "There's been

Chapter 1

The shrill demand of the telephone dragged Helen from the depths of an uneasy slumber. She forced her eyes open. It was still pitch-dark out; not even the faintest thread of light filtered through the wooden slats of her blinds.

The telephone rang again, and Helen rolled over with a groan. What time was it, anyway? She peered at the brass alarm clock that perched on the low oak table beside her bed. Its glowing hands revealed that it was a quarter after three in the morning. But who—

Her mouth went dry, and she grabbed the receiver as the telephone rang a third time. "Hello? Mom?"

"Helen," a male voice barked. "I need you down here right away."

She snapped instantly awake. "Franklin? Where are you?" In the background, she heard the low hum of voices and the clatter of a typewriter.

"I'm at the police station," her boss told her. He raised his voice as a siren began to wail in the distance. "There's been another murder. A bad one. I want you on this, Helen. How soon can you be here?''

Helen rolled out of bed and ran her hand through her short blond hair, her mind already racing. "Half an hour."

"Make it twenty minutes."

"Right," she said crisply. "See you there."

Rain hissed against the pavement as Helen pulled up outside the gray stone building that housed the Evergreen police department. She grabbed her briefcase and umbrella and climbed out of her car. Her low heels tapped against concrete as she hastened up the steps and through the glass doors. The harsh squawk of a police radio sounded from somewhere deep in the building, but the dingy waiting room was quiet and nearly empty.

Helen walked up to the wooden barrier. The uniformed desk sergeant glanced up. "Yes?"

"My name's Helen Stewart. I'm from the county prosecutor's office, and I'm here to meet Franklin Chambers."

"Oh, yeah. He said you'd be coming." The sergeant jerked a thumb over his shoulder. "He's in with Lieutenant Carmel."

Helen thanked him, and he buzzed her through the gate. She strode down the corridor and through a large room filled with desks and telephones. A few detectives stood clustered by the watercooler, speaking in hushed tones. They stared at her suspiciously as she passed, and she gave them a look of cool appraisal in return. She belonged here as much as any of them. She'd fought long and hard to get where she was, to prove that she wasn't anything like her mother, and she wouldn't let anyone take that away from her.

Not anyone.

A glass divider separated Lieutenant Carmel's office from the rest of the room. The blinds that covered the glass were closed, and Helen knocked on the flimsy particleboard door.

"Come in," a deep voice bawled.

She pushed open the door. A man with iron-gray hair and flinty dark eyes sat behind a metal desk. Her boss, Franklin Chambers, sat in a chair in the corner.

Franklin stood as she walked into the office. "Helen, glad you could make it. This is Lieutenant Edward Carmel. Ed, this is Helen Stewart, one of my deputy prosecutors."

"We've met before," Helen said. She leaned over the desk to shake the lieutenant's hand. "It's a pleasure to see you again."

The man smiled, but his eyes remained cold. "The pleasure is all mine." He waved her to a chair. "Did Franklin brief you over the phone?"

She shook her head as she sat down. "Not really. He just said there'd been another murder."

"There has," Franklin said heavily. His eyes were suddenly faraway and he lapsed into silence.

Helen looked at him curiously. In the three years she'd worked for Franklin, she'd never seen him looking other than perfectly groomed. But tonight, his thinning brown hair was disheveled and his tailored suit was rumpled and damp. Deep grooves bracketed his mouth, and there were dark circles under his eyes. Whatever was going on, it had to be something big.

But then, murder was always something big, here in the small city of Evergreen, Washington. There were rarely two murders a month in Evergreen—and this was the second in less than a week.

"Will one of you fill me in?" she asked. "Was the murder victim another prostitute?"

Franklin's gaze swung toward her, and he steepled his fingers. "No. This time the victim's a cop. A detective named Martin Fletcher."

"Marty Fletcher? From Vice?" She glanced at the lieutenant.

"He used to work Vice, but he was transferred to Violent Crimes about a month ago," Carmel said. "In fact, he was working the murder of the hooker who was killed Saturday night. Did you know him?"

"Only slightly. He testified in a few of my cases." Helen paused. "How was he killed?"

"Shot twice in the head."

"Is there any indication this killing is related to the one on Saturday? Have you got any suspects so far?"

The two men exchanged a long look. A tense silence filled the office. The stale air suddenly seemed very warm, almost oppressive, and Helen resisted the urge to fan herself with her fingertips.

"Doesn't look like this has anything to do with the other murder," Carmel said. "But we've got a suspect. Shots look like they were fired from his gun—we'll have a definite answer on that in a few days. And we've got a witness, a lady who saw the shooting and called it in. But there's a problem."

"A problem?" she asked. "It sounds straightforward enough."

Franklin sighed. "There's a problem, all right. A big problem for all of us."

"What is it?"

"It's the suspect. He's a cop."

"A cop? Another cop shot Marty Fletcher?" She couldn't keep the surprise out of her voice.

Carmel nodded. "His own partner, in fact."

"Who is it? Anyone I know?"

Once again, the two men exchanged glances. Franklin gave a small cough. "It's Patrick Monaghan."

Helen's breath seized in her throat. *Patrick.* A shard of memory stabbed through her, memory so fierce, so strong, it sent a crackle of heat racing through her body. It had been a year since she'd seen him, a year since that terrible, magical night they'd made love....

Desperately, she pushed the memory away. "P-Patrick Monaghan?" she asked, hating the uncertainty in her own voice. "Are you sure?"

Carmel's eyes narrowed. "We're pretty damn sure. The evidence is there. And if you don't—"

"Stop it, Ed," Franklin said. "Helen's a good prosecutor. The best young lawyer in my office. I know she won't allow any...personal feelings between herself and Monaghan to affect how she handles the case. Will you, Helen?" He turned to her with a smooth smile.

So Franklin knew about her and Patrick. The realization made her burn with shame. How had he found out? Or had the whole town heard about it? She knew all too well how fast that kind of gossip could spread.

But she'd done everything she could to wipe out her mistake, to prove she was back in control. Surely Franklin didn't think she was still—

She took a deep breath and forced a cool smile to her lips. "Just for the record, there are no 'personal feelings' between me and Patrick Monaghan. But even if there were, I certainly wouldn't let them affect my work."

Franklin gave an approving nod. "Good. I have every confidence in you."

Carmel shoved back his chair and stood. "Monaghan's cooling off in an interrogation room. You want to sit in on the interview?"

Helen's heart thumped. The thought of sitting in the same room as Patrick, of talking to him, of being close enough to touch, sent a hint of panic spinning through her body.

"Has anyone talked to him yet?" she asked, stalling for time.

"Not yet," Carmel said. "Franklin wanted to wait until you got here."

There was no help for it. She was going to have to talk to him. There was no point in delaying it...no matter how much she wanted to.

She made herself get to her feet. "Let's go."

Franklin stood, as well. "I'm going to go home and try to catch some sleep—I've been up most of the night. I'll leave this in your capable hands, Helen."

"I'll give you a full report in the morning."

Franklin nodded, and she opened the door. She stepped out into the main room, but Franklin's voice stopped her. "Helen?"

She swung around to face him. "Yes?"

"This is an important case," he said softly. "A very important case. You know the election's coming up at the end of the year."

She looked at him steadily. "What are you saying?"

"I got elected as the Evergreen County Prosecutor because the people believed I would keep order. A cop shooting his own partner doesn't look good. I want this case wrapped up fast. And I think you're the woman for the job."

Helen gave him a tight smile. Politics. Of course. With the

election coming up, Franklin was even more concerned with appearances than ever.

She knew she should be pleased that Franklin had chosen her to prosecute such an important case. Pleased that her sterling conviction record and the long hours she'd put in on evenings and weekends were finally paying off. But she couldn't help wishing it had been another case. *Any* other case.

"I appreciate your confidence in me," she said finally.

Franklin squeezed her elbow. "Good luck with the interview. I'll see you in the office in the morning."

Patrick Monaghan stared at the smoky glass window at the other end of the interrogation room. His head hurt like hell, and he knew there was blood seeping out from beneath the bandage on his shoulder, but he wasn't about to give whoever was behind the two-way glass the satisfaction of seeing him slump in pain. Especially not if it was that bastard Ed Carmel.

Whatever was going on, Patrick was sure the lieutenant was behind it. Ever since Carmel had taken over the Violent Crimes Unit a year before, he'd done everything he could to make Patrick's life miserable. Carmel hated him, and Patrick knew it.

He just didn't know what new torture Carmel had devised for him.

The door jerked open, and Carmel stalked into the room.

"Speak of the devil," Patrick muttered under his breath.

"What was that?" Carmel demanded.

"Nothing." Patrick leaned back casually and clasped his hands behind his head, ignoring the stab of pain that shot through his shoulder. "But why don't you tell me what the hell is going on?"

"Why don't you tell us?"

The new voice was female, a husky, smoky voice that hit Patrick low in the stomach like a stiff belt of whiskey. It almost sounded like—

His gaze swung to the door. Helen Stewart stood framed in the doorway, holding a black leather briefcase, a raincoat slung over her arm. Her elegant navy wool suit and white silk blouse were immaculate, her face as cool and beautiful at four in the morning as it was in a courtroom at high noon.

The sight of her transfixed him. They hadn't been this close for a year—not since that night they'd spent together, a night that had haunted him ever since.

The memory made his body tighten, and he fought down the instinctive reaction. "Helen?" he demanded. "What are you doing here?"

"I'm here to sit in on the interview. And the name is Ms. Stewart. Not Helen."

She strode into the room with that same athletic grace he'd noticed the first time he'd seen her walking up the courthouse steps. He hadn't known then that she was a distance runner, a natural athlete. But he could have guessed by the way she walked, with such confidence. Determination. The kind of determination it took to run marathons—and win.

She moved the same way now, shutting the door behind her and walking over to the scarred wooden table. She put her briefcase on the table and snapped open the locks. Her movements slow and deliberate, she pulled out a folder and uncapped a gold-tipped fountain pen.

"Well?" she said. "Why don't you tell us your story?"

"My story?" He tried to concentrate on her words rather than on the shape of her beautiful mouth. "What are you talking about?"

"Come on, Monaghan," Carmel said roughly. "What happened out there tonight?"

Patrick looked at Carmel and frowned. "Damned if I know. I'm in the car with Marty, and the next thing I know I wake up in the emergency room at Evergreen General and some doctor is stitching up my head. Where's Marty, anyway? What's this all about?"

Helen jotted a note but said nothing. Carmel stepped forward and yanked out the chair next to Helen's. Its metal legs screeched across the rough linoleum of the floor.

Carmel sat down. "You telling us you don't know where Marty is?"

"Of course I don't know where he is. If I did, I'd be pounding some answers out of him right now."

Helen stiffened and looked up from her notepad. Her blue eyes were hard, raking over him as though he was a stranger. As though they had never kissed, never touched, never shared a night of hot, sweet passion.

"'Pounding some answers out of him?'" she asked.

Patrick's jaw clenched at the cool disdain in her tone. "It's no secret I can't stand him. And he owes me some answers. The doctor told me a bullet had grazed my shoulder. Apparently, I've been shot."

"You have," Carmel said. "Marty shot you."

Patrick shoved back his chair. "What? I know Marty doesn't like me much, but—"

Helen smiled grimly. "It appears he shot you in self-defense. After you shot him. Twice."

Her words exploded in Patrick's mind, and he leaped to his feet. "You're out of your minds. I never shot Marty. Where the hell is he, anyway? I'll kill him for telling lies like that."

"You're too late for that, Monaghan," Carmel snapped. "Marty's already dead."

Patrick froze. "Dead?"

"Sit down, Detective Monaghan," Helen said.

"Not until you tell me what's going on!"

She returned his stare coolly. "You're a suspect in the murder of Martin Fletcher."

"You think I killed Marty?" Patrick demanded incredulously. He planted his hands on the table and leaned forward to look into her eyes. "You don't really believe that, do you?"

Her gaze slid away from him. A tiny flush of color appeared high on her cheekbones.

"You're the only suspect," Carmel said harshly.

Patrick took a deep breath and counted to ten. "You're making a big mistake here, Carmel." He fought to keep the anger, the outrage, out of his voice. Losing his temper now wouldn't do him any good. "I didn't kill Marty."

Carmel's lip curled. "Yeah? Why don't you tell us what did happen, then?"

Patrick ran his hand over his eyes. *Darkness pressing in. Rain hissing against the tires. Marty driving the car down that country road. Wondering where the hell they were going.*

Piercing lights. The raw smell of antiseptic. Pain in his skull. A green robe, the firm hand of a uniformed officer on his arm, a deep voice asking him to come to the station.

"Patr—Detective Monaghan? Are you all right?"

He opened his eyes and saw Helen leaning forward. Her left hand made a little movement on the tabletop, as though she was going to reach for him, but then she snatched it back.

The corner of his mouth tipped up in a smile. So she wasn't quite as indifferent to him as she pretended.

He pulled back his chair and sat. "I'm all right. But I don't remember what happened. I already told you. I was in the car with Marty. We were going to interview some informant of his. Next thing I remember is waking up in the hospital. When the doctor finished stitching up my head, a uniform asked me to come down to the station. So here I am."

"You don't remember," Carmel said, his voice heavy with sarcasm. "How convenient."

Patrick fought the urge to punch the man in the mouth. "No. I don't remember."

Carmel rose halfway to his feet, his hands clenched into fists. "Wonder if a few hours alone with me would bring back your memory?"

Helen shot Carmel a look and gave a tiny shake of her head. He glared at her but sat back in his chair.

She looked at Patrick, her blue eyes direct. "If you don't remember what happened, how do you know you didn't shoot Detective Fletcher?"

"I just know."

She glanced down at her notes. "Do you remember what time you were supposed to meet the informant?"

"Before I answer your question, why don't you answer a few of mine?"

"We're not obligated to answer any of your questions."

"And I'm not obligated to answer any of yours." He looked straight into her eyes. "I want to cooperate, but you're making it very difficult."

Something flickered in her eyes. A hint of—what? Memory? Guilt for the way she'd treated him? He couldn't tell.

"All right," she said finally. "I won't guarantee you any answers, but what do you want to know?"

"Why are you treating me as a suspect?"

"Because you're guilty as sin!" Carmel snarled.

Helen sprang to her feet. "Lieutenant, can I speak with you for a moment?" She stalked over to the door and wrenched it open. After a moment's hesitation Carmel followed her, and they went into the other room, shutting the door behind them.

Patrick stared at the glass. They were back there, talking about him. How many times had he sat behind that mirror, watching a suspect sweat? Hundreds? Thousands?

Now he was on the other side of the glass. Twelve years of working his ass off to keep law and order in Evergreen, and this was where he ended up. Sitting in this ugly little room while Carmel accused him of murder. Carmel...and Helen Stewart.

Patrick closed his eyes and dragged both his hands through his hair. *Helen.* He'd told himself a year ago to forget her—convinced himself he *had* forgotten her—but now that he'd seen her, he knew it was a lie.

He couldn't forget her. No more than he could forget that night.

He heard the click of the door handle, and he opened his eyes. Helen came back into the room, alone. She sat across the table from him, looking all too cool and calm and remote.

Patrick gave her a mocking grin. "What? You left the human pit bull outside?"

"Insulting your senior officer might not be the wisest course under the circumstances. Particularly as he's in charge of the case."

He laughed. "When have I ever done the wise thing? And I remember at least one occasion when you did something...less than wise." His gaze passed over her, drinking in her strong features, the length of her throat, the swell of her breasts under her tailored wool jacket. When he looked back up to meet her eyes, he saw that her face was rigid with anger.

"You're digging yourself in deeper all the time," she said tightly.

His grin faded. "Digging myself into what? Dammit, Helen, tell me what's going on."

She glared at him. "That's Ms. Stewart."

He heaved an exaggerated sigh. "All right. Ms. Stewart. Look, if you explain, I'll be more than happy to cooperate."

"You're not exactly known for cooperation." She flipped open another folder. "You've been reprimanded for insubordination more times than I can count. For disobeying orders. And you told Lieutenant Carmel a week ago that if you had to keep working with Marty, you'd probably end up killing him."

Patrick shrugged. "A figure of speech."

"Quite a coincidence that Marty turns up dead in your company."

"Look, I'll be straight with you. I didn't like Marty. He was a lush, and he was sloppy about his work. I'd only been working with him for three weeks, and he was already driving me crazy."

Helen nodded and made another note. "But?"

"He was still a cop. And we look after our own. I want to see whoever killed him caught as badly as you do." He gave her his most charming smile. "Now, why don't you tell me what's going on?"

She pulled a sheet of paper from her briefcase. "A patrol car responded to a 9-1-1 call saying shots had been fired out on the old highway. When the car got there, the men found you and Marty. Marty was dead. You were unconscious and bleeding, but holding a gun. They took you to the hospital and filed a report."

"That's *it?* This is why I'm a suspect?"

"A witness saw two men, and only two, just before the shots were fired. And it looks like the bullets were fired from your gun."

"They weren't. They couldn't have been." Patrick shot a look at the glass. "You're wasting your time with me. Carmel should be out there searching for the real killer."

"I'm sure Lieutenant Carmel will follow up all potential leads. What did you say Marty's informant's name was?"

"I don't know."

"Where does he live? Why were you meeting him?"

Patrick gritted his teeth. "I don't know. Marty never said anything about him—only that we were going to see him."

"Is there anything else you can tell me about what happened tonight?"

"No."

Helen handed him her card. "If you remember anything else, call me." She snapped her case shut and stood. "I'll be talking to you again once we get the lab results on the bullets."

"You'll be offering me an apology."

"Will I?"

Patrick grabbed her hand. Her fingers were slender but strong, her skin warm and smooth, just as he remembered. He stroked his thumb across her palm, over her wrist. Her pulse fluttered beneath the pad of his thumb, and he knew her heart was racing. Just like his.

A smile of masculine satisfaction curved his lips. "You know me, darlin'. Do you really think I'm capable of murder?"

She wrenched her hand out of his grasp. "You're wrong. I don't know you. I spent a few hours in your company many months ago, and it's something I don't care to remember. I don't know what you're capable of—and I don't particularly care."

It was her lips that gave her away. They trembled just a little as she spoke, giving a hint—just a hint—of the vulnerability Patrick knew was just beneath her tough shell.

"You don't care?" he asked softly.

Helen looked him straight in the eye. "I don't care."

She was lying. She had to be. But before he could say any more, she whirled around and yanked open the door. He heard her heels clicking against the floor, heard her husky laugh in response to some comment Carmel made, and then she was gone.

* * *

Helen's briefcase was so heavy it felt as though it was filled with rocks. The lieutenant had kept on handing her more files. "Here's Monaghan's service files. And the case files he's been working on. And Marty's notes."

She'd made copies of them all and stuffed them into her briefcase, but she was too tired to look at them right away. All she wanted was to go home and catch a few hours' sleep before she went for her morning run and headed in to the office.

The desk sergeant waved good-night as she crossed the lobby. Rain slashed against the glass doors in waves; it was still pouring outside.

Helen pushed open the door and stepped into the night without bothering to open her umbrella. The rain felt cool and fresh against her face. The station had been too warm, filled with the smell of stale cigarette smoke and coffee that had been left too long on the burner.

She was halfway down the stairs before she noticed Patrick leaning against the telephone pole on the far side of her car. He was wearing a brown leather bomber jacket, the collar turned up against the rain. His black hair was soaked, plastered against his skull—he must have been waiting awhile.

For an instant she considered going back inside and calling a cab to meet her out back, but then she squared her shoulders and marched toward her car.

"Helen—wait!"

She heard Patrick's rapid footsteps as he jogged around to her side of the car. He stopped just behind her, close enough that she could smell the warm spicy scent of his aftershave.

Close enough to touch.

She shoved away that thought. "If you need to talk to me, call my office in the morning." She fumbled with her key ring, trying to find her car key, trying to get it into the lock. Her hands trembled and she swore under her breath.

It was the cold making her hands shake like this. And the rain. It didn't have anything to do with Patrick. Not at all.

"I don't want to talk about business." His voice was gentle, caressing.

"There's nothing else for us to talk about."

"There isn't? I need to know, darlin'. Why didn't you ever return my calls?"

Helen managed to insert the key into the lock and pop it open. She put her hand on the door handle, steadying herself against the cold, rain-slick metal. "Because I didn't want to see you again."

"Somehow I find that hard to believe."

She whirled to face him. "Why? You think you're so irresistible? Forget it, Monaghan. You're not my type."

"No?" He grinned, his silver eyes crinkling. "I seem to remember something different."

"It was a mistake."

He took a step closer to her. "Is that what you'd call it?"

Against her will, she felt herself responding to the heat in his eyes, the low, seductive rasp of his voice. Warmth curled through her stomach, a warmth she hadn't felt since that night a year before, since—

She froze.

There was no way she'd let this happen. Not now. Not ever.

Abruptly she turned away from him and wrenched open her car door. "It *was* a mistake," she said, her voice icy. "If you have any new information about Marty's murder, call me. Otherwise, just stay away from me." She slid inside.

"But—"

She slammed the car door and locked it. Patrick stood outside her window for a moment, and then he shrugged and walked off.

Helen sat in the car and watched him go. She kept her hands on the steering wheel, but she felt them shaking. Dragging in a breath, she leaned her head back and closed her eyes.

She couldn't let Patrick get to her like this. Couldn't let him get under her skin, make her lose control...again.

There was far too much at stake. Not just her reputation, but her whole career. Franklin had made it clear that this case was vitally important. If she lost control now, if she blew the case....

Fear shuddered through her, but she clamped down on it ruthlessly. She would not give in to her emotions. She would *not*.

Helen opened her eyes and started the engine. A movement off to her right caught her gaze, and she turned to see what it was.

The door to the police station opened. A woman in a skintight purple dress stumbled through it, clinging to the arm of a tattooed man. She teetered down the stairs on her high heels, and paused on the sidewalk to pull the man's head down to hers for a long, lascivious kiss.

Helen swallowed convulsively and averted her eyes. She put the car in gear and pulled out onto the street, heading for home.

"Control," she said out loud. "I have to keep control."

Chapter 2

Patrick's head pounded as he was abruptly jerked awake. *Thump. Thump. Thump.* He grimaced and flung his arm over his eyes, trying to block out the light. Damn, he wished he hadn't woken up. He'd been dreaming about Helen. In the dream she'd been smiling at him and explaining that she'd really meant to call him all along. Now, if he could just go back to sleep....

Thump. Thump. Thump.

The pounding wasn't just in his head. There was somebody banging on the door of his apartment.

"Go away," he growled, pulling his pillow over his head.

The pounding continued, and his brother's voice filtered through the heavy oak door. "Dammit, Patrick, I know you're in there. Open the door already!"

It was Adam. And knowing Adam, he would stay out there pounding all day. Patrick let out a groan of frustration. It looked like he wasn't going to get back to that dream after all.

"Patrick?"

"Coming!" he shouted.

He pushed himself upright in bed and looked down at himself

in distaste. His T-shirt was still stuck to his shoulder with blood, and his mouth felt as if it were full of sawdust. By the time he'd driven home last night, he'd been so beat he'd just swallowed a handful of aspirin, yanked off his jeans, and fallen into bed.

He grabbed a pair of gray police department sweatpants off the back of a chair and pulled them on before he went to the door, undid the bolts, and opened it wide to admit his visitor.

Adam strode into the room. He wore a charcoal-gray suit and a white shirt. His subdued tie bore the unmistakable sheen of silk. His black hair was short, like Patrick's, but it was brushed back neatly, instead of sticking out in all directions. Patrick gave a wry smile. As children, they'd often been mistaken for twins, but sure as hell nobody would make that mistake now. Adam *looked* like a lawyer, and Patrick—well, he looked like what he was, too.

Adam stopped in front of the window and swung around. "You look like hell, little brother."

Patrick closed the door and leaned back against it, folding his arms over his chest. "You come all the way over here to insult my looks?" he asked lazily.

A muscle twitched in Adam's cheek. "I heard a rumor you'd been arrested."

"I haven't. But I'm sure Carmel is working on it overtime. He wants to get me so bad he's almost frothing at the mouth."

"I should've known you'd be joking about it. But from what I heard, you're under suspicion of murder. If that's true, it's no laughing matter."

Patrick shrugged, wincing at the pain in his shoulder. "If you want to lecture me, feel free, but could you wait until I've had a shower and a cup of coffee, at least?"

"I guess so," Adam said grudgingly.

Patrick walked over to the corner of the room that served as a kitchen. His apartment had once been a warehouse, and it was basically one large room. A curving wall of glass blocks shielded the kitchen from the living area, and his bed was hidden by screens, but the bathroom was the only room closed off by a door.

He rummaged in a cupboard for his battered percolator and got the coffee out of the freezer. He filled the pot with water, dumped in a healthy amount of coffee, and turned on the gas. "Keep an eye on the coffee, will you?"

Adam grunted in response, and Patrick headed for the shower. Twenty minutes later they sat under the window at the scarred pine table. Adam nodded thoughtfully as Patrick filled him in on the details of the previous night.

"I still don't understand why they didn't keep you in the hospital overnight," Adam said when Patrick had finished.

Patrick laughed. "They wanted to, but I walked out. You know how much I hate hospitals. Besides, it's just a concussion. There was lots of blood, but the cut in my head wasn't deep. And the bullet only grazed my shoulder." He took a sip of his coffee and grinned at Adam over the rim of the thick stoneware mug. "It's the luck of the Irish, I guess."

Adam scowled. "Don't even joke about it. Six inches lower and you'd be dead. You know anyone with a reason to kill you?"

"Take your pick. Ex-cons. Guys I've busted." Patrick took another swallow of coffee. "Ed Carmel, for that matter."

"Carmel? I know he hates your guts, but enough to kill you?"

"I wasn't really serious."

"He's got it in for you, though."

"Tell me about it. The look on his face when he took my badge and gun and told me I was suspended was pure glee."

"And you talked to that guy?" Adam demanded. "You let him question you?"

"I've got nothing to hide."

"Patrick, you're a cop. You know damn well you should have called your lawyer."

"I don't have a lawyer."

This time, Adam swore. "You got a buck?"

"What for?"

"Just give me a dollar."

Patrick stood and grabbed a can off the top of the fridge. He shook out four quarters. They clattered onto the table.

Adam slid them into his hand and stuck them in his pocket. "There. That's my retainer. You now have a lawyer."

"I already told you I don't need one. The whole idea that I

could have killed Marty is crazy. Carmel's just going to ride my ass for a few days, and then the whole thing will blow over.''

''What about the prosecutor? Didn't you say it was Helen Stewart?''

''Yeah.'' The thought of her made his mouth curve in a smile. ''I did.''

''She's got a reputation for being tough. Almost ruthless. She have it in for you, too?''

''No.'' His lips twisted a little as he remembered the things she'd said in the rain last night. ''At least, I don't think so. But with women, who can really tell?''

Adam shook his head. ''You said you knew her before. How?''

How? Memories skidded across Patrick's senses. The scent of the ocean on her skin. The whisper of her fingertips across his hair. Her gasp of shock and pleasure when he'd tipped back her head and kissed her for the first time.

''Oh, no. No.'' Adam clapped his hand over his eyes. ''Tell me it's not what I'm thinking.''

''What are you thinking?''

''You slept with her, didn't you?''

''That's a hell of a question to ask, brother.''

''So what happened? She doesn't seem like the type to have a casual affair.''

''What makes you think it was casual?''

''Come on, Patrick. Ever since Jessica—''

Patrick's jaw hardened. ''Let's not mention that name.''

''Okay. Fine. But you have to admit that since your divorce, all your relationships have been casual. As soon as a woman starts to get too close, you find some excuse to dump her.''

''Yeah, well, it wasn't like that with Helen.''

''No? What was it like?''

He deliberately set his coffee cup back down on the table. ''She was the one who broke it off with me.''

''Really?'' Adam's dark eyebrows rose. ''That's a first.''

Patrick shot him a look. ''Not exactly.''

''Other than Je—'' Adam coughed. ''Other than...your ex-wife, it is.'' He paused. ''So. Why did Helen break it off?''

"She never told me why." Patrick couldn't keep a tinge of bitterness out of his voice. Her words from last night came back to him again, stronger this time.

It was a mistake. You're not my type.

What was her type? One night last winter when he'd been walking home from the bar, he'd caught a glimpse of her outside the opera house. She'd been getting into a Mercedes with a man whose cool blond looks were a match for her own. A man who looked as if he'd be perfectly at home in a boardroom, on a golf course, or in a fancy French restaurant.

Just like the man Jessica had married after their divorce—the man with whom she'd just had a child.

The old anger curled through his gut, and Patrick gritted his teeth. He wouldn't think about that. Wouldn't think about Jessica's perfect husband and her new baby. And he wouldn't think about Helen's rich friend, either.

Because even if he wasn't her *type,* even if he wasn't the kind of man she wanted on her arm at the opera, there was still something between them. Last year they'd generated enough sexual heat to melt the North Pole in January. And she still wanted him. He was sure of it....

Adam's voice dragged him back to the present. "Just as long as Helen doesn't have any reason to hate you."

"She doesn't. Trust me."

"Good. If both Carmel and the prosecutor had it in for you, you'd really be in trouble."

Patrick stared at him. "You're not serious. I didn't kill Marty. It wouldn't matter how much Helen or Carmel or anyone else hated me—it wouldn't change the facts of the case."

"We'll see," Adam said. "But for now, you should keep your head low. And do me a favor. Go see your doctor. I don't like the sound of this memory thing."

"I've got an appointment this afternoon. But the doctor at the hospital said concussion often brings on minor memory loss. It usually affects the few minutes before the injury."

"Which is exactly what you can't remember."

"Right. It's just—gone."

"Do you know if it's going to come back?"

Patrick shrugged. "It might or it might not, according to the doctor at the hospital. I'll ask my own doctor more about it this afternoon."

"You do that." Adam shoved back his chair and stood. "I've got to get back to the office. Take it easy, Patrick. And for God's sake, don't talk to anyone from the P.D. or the prosecutor's office, okay? Not without calling me first."

"Okay, okay. I won't—"

A knock sounded at the door.

Adam tensed. "Are you expecting someone?"

"No." Patrick stood as the knock sounded again. He grinned at Adam as he walked toward the door. "Some of us don't plan our social schedule weeks in advance. Some of us are actually spontaneous."

He opened the door. Two uniformed police officers stood there. Jefferson and Larkin, two of the rookies on the force. He'd played pickup basketball with both of them. Dispensed advice when they'd asked for it. Jefferson had even confided his troubles with his girlfriend to Patrick.

He held the door open wide. "Hey, guys, come on in. I just put on some coffee."

Jefferson's Adam's apple bobbed. "I'm sorry, sir, but we're here on official business."

Patrick blinked. "What?"

Suddenly Adam was behind him. "I'm Detective Monaghan's lawyer. What do you boys want?"

"We have orders to escort Det—er, Mr. Monaghan, to the station to participate in a lineup."

"And if he refuses?" Adam asked softly.

Larkin's face went red and he looked down. "Then we've been told to arrest him."

"You're kidding," Patrick said.

"It's no joke, sir."

Patrick swore, the word hissing out from between his teeth. "Carmel really does have it in for me."

Jefferson gulped. "I wouldn't know about that, sir. Will you—will you come voluntarily?"

"I don't have much of a choice, do I?"

"No, sir," Larkin said. "You don't."

Patrick's mouth twisted in a wry grin as he looked over his shoulder at Adam. "I guess maybe I do need that lawyer after all."

Helen squeezed her car into a spot half a block from the police station. As she climbed out of the car, a gust of rain blew into her face, sharp and cold. She gritted her teeth. Was it ever going to stop raining?

She'd grown up in Seattle, only seventy miles south of Evergreen. She knew she should be accustomed to the rain, but today the relentless grayness of the late fall seemed more than usually depressing.

"Get a grip, Stewart," she muttered under her breath. "You were the one who wanted to stay on the West Coast."

She snapped open her umbrella and stepped onto the crosswalk.

A rusty blue convertible screeched to a precarious halt only a few feet away. The police car right behind it almost slammed into its rear bumper. Helen started and jumped back. Her heel skidded on the rain-slick pavement, and she nearly fell. Her briefcase slipped out of her hand and crashed to the ground. She barely managed to hang on to her umbrella as her other arm windmilled, trying to keep her balance.

She straightened, anger pulsing through her. "What do you think you're doing?" she yelled, whirling to glare at the driver.

A pair of eyes the color of rain met hers. Patrick.

Helen froze.

Ever since she'd seen Patrick last night, she hadn't been able to stop thinking about him. Not the case, but *him.* Seeing him had brought so many dangerous memories to light. Dangerous memories…and dangerous feelings.

Every time she closed her eyes, she saw his face. It was scorched into her memory like a brand. Even on her morning run, she'd thought of him, and her damp skin burned with the memory of his touch. She'd run harder, faster, trying to forget. But the trickle of sweat down the side of her neck only made her remember the way he'd kissed her there, and the ache of her muscles reminded her of another, sweeter, kind of ache.

Back at the office she'd found herself staring at the black-and-white photo in his personnel file, remembering details long suppressed: his infectious grin, his exuberant laugh, the strange joy she'd felt as they'd walked on the beach that night.

She'd struggled to keep her mind on the facts of the case, but it kept slipping to the man. And what she knew of him wasn't easy to reconcile with the facts. Sure, Patrick was no saint. He was charming, reckless and unpredictable. But a murderer? Could he really have shot another man in cold blood?

Helen tightened her lips. She'd assured Franklin that her personal feelings weren't going to interfere in her handling of the case. And they wouldn't. She would control them as she always had.

Almost always.

"Are you going to stand there in the road all morning?" Patrick's voice had a hint of laughter in it.

Helen jerked up her head. Patrick was leaning out the window of his disreputable car, a grin on his handsome face. To her horror, she felt herself begin to blush. What was wrong with her, standing in the road and staring at Patrick while rain seeped into her shoes and the wind blew her hair into a sodden mess?

Gathering the remains of her dignity, she shot him the glare that had reduced seasoned defense lawyers to ashes in the courtroom. "You were the one who nearly ran me over, Monaghan." She leaned down and grabbed her briefcase, her chilly fingers fumbling with the handle.

"I'm sorry," Patrick said. He opened his car door and unfolded his legs from the ridiculously tiny interior.

Heedless of the pouring rain, he left his car door open and strode toward her. Traffic was starting to pile up on the street behind his car. Horns blared, but Patrick ignored them.

He reached for her, his grin fading into a look of concern. "You all right, darlin'?"

She retreated a step. She couldn't let him touch her. Couldn't risk a return of that sizzling heat that had ignited between them before. "I'm fine. And I'm not your darling."

He came closer. "I didn't mean to scare you."

"You didn't," she said hastily. The spicy scent of his after-shave, mingled with the crisp smell of the rain, wafted across her senses. She gulped as a fresh surge of memories raced through her. It had been raining that night, too. He'd smelled just the same way when he'd pulled her into his arms and kissed her before she could raise the wall of icy control that usually kept her safe.

"Helen?" He frowned slightly. "Are you sure you're okay?"

Another horn blared, punctuated by an angry shout. "Get your car outta the way, pal!"

It was enough to break the spell. Helen yanked her gaze away from Patrick's pewter eyes.

"You'd better get back in your car," she said, her voice low. "You don't want to be late for the lineup." Turning, she headed for the police building.

It was all she could do to force herself not to run.

Helen grimaced as she looked at herself in the cracked mirror. Her face was pale—too pale. She washed her hands and brushed back her short hair. The woman in the mirror stared back at her, her mouth a little uncertain, a little vulnerable. Where was Helen Stewart, the tough, ruthless prosecutor? The woman her colleagues referred to as the Ice Queen behind her back?

This woman looked more like the girl she'd once been. The girl who hadn't yet had her illusions shattered. The girl she'd sworn never to be again.

Savagely, Helen grabbed a tube of lipstick from her briefcase and slashed some on. It didn't help. Instead of looking cool and sophisticated, she looked like a ghost with red lips.

And would Patrick think she'd dolled herself up for him?

"Forget it," she muttered. She grabbed a piece of paper towel and blotted the bright lipstick. When she was done, she wadded up the towel and threw it at the overflowing garbage can in the corner.

And missed.

She stared at the crumpled ball lying on the floor. Nothing was going right today. Nothing.

Resolutely, she walked across the washroom, picked up the paper, and deposited it neatly in the garbage. She couldn't hide in here all day. It was time to get out there and face the witness—the witness whose testimony could put Patrick behind bars. The thought made her neck muscles tighten with tension, but she squared her shoulders and headed for the door.

She strode out of the washroom and down the hall to the room where the witness waited. Lieutenant Carmel looked up as she pushed open the door.

He scowled at her. "It's about time you got here."

She fought the urge to snarl back at him. Instead she ignored him and turned to focus on the witness.

Tammy Weston sat on the low couch in the corner, her hands clenched together so tight her knuckles had turned white. She was wearing a white nurse's uniform, and her head was bowed so that Helen could see the dark roots that clashed with the red blaze of her hair.

Helen crossed the room. "Ms. Weston? I'm Helen Stewart, the prosecutor assigned to this case."

The woman's head came up, and Helen saw that her lips were tight and angry. "What's this all about? The cops came and got me from the hospital in the middle of my shift. And he—" she gestured angrily at Carmel "—won't tell me a damn thing."

"We asked you here so you could try to identify one of the men you saw last night," Helen said.

Tammy's narrow lips thinned. "That so? Well, I don't want to do it. I didn't think I'd have to."

Helen bit back a sarcastic comment. Lots of people who reported crimes didn't want anything more to do with them, and it looked as if Tammy Weston was one of those.

Great. It was just one more thing to worry about.

Pulling up a chair, she sat and looked Tammy in the eye. "Ms. Weston, you told the police that you were driving home from the hospital on the old highway when you saw two men arguing by the side of the road, is that right?''

"Yeah. I already told all that to the cops.''

"I know. But bear with me for a minute. Shortly after you drove by, you heard shots. You looked in your mirror and saw one of the men fall?''

Tammy shifted irritably. "If you already know what happened, why ask me again?''

"Because we have to be clear on exactly what happened. The man who fell was a police officer—and now he's dead. We need you to identify the man who was with him.''

"I know he's dead. But I don't want to identify anyone!''

Helen pinned her with a glare. "You just agreed that you witnessed a murder. If you don't cooperate now, I'll subpoena you to the grand jury and put you on the stand. If you refuse to make the identification there, you'll be in contempt of court. You could go to jail, Ms. Weston.''

"Jail? You can't do that to me!''

"I can,'' Helen said coldly. "And I will.''

Tammy slumped into the sagging couch. "Okay, okay. I'll do it.''

Suddenly the door opened. Helen looked over her shoulder and saw a tall, dark-haired man walk into the room. She'd never actually met him before, but she knew he was Adam Monaghan, the well-known defense lawyer. Patrick's brother.

The sight of him made her mouth go dry. The brothers had to be very close in age. Was their relationship close, as well? How much did Adam know about her and Patrick? There was no way to tell. Unlike his brother, his thoughts didn't show on his face.

"You must be Helen Stewart,'' he said.

"That's right,'' she said, careful to keep her voice cool and professional. "Adam Monaghan?''

He nodded and shook her hand briefly. "I want to make it clear that my client has agreed to this lineup solely for the purpose of elimination.''

"Can we get on with it?'' Carmel interrupted. "I'm a busy man. Unlike you fancy lawyers, I've got work to do.''

"Fine," Helen said tightly. "Let's go ahead."

Carmel spoke into the microphone that was mounted on the wall by the two-way mirror. "Bring 'em in!"

Helen took a deep breath as a line of dark-haired men filed in on the other side of the glass. Patrick was fourth, and her heart gave a little jump at the sight of him. He flashed a quick grin in her direction. She knew he couldn't see her through the mirror, but it didn't matter. Heat flooded through her body—heat and something dangerously like desire—and she had to fight the crazy urge to smile back.

Her heart thumping, she forced her gaze away from him. What was wrong with her? There was no way she should let Patrick's smile—or anything else about him—affect her like this.

She stepped back and turned away from the glass, trying to recover her composure.

She nodded to Tammy. "Okay, Ms. Weston. Come and take a look. Tell me if you can identify the man you saw last night."

Tammy got to her feet. In the silence of the little room, the faint creak of her nurse's shoes seemed very loud. She stepped up to the glass.

"Number four," she said flatly.

Helen sucked in her breath. For an instant the room darkened and she fought a wave of dizziness. "Are you absolutely sure?"

Tammy was already turning away. "I'm sure. Now can I go back to work?"

"Of course." Her voice sounded hoarse and strange, even to her own ears. She swallowed hard and nodded to Lieutenant Carmel, who took Tammy's arm and led her out of the room.

For a moment Helen just stood there. She could feel Adam Monaghan's curious gaze on her face, and she knew she had to somehow get moving, but her limbs felt heavy and frozen, her hands ice-cold.

Finally she made herself move. Stepping over to the microphone, she flipped it on. "All right, gentlemen. We're done."

A uniformed officer opened the door on the other side of the glass, and the men filed out.

Helen turned to Adam. "Your client is free to go," she said, her voice cracking. She paused and cleared her throat. "For now."

The door was flung open, and Carmel strode back in. "Helen. I've gotta talk to you." He waved some sheets of paper in the air. "We've got him now! These just came in—take a look."

Adam stepped forward. "Oh? I assume you're discussing my client?"

Helen snatched the papers away from Carmel before he could say any more. She scanned the top one quickly. It was a lab report on the bullets that had been retrieved from Marty Fletcher's brain. They were both perfect matches with a test bullet that had been fired from Patrick's gun.

Her throat closed, and she forced herself to flip to the other piece of paper. The tests for gunshot residue on Patrick's hands had come up positive. He had fired a gun last night. There was no doubt of that.

The words on the page swam before her eyes and bile rose in her throat. Positive. Gunshot residue. Matching bullets. How was it possible? How could Patrick have done this? It was a nightmare…a nightmare that was rapidly becoming all too real.

"He fired his gun, shot Marty in the head. We've proved it now." Carmel gave Adam a look of pure triumph. "You go tell your brother we're gonna arrest him."

"No!" Helen blurted. The word flew from her lips before she could stop it. "I mean—"

Carmel spun around. "*You.* I should have known you wouldn't want him arrested. You have the hots for him, don't you? You and every other woman for a hundred miles."

A hot wave of fury washed through her body, fury that threatened to engulf her. She wanted to shout, she wanted to scream, to deny his words.

Control, she told herself frantically. Control.

She dragged in a deep breath. She had to keep her cool. But she couldn't back down now. If she did, it would be practically admitting that Carmel's words were true, that she didn't want Patrick arrested because she had feelings for him.

And that wasn't the case, she told herself fiercely. Logic dictated that they shouldn't arrest him yet. Logic, pure and simple. After all, if they went to trial with the wrong judge, a premature arrest could result in important evidence being excluded. The case might even get thrown out.

She couldn't take that risk. Not with a case as important as this one.

She took a step closer to Carmel and looked him straight in the eye. "I'm in charge of prosecuting this case, Lieutenant. And you'll do as I say. We're going to wait for an arrest warrant. If we start the paperwork right now, we can probably get Judge Gove's approval by morning."

Suddenly the door banged open. "Adam? Are you ready to go?"

The deep voice was Patrick's. It slid down Helen's spine, sending slivers of heat dancing through her. She turned to face him just as Carmel did the same.

"You! Get outta here!" Carmel clenched his fists, his face darkening to purple. "Murderers don't get the run of the police station."

Patrick's silver eyes narrowed and his lazy smile vanished. "What did you say?" he asked, his voice low and dangerous.

Adam stepped toward him and took his arm. "Time to go, Patrick," he said swiftly. He turned back to Helen. "Call me when the warrant comes down. I'll arrange for him to turn himself in."

"Warrant!" Patrick spun around. "What are you—"

"Later," Adam snapped.

Patrick shrugged away his hand. "Helen?"

The cold fury in his voice ripped through her, and she gulped. "I'm applying for a warrant to arrest you. For murder."

The look in Patrick's eyes made her want to crumble. Suddenly she realized that she'd rarely seen him when he wasn't smiling. There was usually humor in his silver eyes, along with a dancing light of mischief and reckless charm.

But now he looked like a man who'd been cast abruptly into hell.

And she felt like the devil who had put him there.

Chapter 3

The M.G.'s wipers swished across the windshield. Rain hammered down on the cloth roof. Patrick hadn't gotten around to patching the tiny crack in the roof, and cold water seeped through it to trickle down his cheek.

"I don't believe I'm doing this," he muttered as he turned onto Ocean Drive. "No way she's going to listen to me. I should just turn right around and head over to Callahan's for a drink."

But he couldn't. Not so long as there was a chance of convincing Helen to hold off on the arrest.

A fist of tension tightened in his stomach. Until this afternoon he hadn't taken this whole thing seriously. Not at all. But now...now, he just hoped Helen would listen to him. Hoped their past meant *something* to her.

It had to, he told himself grimly. It just had to.

Patrick braked the car in front of Helen's building and peered up through the bare tree branches toward her apartment. Light filtered out from between the slats of her blinds. Relief threaded through him. At least she was still awake.

He found a place to park a block away and jogged back through the rain, reaching the entrance to her building just as a well-dressed couple was leaving. They held the door open for him, and he walked inside.

He crossed the lobby, glancing around curiously. His wet shoes squeaked against a gleaming hardwood floor. Giant plants were scattered artfully around. Several long skylights overhead would let in the sun, if it ever stopped raining. The room had the feel of a conservatory—green, hushed, and very expensive.

It had been years since he'd been in a building like this one. On a social call, at least. None of the guys from the department could afford to live like this, and the women he usually dated were way too down-to-earth.

He bet everyone in Helen's building was a lawyer or a banker. The kind of people who sat around discussing vintage wine and stock options and their latest trips to Europe.

The kind of men who were probably her *type*.

Patrick's jaw tightened at the thought. This was Helen's world. Was it really any wonder she hadn't stuck around that night? That she hadn't wanted to get involved with a cop whose name proclaimed his Irish Catholic background, who was proud of his working-class roots, and who hated opera and snooty restaurants and all the other things that seemed to go along with money and power and success?

Jessica hadn't been able to forgive him for those things, either. For failing to meet her expectations of what a man should be. She'd walked away, too—but not before she'd destroyed his most cherished dream....

Patrick curled his hands into fists and shoved the thought of Jessica out of his mind. "Forget it, Monaghan," he said under his breath. "It doesn't matter. Just get on with it."

He punched the elevator button and rode to the third floor in silent luxury. When he stepped out of the elevator, he turned right and headed toward Apartment 312. His feet sank noiselessly into the plush carpeting on the hallway floor. Perfect for a surprise attack, he thought wryly.

As he knocked on Helen's door he heard the faint sound of music coming from inside. Violins. His lips twisted. God, he hated classical music. He'd heard enough of it with Jessica to last him a lifetime. And then some.

He knocked again, louder this time, and the music switched off. Footsteps echoed faintly.

"Who is it?" Helen's voice sounded suspicious.

"It's Patrick."

Silence.

He braced himself against the door frame with one hand and knocked again with the other. "Helen?"

Her voice was muffled, but he heard the tension and anger that threaded through it. "Go away, Patrick."

"I have to talk to you. About the case."

"Now?"

"Yes, now." He tried to keep the frustration out of his voice. "Helen, I—"

Behind him, Patrick heard another door opening. He looked over his shoulder and saw a well-fed man wearing a heavy brocade robe standing in the door to Apartment 311. He was scowling.

"Must you carry on your conversation in the hallway? And at this time of night?" the man demanded. "Some of us are trying to get to sleep."

Patrick shrugged. "Sorry I woke you."

The man glared at him. "Just keep it down. Or I'll call the cops." He banged his door closed.

Patrick turned back to Helen's door and knocked again. "Helen? I'm not going away. I told you—"

A chain rattled. He heard a lock click, and then Helen pulled open the door.

He stared at her. She looked beautiful. And completely unlike the cool, professional lawyer she'd been that afternoon. Her hair was tousled, her face devoid of any makeup. She was wearing a heavy, cable knit sweater, the creamy wool thick and bulky over her slender frame. Her legs were encased in leggings the color of heather, and her feet were bare.

He looked down at her feet. They were long and narrow, and

her toes were knobbly at the ends. To his amazement, a shaft of heat shot straight to his groin.

What was happening to him? They were just *feet,* for God's sake.

He yanked his gaze back up to her face, feeling off balance with a woman for almost the first time in his adult life. "Uh, hi, Helen."

"Patrick." She grabbed his arm and pulled him inside, slamming the door behind him. "What are you doing here?"

"I told you, I have to talk to you about the case." He rubbed his hand over his arm where she'd touched him. He could almost swear he still felt the warmth of her hand, even through the layers of cotton and leather.

"You should've called my office in the morning." Helen stepped back a pace and dragged her fingers through her hair in what he could tell was a nervous attempt to tidy it. For him? If he meant absolutely nothing to her, surely she wouldn't try to fix her hair.

A spark of hope ignited in his chest.

"By tomorrow morning it might have been too late," he said. "I caught your boss on the news. He said an arrest was expected tomorrow."

"That's right." Her voice was low.

He looked her in the eye. "You're making a big mistake."

"Am I?"

"You don't really believe I'm a murderer." He gave her his most charming smile. "I know you don't."

She folded her arms across her chest. "Really. And you know so well what's going on in my mind."

He could tell by the hard look on her face that she wouldn't appreciate it if he suggested she had any kind of feelings for him. And making her angry was definitely not part of his plan.

Instead, he chose the logical approach. "If you believed I'd shot Marty, you wouldn't have let me into your apartment."

"Letting you in has nothing to do with what I believe. The last thing I need is Gary across the hall calling in the cavalry and having the cops find you hanging around my door."

"Why would you care?"

Color spread across her cheeks, and she looked away. "Franklin knows we were…involved last year. If he heard you'd been seen at my apartment, he might think—" She ground to a halt. "It wouldn't do my career any good."

"Your career is the only thing that matters to you? Even more than your safety?" He watched her closely. This might—just might—be a way of getting her to listen to him.

Her gaze snapped back to his. "My feelings about my career are none of your damn business!"

Bingo.

"Helen, we have to talk. Having me arrested and pursuing prosecution could end up ruining your career."

"If anyone finds out I've talked to you, that could ruin my case. *And* my career."

Patrick stared into her eyes. "It's up to you. You're taking a risk either way. But if you talk to me now, nobody has to find out. And if you don't…"

Her lips tightened. "Are you threatening me?"

"No," he said bluntly. "I'm just pointing out the facts."

"What are you saying?"

"That's exactly what I want to talk to you about."

She stared at him for a long moment. He saw the play of emotions on her face, emotions she couldn't quite hide.

He took a step closer to her. "Please."

Their eyes caught, and Patrick's breath snagged in his throat. What was it about her beautiful blue eyes that made him feel this way? As though there was something far more at stake than whether or not she would talk to him tonight?

Just when he thought he couldn't stand it anymore, she broke the gaze and turned away. "All right. I'll give you an hour. No more."

Relief flooded through him. He was past the first hurdle. She would listen to what he had to say. Now all he had to do was convince her that he was telling the truth.

He shrugged out of his jacket and left it hanging on the carved wooden rack behind the door. Helen led him through her foyer and down a short hall. A kitchen opened onto the left; he caught a glimpse of tiled countertops and gleaming appliances before she whisked him into the living room.

Patrick glanced around. The room had a kind of rich, understated elegance that immediately made him feel uncomfortable. Out of place. Damn, he wished he could take Helen down to Callahan's and talk to her there.

The corner of his mouth tipped up at the thought. Yeah. And he could just imagine how much Helen would like the place, too. Probably about as much as he liked the opera.

The faint boom and crash of the ocean made him glance toward the window. It was open a crack. He crossed the room and looked out over the black, foaming water.

"Sit down," Helen said sharply.

He turned away from the window and sat on her butter-yellow leather sofa. It was soft and luxurious—so different from his own battered couch—and he leaned forward to keep from sinking into it too far. Papers were strewn over the coffee table in front of him, and he angled them a glance. She'd been working, obviously. On his case? Or—

She swept the papers out from under his nose. An antique rolltop desk stood in one corner of the room, and she dumped the papers onto the work top and banged down the cover.

"Don't do that again." She sat in a morris chair across from the sofa, keeping the coffee table between them like a barrier. Tension crackled in the air.

Trying to relax the atmosphere, he stretched out his legs and tossed her a lazy smile. "Nice place you've got here."

He didn't miss the little flash of pride on her face before she covered it with a frown. "How did you know where I live?"

"Looked you up in the phone book."

"You can't have. I'm unlisted. What did you do? Follow me home from work?"

"Nope."

Her lips tightened. "Don't play games with me, Monaghan. How did you know where I live?"

"I've known since last year." He weighed his words carefully. "I got one of the guys at the station to look you up."

Her face went rigid. "Why? So you could gloat every time you drove by? Do you do this with all your conquests?"

He felt the fuse of anger that had ridden deep within him since he'd woken up alone that morning a year before suddenly ignite. First she dumped him without a word, then she insisted that what had happened between them was a *mistake,* and now this?

The words spilled out before he could stop them, before he could tell himself he didn't care, it didn't matter. "You want to know why I looked you up? It was because I went to bed one night with a woman in my arms, and when I woke up in the morning she was gone without a trace. No note. No phone call. I didn't know what happened to you. It scared the hell out of me."

"I'm supposed to believe that?"

"Damn right. I called the station and got your address and went tearing out of my place like a fool. I didn't know if you were ill, or if you went out for a cup of coffee and got mugged, or what. And when I got here, I saw you standing by your kitchen window." He gave a harsh laugh. "You were watering your plants."

Helen looked down. "Oh."

Patrick's jaw tightened as the memories flooded through him. That night he'd thought— Hell, he didn't know exactly what he'd thought, but he hadn't expected her to disappear like that.

At first he hadn't thought—hadn't believed—she really meant it. So he'd called her. Left messages on her answering machine at home, on her voice mail at work. And she'd ignored him.

He'd told himself he didn't care. That he'd forgotten her, that it didn't matter anyway. After all, it wasn't as if he wanted a serious relationship.

No. Jessica had cured him of that.

With an effort, Patrick brought his temper under control. "I didn't come here to talk about the past. I came because if you get that warrant, I'm going to be arrested tomorrow. Probably indicted by the end of the week. And if you go through with it, your career will be ruined." He looked her in the eye. "I'm innocent, Helen. You have to back off."

"You're right, you probably will be indicted by the end of the week. Franklin wants this case sewn up fast." She spoke coolly. "But I fail to see how doing it will hurt my career."

"No? Who'll take the fall when it comes out that the wrong man has been charged with the crime? Franklin...or you?"

"That won't—"

"Come on, Helen. Chambers loves the spotlight. Can't you hear him on television? 'I regret that an overzealous young prosecutor overstepped the bounds of justice and acted hastily in her pursuit of Detective Monaghan. I had no personal knowledge, et cetera, et cetera.' He'll throw you to the dogs without a second thought."

"Only if you get off. But I'll get a conviction. Don't you doubt it."

"And this case will make your career, right?" Patrick leaned forward. "But what about the cost? What if you convict an innocent man?"

Helen's mouth flattened. "We've got an eyewitness who says you and Marty were the only people out there on the highway last night. A lab report confirming that the bullets in Marty's brain came from your gun. Gunshot residue on your hands. And you claim you can't remember what happened. Innocent?" She shook her head. "I've rarely seen more compelling evidence of guilt."

He shot her an assessing look. "But what does your gut tell you?"

She stared at him as if he was speaking Urdu. "My gut?"

"Your instincts." He waved a descriptive hand. "Your feelings."

She stiffened. "When it comes to my work, I don't have feelings. I use logic. Not emotion."

"And was it logic that made you let me into your apartment?" Patrick reached across the coffee table and grabbed her hand. Electricity coursed through him as his fingers closed over hers. She gasped, and he knew she felt it, too—felt the fire that had brought them together a year ago, the fire that still sparked between them even now.

"Is this logical?" he demanded.

She tried to wrench her hand away from his, but he hung on. A tremor ran through her body, and an answering flash of heat shot through his. God, he wanted to kiss her. To run his hands into her hair. It would feel like silk, raw silk sliding over his rough hands, and—

"Don't touch me!" Her voice was high, almost panicked. She jerked away from him and leaped to her feet.

He stared at her in confusion. Was that fear he saw in her eyes, in the rapid pulse at the base of her throat? Or was it something else?

He shoved himself off the couch. "Helen—"

"Stay here. I'm going to get a glass of water." She whirled away and disappeared down the hall toward the kitchen.

Helen ran the water for a good five minutes before she filled one of the heavy crystal glasses she'd bought herself last year as a Christmas present. She lifted the glass to her lips and took a long swallow. The water was cold and soothing as it slid down her throat.

She stared out over the sink, past the window ledge filled with herbs in clay pots, toward the darkened street below. A lone brown sedan sat beneath the streetlight by the entrance to her building. Probably in exactly the same spot Patrick had sat when he'd looked up at her from the street that morning.

That morning. The morning after the first—and last—time they'd made love.

Helen sucked in her breath as the memories washed over her. Memories of Patrick's laughter as he lifted his face to the rain. Of the feel of his warm hands on her wet, bare skin. Of his voice, low and rough and urgent as he'd lifted her against him. Of wanting...*wanting*....

She thought she'd put those feelings—those crazy, dangerous feelings—away forever. But she'd been wrong. They were creeping up on her again, threatening her sanity, threatening everything.

Sharp, bright fear stabbed through her. Dear God, she couldn't let her emotions take over. Couldn't risk losing control. She couldn't risk becoming like her mother, the way everyone had always said she would.

The memories burned like acid. *"Helen's a tramp, just like her mom." "Hey, Helen, you wanna have a few drinks and a good time?" "Come on, babe, you gave it to Joe...."*

Desperately, she shoved the memories away. Taking a gulp of water, she struggled to think clearly, to come up with a plan.

"I should throw Patrick out," she said out loud. "Right now. Before anyone finds out I've talked to him."

But...but what if he really was innocent? Helen's fingers tightened on the cold, smooth glass. Patrick had been right about Franklin. If anything went wrong with the case, she'd get all the blame. It could destroy her career in one stroke.

Helen squeezed her eyes shut. She couldn't let that happen. Her career was all she had—it was what she'd worked for all her life. To get out of Seattle's slums. To graduate from high school, college, law school. And she'd made it. She was a good lawyer, a good prosecutor—good enough to become the head prosecutor of a county one day.

If she didn't listen to Patrick, she risked losing it all.

She was going to have to talk to him. And that wasn't emotion, she told herself grimly. That was logic.

Squaring her shoulders, she set her glass down on the counter and headed back into the living room.

Patrick stood looking out the window, his legs spread, his hands shoved deep in his pockets. His shoulders looked very broad, the line of his back straight and lean. Untidy black hair brushed the collar of his shirt, and she felt the sudden wild urge to brush that hair aside, to stand on her tiptoes and press her lips to the back of his strong neck.

Her heart thumped crazily and a wave of heat climbed her face. What was wrong with her, anyway? She had to get a grip. Concentrate on the case.

She strode the rest of the way into the room and halted a few feet from the window. Clearing her throat, she looked pointedly at her watch. "You've got another half hour, Monaghan. If you have any proof you're innocent, you'd better start talking. Fast."

Patrick turned to face her. He looked at her carefully. "Are you okay?"

Suddenly she remembered the way she'd jerked away from him and charged out of the living room. Did he know why? The thought sent a burst of humiliation twisting through her. "I'm fine," she snapped. "Just get on with it."

His expression changed, hardened. "Okay. I don't have any proof. But I am innocent. I'm sure I'm being set up."

"By whom?"

He shrugged. "By Carmel. Or whoever was out there with me and Marty last night."

"Why would Carmel want to set you up?"

"He hates my guts."

"Why?"

Patrick spread his hands. "He thinks I slept with his wife."

"And did you?" As soon as the words were out of her mouth, she wanted to cut out her tongue. The last thing she wanted was for Patrick to think she gave a damn who he slept with.

He shot her a look of pure outrage. "Of course not! What kind of guy do you think I am? I don't mess around with married women."

"So why does Carmel think you did?"

"Amanda told him so. Carmel was having an affair and she wanted to make him jealous."

He was telling the truth. She was sure of it—his face was so easy to read. Relief filtered through her, loosening the tension in her shoulders, but she kept her expression cool, as though it didn't matter to her. Which it didn't, she told herself sternly.

She forced her mind away from Patrick's love life. "You mentioned someone else being out there on the highway last night. Have you remembered something new?"

"No, I wish I had. But if Carmel isn't setting me up, faking the lab reports and so on, there must have been someone else there. I had a concussion and a cut on my head. Someone must've knocked me out and then used my gun to shoot Marty.''

''How would that explain the gunshot residue on your hands?''

His brow furrowed, his silver eyes narrowing in concentration. ''Maybe I shot at my attacker.''

''Patrick, there was an eyewitness. She saw only two men.''

''She could be lying.''

Helen's mind spun back to Tammy Weston. She'd been tense. Angry. Hostile. And what was it she'd said? Something about thinking she wouldn't have to identify anyone?

Helen rubbed her cheek. Maybe…maybe somebody had paid Tammy to phone in a false report. And hadn't told her she'd have to be involved after that. Helen's heart began to beat a little faster. It was possible. Just possible.

She looked at Patrick, at his handsome sculpted face and laughing eyes, and she knew that she wanted it to be more than possible.

She wanted it to be true.

She swallowed hard. ''So you think someone came up with this elaborate plot to kill Marty and pin it on you. Why?''

Patrick rubbed his hand over his shadowed jaw. ''I've been wondering if it could be related to the case we were working on.''

''What case? I left all your files at the office.''

''It was a murder. A hooker called Jamie Lee Turner. Somebody strangled her on Saturday night down at the Lucky Seven Motel.''

Helen frowned. She vaguely remembered Carmel mentioning that Patrick and Marty had been working on the Turner murder, but she'd pushed it to the back of her mind. Somehow it just hadn't seemed that important.

''What could that case have to do with Marty's murder?'' she asked.

''I don't know. But somebody killed Jamie Lee Turner. Maybe we were getting too close to the killer, and he decided it was time to get rid of us.''

"Get rid of you both? But you're still here, Monaghan. Whoever was out there Monday night only got rid of Marty."

"That might have been a mistake. He could've meant to kill me, too."

A ribbon of fear raced through Helen, chilling her to the bone. She pictured Patrick lying on that dark highway, blood seeping out of his head. The cold in her heart intensified, the room receding into darkness. A gust of sea wind blew through the window and she shivered violently.

"Helen? Are you okay?" Patrick put his hand on her shoulder. Instantly heat flooded through her body, dispelling the icy-cold fear. Through the heavy wool of her sweater, she felt each of his fingers, felt them as clearly as though he was touching her bare skin. His thumb brushed the side of her neck, a feather-light touch, and her stomach lurched with longing.

Violently she twisted away. "I'm fine. Just a bit cold." She banged the window shut. Turning back to face Patrick, she realized that he was as close as ever. Too close.

"So what do you think?" he asked.

Think? When he was standing so close to her, she couldn't think at all.

Hastily, she backed up a few steps, fighting for control. "I think everything you've said is pure speculation. You don't have proof of any of it, do you?"

Patrick shook his head. "Not yet."

She crossed her arms over her chest. "And you want me to hold off on the arrest until…what? You come up with evidence that aliens killed Marty?"

His face hardened. "No. All I'm asking for is twenty-four hours. To see what I can come up with."

"What do you think you can accomplish in twenty-four hours?"

"A lot."

Helen sighed. "Give me one good reason why I should agree to this."

Patrick stepped forward, closing the gap between them. He bent his head toward hers, a spark of heat flaring deep in his eyes.

Something deep inside her—something primal and female and altogether dangerous—shuddered to life.

"Logic," he said, his warm breath caressing her cheek. "If you move on an innocent man, you could jeopardize your career."

"Right. Logic." The words came out so low and husky that she barely recognized her own voice.

His sculpted lips curved in a hint of a smile. "So will you do it? Give me another twenty-four hours?"

His deep voice slid over her nerves, and she closed her eyes briefly, struggling for control. *Logic. Emotion. Her career.*

Her career.

She opened her eyes. "Okay. I'll give you twenty-four hours."

Patrick's face broke into a huge smile, a smile so infectious, she had to fight the urge to grin back at him.

Instead she shot him a steely look. "But if you don't come up with anything solid by then, I'm going for the warrant. And I'll be doing some checking of my own. If I find out you've lied to me about *anything,* the deal's off. I'll have you arrested like that." She snapped her fingers.

Patrick grinned. "Yes, ma'am."

"And one more thing. I want you to promise me that for now, you won't tell anyone we've talked. Not even your brother."

His grin faded, and his silver eyes turned serious. "Of course I won't. Don't worry. Nobody has to find out."

Early the next morning Helen unlocked the front door to the county prosecutor's office suite. Flipping on the light, she turned to the glowing box on the wall and punched in the code to deactivate the alarm system. The box bleeped twice. Somebody else had already turned it off.

"Hello?" she called. "Anyone here?"

Silence.

Whoever had come in earlier had probably just dropped off their briefcase and headed down to the ground-floor coffee shop. As she walked down the hall to her own office, Helen glanced at the clock on the wall. Quarter to seven. No wonder no one else was working yet.

As usual, she would be the first one at her desk.

She hadn't slept well. After Patrick had left, she'd gone to bed and tossed and turned restlessly, worrying that someone might have seen him, might somehow find out they'd talked. When she'd finally fallen asleep in the small hours of the morning, she'd dreamed of Patrick—dreams that made her wake with her heart pounding, her body slick with sweat and aching with need.

After that, she'd given up on sleep. She'd gone for her usual five-mile run and then showered and headed down to the office. Her mind—and her body—were in turmoil, and work was the only thing that would help her regain her balance.

Work had always been her savior, her lifeline. It had been since she was a child. So often she had come home from school to find her mother half drunk and making out with some strange man. Sickened and ashamed, she would run—run to the public library, where she'd bury herself in homework and books.

Her mother had jeered at her. "What're you doin' with all those books? You think you're hot stuff, doncha, baby? Well, you're no better'n me. You'll see. Just you wait."

Helen grimaced at the memory. She must have heard those words a thousand times; her mother had been saying them since she was born. But she'd proved Lana wrong.

Hadn't she?

"Stop it, Stewart," she muttered as she fumbled with her keys. "There's no point in thinking about it."

Because she *had* proved Lana wrong. She had a great career. A beautiful apartment. Everything she'd ever wanted.

Sure, other women might want husbands and children—might want love—but she never had. She'd focused all her energy on her career. And that was exactly how she wanted it.

She frowned down at her keys and finally found the right one. Unlocking her office door, she flipped on the light.

And froze.

Her office was a shambles. There was paper everywhere. The file drawers that lined one wall had all been yanked open, their contents dumped out on the floor. Her desk had been upended, her chair knocked over. Even her prized Persian rug had been ripped off the floor and flung carelessly into a corner of the room.

''Oh, my God,'' she whispered.

Hot tears stung her eyes as she walked into her office, her feet crunching against the piles of paper on the floor. The room was icy-cold, and she saw that the window was open. Rain had spilled in, and water ran down the wall and puddled on the floor next to the shattered remains of a crystal vase.

Bile rose in Helen's throat. This was her workplace. Her sanctuary. And somebody had systematically torn it to shreds.

Her eyes blurring with tears, she scanned the room. What had they wanted? Her computer was still there, lying smashed on the floor. An expensive signed print still hung on the wall.

Helen squeezed her hands into fists. Whoever had broken into her office wasn't any ordinary thief. He—or they—had definitely been after something in particular.

But what?

Chapter 4

Helen rocked back on her heels and surveyed the piles of paper on the floor. The police had come and gone, leaving black fingerprint dust, wet footprints, and a small raft of cardboard coffee cups behind. She and David Holt, one of the clerks, had been working for hours to clean up the mess.

Righting the furniture and sweeping away the water and broken glass had been the easy part. Sorting out the masses of files and paper was something else altogether.

"How's it going over there, Dave?" Helen asked.

"Not too bad." Dave was crouched in the corner, surrounded by several precariously leaning piles of files. His wire-frame glasses had slid down his nose, and his tie was askew. "I think I've got most of the files for the Wilson case back in order."

"Good." Helen ran a tired hand through her hair. "Any sign of those police files yet?"

"Nope. I've gone through this stuff three times, and I can't find them. Are you sure you didn't take them home last night?"

"I'm sure." She frowned at the heaps of paper. "They've got to be here somewhere."

She was positive she'd left the files relating to Jamie Lee Turner's murder right on top of her desk. All the files Carmel had copied for her had been there: Patrick's personnel files, Marty's notes, the case files for the Turner murder.

She and Dave had unearthed the personnel files, but they couldn't find the case files or Marty's notes. So where were they? Jumbled in with the mess of paper on the floor?

Helen bit her lip. It would take days to systematically sort through all the paper. Too long. She needed those files right away, needed them to check Patrick's story.

Needed to prove to herself that she'd done the right thing—the logical thing—by postponing the arrest. That it wasn't the crazy feelings that sprang between them each time they touched, those dangerous flashes of heat, that had made her agree to Patrick's request.

She stood and walked over to her desk. "Keep up the good work, Dave. I'll see if I can get another copy of those files."

Sitting down at her desk, she flipped through her Rolodex card file. Calling Carmel was the last thing she felt like doing. When she'd told him earlier that Patrick's arrest had been postponed, he'd all but accused her of having an affair with Patrick. And she'd come dangerously close to losing her temper in return.

She didn't want to deal with him again. Not today. Not when her control was already stretched so thin and tight. But there was no help for it. She had to have those files.

Gritting her teeth, she picked up the phone and dialed Carmel's number.

He answered immediately. "Carmel."

"Lieutenant. It's Helen Stewart. I need another copy of those files you gave me Monday night."

"All of them?" he demanded.

"Not quite all. I don't need the personnel files. Just the case files on the Turner murder and Marty's notes."

"What happened? You lose them already?"

She tightened her lips. "No, I didn't lose them. Someone broke into my office last night and tore through every piece of paper I have. It'll take days to deal with the mess, and I don't have that kind of time."

"Okay," he said grudgingly. "Hang on."

She heard a clatter as he dropped the phone, and then sounds of paper shuffling. A muffled string of profanity made her wince, and then Carmel came back on the line.

"I can't find the files. Someone must've moved them off my desk. I'll call you back when I find them."

"I need those files right away."

"Yeah, yeah. Look, I'll ask around and call you back in a couple minutes."

"I'll be waiting for your call."

He hung up without a response. Helen stared at the receiver for a long moment before she put it down. Unease curled through her stomach. She couldn't find the files. Carmel couldn't find the files. What if... But there was no point in speculating about it until Carmel got back to her.

She sighed and tapped her pen against her desk, staring out the window. Rain dripped down the pane. Across the street, a woman wearing a bright yellow slicker hurried out of a store, hustling a child carrying a miniature umbrella.

The phone rang, and she grabbed it. "Helen Stewart."

"It's Carmel." He paused. "Look, I, uh..."

The unease in her stomach twisted into a painful cramp. "You can't find the files."

"How'd you know?"

"It doesn't take a genius, Lieutenant Carmel. Someone breaks into my office. My files go missing, but after all, they're only copies. Why am I not surprised the originals would vanish, too?"

"Hey!" Carmel's outraged bellow crackled across the line. "I didn't take them, if that's what you're suggesting."

"You're mighty quick to defend yourself against something you haven't been accused of. Guilty conscience, Lieutenant?"

"I told you, I didn't take the damn files!"

"So someone broke into the police department, got past the desk sergeant, through the bull pen, and into your office without anyone seeing them?"

"How the hell should I know?"

She kept her voice cool and professional. "Those files had better turn up. I want every drawer, every filing cabinet, every desk searched until they're found." If by some miracle he was telling the truth, they had to be there somewhere.

Carmel's breathing was hard and heavy. "It's a waste of time. We're not gonna find them."

Her eyes narrowed. "No? You seem very certain for a man who doesn't know where they are."

"Just don't tell me how to do my job, lady!"

The taut wire of her control finally snapped. "And don't you get in the way of my case! If you do, I'll see you lose your precious job! Go find those files, Lieutenant. I'll expect them on my desk by tomorrow morning." She banged down the phone.

From the corner of the office, Dave looked at her strangely. "You okay, Helen?"

She sucked in a shaky breath. "I'm all right. But will you give me a couple of minutes, please?"

"Sure thing. Time for a cup of coffee, anyway." He got to his feet and ambled out of her office.

Helen stared at the piles of paper on the floor.

They weren't going to find the files anywhere. Not here. Not at the police department. She would bet her life on it.

It was incredible, but it looked as though someone had broken into her office with the express purpose of stealing those files. And judging by his response, that somebody was very likely Lieutenant Edward Carmel.

Her hands shaky, Helen grabbed the phone book. She looked up the number she wanted, picked up the phone, and dialed.

He answered on the first ring. "Hello?"

The sound of his deep voice sent a rush of relief racing through her, a feeling she didn't want to analyze too closely.

"Patrick," she said. "We have to talk."

Patrick parked his car in the gravel lot above the stone retaining wall. The rain had finally stopped, so he didn't bother rolling up his window before he headed down the uneven steps that led to the beach.

He saw Helen in the distance, walking along the edge of the surf. Her blond hair shone like a beacon against the pewter-gray of sea and sky. Even at this distance, he felt a tug of desire at the sight of her.

He cupped his hands around his mouth. "Helen?"

The wind whipped away his voice, so he headed across the beach, following the line of slender footprints Helen had left in the sand. "Helen!"

She still didn't hear him. The tide was just turning, and surf boomed and crashed against the shore. Wind gusted across the beach, blowing wet sand and strands of kelp before it.

He caught up to Helen and touched her shoulder.

She whirled around, fists clenched, prepared to strike.

He held up his hands. "It's just me."

"Patrick." She took a deep breath and unclenched her hands. "You scared me."

"I called you, but you didn't hear me."

She glanced out at the sea. "It's pretty wild out here today." She turned her gaze back to him. "Thank you for coming."

"How could I resist?" He grinned, trying to make light of the elation he'd felt when she called him. "Beautiful women don't invite me to secret assignations on lonely beaches every day."

Helen's lips tightened. "Don't joke about it. I think you might be in danger."

"Danger?" He glanced around. The beach was deserted. The rain had only stopped a few minutes ago, and the wind still whipped the waves into a frenzy. Nobody else was crazy enough to be out here on a day like this.

"Not here," Helen said quickly. "That's why I wanted you to meet me here. Where nobody would see us."

He couldn't resist teasing her just a little. "And I thought it was because you'd finally given in to my irresistible charm."

"This is serious, Patrick. I think you might have been right last night. About Marty's murder being related to the case you were working on. And maybe even about you being in danger."

She was trying to sound cool and unconcerned, but Patrick detected the fear in her voice. Instinctively, he wanted to comfort her, to pull her into his arms and soothe her. And to do more than soothe her. To kiss her beautiful trembling mouth, to taste the salt of the ocean on her skin.

To make her remember just how good it had been between them.

A bolt of heat shot through him at the thought. His reaction was physical, immediate, and he controlled it with difficulty. This was definitely not the time to kiss her. Not when she obviously had something important to tell him.

Not when she had an excuse to push him away—again.

He tried not to look at her mouth. "What's happened?"

"Someone broke into my office last night. Not any of the other offices in the suite, just mine."

"And?"

"The files are gone. All the files relating to Jamie Lee Turner's murder. As far as I can tell, nothing else was taken—just the files. There must have been something in them. Maybe something that could incriminate somebody."

For the first time since Helen had said she was applying for a warrant, he felt a surge of real hope. This was the first tangible evidence that his hunch was right.

He dragged his hand over his jaw. "So Marty's murder does have something to do with the Turner case."

"It also has something to do with Lieutenant Carmel."

"What do you mean?"

"My files were just copies. Carmel had the originals—and they've mysteriously 'disappeared.'" Her voice was grim. "Whatever is going on, Carmel is up to his neck in it."

Patrick swore under his breath. "I thought he had something to do with this."

"But how? Was he involved in Jamie Lee's murder? Or is he just setting you up? But if that's the case, why would he care about the Turner files?" She shook her head. "I don't understand what's going on. And I hate the idea that someone is using me to prosecute you when you're innocent."

Innocent. The word made Patrick's heart leap, the blood sing to his head. Helen believed in him. She actually believed in him.

His face broke into a big smile. "So what did your boss say about it?"

"I haven't told him."

"What?" His smile faded. "Why not?"

"Patrick, there is a mountain of evidence against you. Weighed against that, a break-in and a few missing files aren't all that significant."

"But you know I'm innocent."

"Yes," she said slowly. "I do. Even before the break-in, I had my doubts that you killed Marty. But that's not the point."

"Then what is the point?"

She crossed her arms over her breasts. "If I go to Franklin without any hard proof and tell him you're innocent, do you know what he'll say?"

"No."

"He'll say that I'm allowing my personal feelings to affect my judgment, and he'll take me off the case."

Sudden anger twisted through his gut. Was it only seconds ago that he'd thought she believed in him? What was it with her, anyway? Every time he started to think she gave a damn, she turned right around and slapped him down.

And the worst part of it was that her rejection—the reminder that he didn't mean anything to her, that he wasn't her *type*—actually hurt.

Dammit, he was a fool, he told himself bitterly. He knew better than to care what she—or any other woman—thought of him. To care whether he measured up in her eyes or not. After Jessica had killed their future and destroyed their marriage, he'd sworn he wouldn't give any woman that kind of power over him again. Especially a woman like her: a lawyer, a woman who cared more about success than anything else, even—

"Did you hear me, Patrick?" Helen put her hands on her hips. "I said, he'll take me off the case."

Patrick gave a sarcastic laugh. "And we all know you wouldn't want that to happen. God forbid you should do anything to hurt your career.''

''It wouldn't do you any good, either. Another prosecutor would have you arrested in a New York minute.''

''Whereas you've given me twenty-four whole hours. I guess I should be grateful you didn't already have me arrested. It would have looked great on the evening news, wouldn't it, darlin'?''

Helen's chin jerked up. ''I'm not like Franklin. I don't care about the press. I want to do what's right.''

''As long as it doesn't hurt your career.''

Her eyes blazed. ''I've already admitted my career is very important to me. What's wrong with that?''

''There's something wrong with it when you have an innocent man arrested for a crime you know damn well he didn't commit.'' Patrick spun on his heel and began to walk away.

''You're not going to be arrested!'' she shouted.

He froze. ''What?''

''I said, you're not going to be arrested.'' She walked toward him, her feet slapping against the sand. ''I called Judge Gove and told him to put the arrest warrant on indefinite hold. I'll be working on the case, and as soon as I have a solid line on another suspect, I'll cancel the warrant altogether.''

Suddenly he felt like a total fool. ''Hell. I thought—''

''I know what you thought. But you were wrong.''

The surf boomed, and ocean spray swirled into the air as they stood there. Patrick looked into Helen's face. He read frustration. Determination. Anger.

Reluctant admiration swept through him. She really was dedicated to her career, but she'd told the truth about wanting to do what was right. It had been a risk for her to call Judge Gove. Another prosecutor would have arrested him—innocent or not— and tried to climb to glory on his back.

But Helen hadn't.

He stretched out a hand to her, but she stepped backward. ''Helen, I'm sorry. I shouldn't have lost my temper.''

''No, you shouldn't have.''

He gave a rueful smile. ''I always did have a temper.''

"Oh?" she said coolly.

He nodded. "When I was a kid, I went to Catholic school, you know?" Somehow he wanted to talk, to try to make things right between them. "The kids from the public school used to come by the school yard and call us dirty micks. And worse. Adam always walked away from it. He worked hard. Beat the kids from the public school at debate. And sports."

"And you?"

He shrugged. "Got in a few brawls. One time I heard a guy from the public school call my sister an Irish slut, and I broke his nose."

She was trying to look disapproving, but he didn't miss the spark of interest in her eyes. "What happened then?"

"The principal gave me the strap. Got home, and my dad gave me a talking-to I'll never forget. And then there was confession. Father O'Malley made me spend every Saturday morning for a month in church saying rosaries as a penance."

A tiny smile appeared on her lips. "And you never got into any fights again?"

"Learn my lesson so easily?" He spread his hands. "You've got to be kidding."

"I should have guessed. You probably kept on punching boys in the nose, didn't you?"

"That's why I became a cop."

Her smile became a full-fledged grin. "So you could punch other guys without getting in trouble?"

"No. Because I wanted to put things right."

"What do you mean?"

He paused. Why was he telling her all this? What made him think she would understand? Jessica never had, that was for sure.

But something in the way Helen looked at him, something in her direct blue gaze, made him want to try to explain. He didn't understand it, but the words came out of his mouth almost before he could stop them.

"I got in those fights because I lost my temper. But the reason I lost my temper— It was because I saw the injustice of it. The boys from the public school would stand on the other side of the fence taunting us, harassing the girls. It was wrong of them. And I wanted to make them stop.'' He shook his head. ''My method was all wrong, but my heart was in the right place.''

''You wanted to make the world a better place,'' she said slowly.

''You make it sound more noble than it is.'' He shoved his hands deeper into his pockets. ''It's just—this is who I am. I always hated injustice and cruelty. I wanted to stop it. So I grew up and became a cop.''

She nodded, her eyes serious. ''I think I understand.''

Her words struck him to the core. It was crazy, but for an instant he thought she really did understand. He felt her level gaze deep inside him...almost as though she could see through his leather jacket, through his shirt and his skin, and right into his heart.

The realization made him stiffen. What was he doing? The only woman to whom he'd ever bared his soul was Jessica. She'd seen him, seen his most secret thoughts and hopes and dreams—and she'd rejected him. And not just him, but everything he had given her....

Three years ago he'd vowed never to trust a woman like that again. Not ever. He wouldn't risk putting himself through that kind of fury and pain all over again.

But now, here he was, telling his innermost thoughts to Helen—who'd already walked away from him once. Who'd made it more than clear that no matter how much her body wanted him, the rest of her definitely didn't.

Patrick squeezed his hands into fists. What the hell was wrong with him, anyway? Wanting Helen was one thing. Wanting her, he could handle. But this?

If he knew what was good for him, he'd better back off this conversation. Fast.

He forced a casual smile to his face. ''So, darlin', now you know all my darkest secrets.'' He kept his tone light, as though they'd been discussing nothing more important than office gossip or football scores. ''I have a terrible temper. Always have, always will.''

Her gaze was searching. "And you love being a cop."

He shrugged, deflecting her gaze. "That's right." Seizing the opportunity, he turned the conversation away from himself. "So the sooner the real killer is caught, the sooner I get back my badge and my gun, the better."

"Better for me, too. Franklin is anxious to get this case wrapped up as soon as possible because of the election."

"How did you explain postponing the arrest?"

"I haven't yet. I've got a meeting with him this afternoon." She bit her lip, that full lower lip that made him want to kiss her. "He's going to want *somebody* arrested. Soon."

He dragged his gaze away from her mouth. "We'd better get started with the investigation, then."

She raised a cool, blond eyebrow. "'We?'"

"We."

The sea crashed, water racing up the sand. Patrick caught Helen's hand and pulled her away from the surging water. Electricity surged through him as their palms met. Her skin was cool and damp, but the feeling that coiled through him was anything but cool.

No, it was definitely hot. Verging on explosive.

He tightened his fingers on hers and tugged her a little closer. He heard the sharp intake of her breath, and she moistened her lips.

He almost groaned out loud.

And then she pulled away from him. Not hard and fast, as she had before, but slow and almost reluctant. He would have reached for her again, but she began to speak, her voice husky and a little breathless.

"I'm the prosecutor assigned to this case. It's my job to make sure all the evidence is in place. But you can't be involved in that."

"It's my job, too, Helen. I'm a cop. Carmel took away my badge and my gun, but that doesn't make a difference to what I am in here." He tapped his chest. "Besides, it's my life you're talking about."

"That's beside the point."

"Is it? Admit it, you need my help. You can't get the police involved in the investigation if you're hiding the truth from Franklin. And you can't do it alone. You need me."

She stiffened. "I don't need anything from you!"

"No? What about information? You said you'd lost the files on the Turner murder. I'm the only person who can tell you about that investigation."

She lifted her chin. "Okay. I need information. But that's all."

"No. You need a partner to help with the investigation."

"If anyone saw me with you—"

"They won't." He took a step closer. "We'll be careful."

She shook her head stubbornly. "No, Patrick."

"It makes sense." He ran his finger down her cheek. "We want the same thing."

She batted his hand away. "This is business. It's not personal."

His lips curled in a smile. "I never said it was personal."

"Didn't you?"

"No. I said we wanted the same thing. You want to advance your career by catching Marty's killer and prosecuting him. I want to clear my name and be reinstated on the force—by catching Marty's killer. You see? We do want the same thing after all."

Helen stared at him for a long moment, and then her thick golden lashes swept down, hiding her eyes. The wind gusted again, swirling around them, blowing her hair across her face.

"All I want from you is information," she said, her voice low. She checked her watch. "I have to get back to the office for my meeting with Franklin. But I want to meet with you later."

"I'd be happy to meet you. For dinner."

She shook her head. "I told you, I don't want us to be seen together in public."

"I wasn't asking you to have dinner with me in public."

Her head snapped up, her eyes hard. "If you think I'm going to your apartment, you're wrong."

Patrick grinned. "You think I'll try to seduce you?" She glared at him, and he laughed. "Don't worry. I wasn't asking you to my place. I thought you could come to my parents' house."

Her eyes narrowed. "Why?"

"My father was a cop for forty years. He's retired, but he's still the best cop I know. He might have some ideas."

"But—"

He made an exasperated sound. "Trust me, Helen. No one from your office will see us in my parents' neighborhood. They live on South Commercial." It was where he'd grown up, in the south end of town. A tough, tight-knit neighborhood that was definitely on the wrong side of the tracks. There were no lawyers there, that was for sure. No doctors or bankers, either.

Helen hesitated, and Patrick's jaw hardened. So she didn't want to come to his parents'. He should have guessed. After all, how many times had he been through this with Jessica?

The old anger twisted deep within him, and he crossed his arms over his chest. "What, isn't the South End good enough for you, darlin'? I bet your family lives in some nice fake Georgian out by a country club, don't they? Your father's probably…let me guess. A stockbroker. And your mother's a Realtor."

She recoiled as if she'd been struck. "You couldn't be farther from the truth, Monaghan," she said, her voice bitter.

"No? What is the truth, then?"

She didn't answer his question. A drop of rain plopped down, striking Patrick in the forehead.

Helen glanced up at the sky. "It's starting to rain again. And I've got to get back to the office."

"What about—"

Helen shot him a level look. "Give me the address. I'll be there at six."

"Helen! What's going on with the Monaghan case? The press have been hounding me, and I need to give them a statement."

Helen closed the door behind her and crossed the Aubusson carpet that graced the floor of Franklin's huge corner office. She sat in a leather chair and glanced at Franklin across the glossy expanse of his cherrywood desk.

His forehead was creased—a sure sign that he was more than usually worried. He almost never let himself frown. Helen suspected he didn't want to speed the aging process. After all, frowns might lead to wrinkles. And wrinkles didn't look good on television.

She managed to smile at her boss. "I wanted to meet with you earlier, but you were out."

"I had a meeting with Judge Gove. He mentioned you'd called him to postpone the arrest...again. Why?"

She looked at him coolly. "If we move too quickly, we might be gambling with our chances of a conviction."

"I see." He clasped his hands and steepled his fingers. "How long do you think you'll need? I have to tell the press something. All they know is that a cop killer is on the loose. The public needs reassurance. I want them to know they're safe."

And that he was the one who made them safe, she thought wryly. Politics again. But as much as she disliked it, she knew she had to play the game.

She folded her hands over her knees. "The public also needs to know that when the killer is arrested, he'll spend the rest of his life behind bars. I can make that happen. But I need a few more days."

She knew she'd hit the right note, because Franklin flashed her his famous magnetic smile. "All right. As I've said before, I have every faith in you." He leaned forward confidentially. "You know Alex will be leaving us shortly to go into private practice. When he goes, I'll need a new executive deputy prosecutor. I've got my eye on you, Helen. You win this case, and I'll know I was right in my assessment of your abilities."

Helen's eyes widened. Executive deputy prosecutor? It was the best job in the office. And to get such a job before her thirtieth birthday would be a coup indeed.

But Franklin's offer was clear. She had to win the case—and fast—to get the job.

She could do it. She *had* to. Not just for herself, or for her career, but for justice—to keep an innocent man out of jail.

And for Patrick.

She'd glimpsed something in him today that she hadn't suspected. Beneath the charming rogue was another man altogether.

A man who took the idea of justice seriously, a man who wanted to set the world right.

She'd taken a closer look at his personnel file when she'd gotten back to the office. There were the reprimands for insubordination. Disobeying orders. Memos from superior officers complaining about his blazing temper, his recklessness.

And six citations for outstanding bravery, hundreds of perfect arrests. Several letters from crime victims who'd written to the department to praise his handling of their cases.

Yes, there was more to Patrick than met the eye. Much more.

"Helen? What do you think about my offer?"

Helen dragged her thoughts away from Patrick and saw that Franklin was watching her carefully. She lifted her chin. "I'm going to win this case."

Approval flared in Franklin's eyes. "I know you will. You're a very talented lawyer. And after the excellent job you did on the Irving case, I knew you'd be perfect for this one."

Helen frowned slightly. The Irving case? Billy Irving was a handsome salesman she'd prosecuted for larceny after he'd embezzled almost a million dollars from his firm. He'd tried to hide the money by depositing it in the names of his girlfriends—all three of them—but one of them had found out about the others and turned him in. Helen was proud of the conviction, of course, but it was as different from a murder case as night to day.

"Thank you, Franklin," she said, "but I'm not sure I see the connection between the Irving case and this one."

"Don't you remember what you said to me after Irving's sentencing? When everyone was saying that Judge Zedillo had gone too far? You told me that a man like Irving who was so free and easy about sex deserved whatever he got." He chuckled. "And you certainly went after him with everything you had. I know you'll do the same with that womanizer Monaghan."

Monaghan. Helen's smile froze on her face. It was on the tip of her tongue to tell Franklin that she wasn't going after Patrick—womanizer or not—but she forced the words back. She couldn't risk being thrown off the case. Not now.

Besides, Franklin wouldn't care who they arrested. As long as they arrested somebody, and he could go on the news and tell the people of Evergreen County about it.

Politics. It was all politics to him.

Hiding her distaste, Helen stood. "I'll let you know as soon as we're ready for the arrest."

With a brilliant smile, Franklin walked around his desk to shake her hand. "Thank you. And keep me posted on any new developments. We have to keep the public happy."

"And safe," she said.

His thousand-watt smile flashed even brighter. "Of course."

Chapter 5

Helen stood in front of her closet, staring at her clothing. On the right, a row of suits—navy, gray, black—marched in a solid line. On the left hung several plain silk blouses and the sober dresses she wore to work functions.

"I can't wear work clothes to a family dinner at the Monaghans's," Helen muttered. Pushing the suits aside, she reached into the back of her closet for the few items that qualified as informal. A colorful broomstick skirt she'd bought on impulse two years ago and never worn. Two pairs of ancient corduroy pants and a faded print blouse. A tunic made of rose-colored raw silk.

"Okay, the cords." She grabbed the brown pair off the hanger, grimacing as she saw a paint stain splashed across one thigh.

No. They were beyond casual. Definitely sloppy.

She put her hands on her hips and sighed, rolling back her head to get the kinks out of her neck. "Come on, Stewart. You're going to be late if you stand here much longer."

Reaching into the closet, she grabbed the broomstick skirt and rose tunic. She pulled the tunic over her head, the raw silk sliding seductively over her skin. The skirt whispered against her ankles as she turned to look at herself in the mirror.

She swallowed rapidly at the sight of her reflection. The long, floaty skirt was colorful and romantic, and the rose of the top brought out the natural pink in her cheeks. With her blond hair a little tousled, she looked young. Almost pretty.

Helen stared at the mirror. What would Patrick think? Not that she really cared, of course.

"Right, Stewart," she said under her breath. "That's why you just stared into your closet for twenty minutes."

The telephone rang. Still eyeing herself in the mirror, she picked it up. "Hello?"

"Hi, baby," a familiar voice rasped. "It's me."

Helen's neck muscles tightened. "Hi, Mom." She'd made her weekly call to Lana just a few days ago, so it was unlikely her mother was calling just to chat. Not that she ever did. "What's up?"

"You gotta len' me some money." Lana was slurring her words, but not too badly considering it was after five. "It's a 'mergency."

Helen sighed. They must have had this conversation a thousand times. "What kind of emergency?"

"It's my...uh, my lan'lord. He says he's gonna throw me out if he doesn' get some money. Tonight."

"Well, you just tell him to call me. You know I pay him your rent every month, so he has no reason to throw you out." Helen glanced at the clock. "Look, I'm in a hurry. Can I call you back tomorrow?"

"Too busy to talk to your ma?" Lana's voice rose. "Think you're too good for me, doncha?"

"No, I—"

"Well, I got things to do, too. Fact, I'm gettin' dolled up for a date right now. Guess he won't mind spendin' a little money on me, either."

"Mom—"

It was too late. Her mother had already hung up.

Slowly, Helen put down the phone. She felt sick, sick and

defeated and about a hundred years old. Raising her head, she
looked at herself in the mirror. Was it only a minute ago she'd
thought she looked young? *Pretty?*

Her mouth twisted bitterly. Pretty? She didn't want to look
pretty. To doll herself up. Not for Patrick. Not for anyone.

Helen jerked the tunic over her head and pulled off the skirt.
She stuffed them both into the bottom of her laundry basket and
reached into her closet.

It would just have to be a suit after all.

Twenty minutes later Helen walked up the path that led to the
Monaghans's bungalow. A neatly clipped hedge surrounded the
tiny front yard, and flower beds lined the path. An earthy scent
of grass and rain hovered in the air, and a warm light shone from
the three glass panels in the front door. The door itself had been
painted red, an incongruous touch that somehow made the small
house seem even more welcoming.

Helen's throat tightened. As a child, this was the kind of house
she'd dreamed of living in. The kind of home she'd longed for.
And instead, she'd had one-room apartments. Roach-infested
hotel rooms. Lana hadn't cared, as long as she had the two things
that were most important to her. Booze. And men.

Angrily, Helen pushed the memories away. There was no point
in thinking about the past. She'd escaped all that, left it behind
her. Maybe her mother would never change, but she had proved
she was nothing like Lana.

Nothing.

Straightening her spine, she mounted the steps. She shook her
umbrella closed, juggled the sheaf of irises into her other arm,
and knocked on the door.

Almost immediately the door swung open. Music and laughter
spilled into the night. A small boy grinned up at her from the
doorway, revealing a large gap where his front teeth should have
been.

"Hi!" he chirped. "Are you here to see my grandma?"

Helen's heart seized. She knew Patrick had been married before, but she hadn't known he had a child. The little boy was the

image of Patrick. His tousled black hair mimicked Patrick's perfectly, and his eyes were the same silver-gray. Even his stance, legs spread, fists shoved deep in his pockets, was achingly familiar.

"You must be Helen." A woman with black hair liberally streaked with gray appeared behind the boy. She put her hand on his shoulder as she offered Helen a vibrant, welcoming smile. "I'm Bridget Monaghan."

Helen felt an answering smile being pulled from somewhere deep inside her. Patrick's mother was a small woman, but she positively exuded energy—almost as much as the little boy who bounced from foot to foot.

"It's a pleasure to meet you, Mrs. Monaghan."

"Oh, please, call me Bridget. Nobody's called me Mrs. anything since I retired from teaching last year."

"And I'm Tommy!" The little boy gave Helen another huge smile.

Bridget ruffled the boy's hair. "Tommy is Patrick's nephew."

"Nephew?" Helen let out her breath. "He looks so much like Patrick, I thought...."

A brief flash of emotion—something almost like pain—appeared in Bridget's eyes. "No," she said quietly. "Patrick has no children of his own. Just nieces and nephews."

"Like me!" Tommy piped up.

Helen smiled and squatted so they were at eye level. "Hi, Tommy."

"What's your name?"

"Helen. Helen Stewart. I'm a friend of your uncle Patrick's."

He nodded seriously. "So you're *that* lady. My mom said maybe you're gonna marry him."

Helen's cheeks flamed. Bridget stifled a laugh and said, "Tommy, it's not polite to—"

Another door swung open at the end of the hall. The smell of fresh bread seeped into the hallway along with a burst of laughter, and Patrick appeared, wiping his hands on a dish towel. He looked at her, crouched on the floor by his nephew, and his face split into a smile. "Helen."

She got to her feet, swallowing hard. Patrick was wearing black jeans that hugged his lean hips, and a hunter green T-shirt that left his muscular arms bare. Too bare. She could see the bulge of his biceps and the dusting of black hair on his skin, and her stomach flopped over. She remembered running her hands up his arms, remembered the contours of muscle and the soft rasp of hair, and—

She jerked her gaze back up to his face, and he gave her a welcoming grin. She felt the impact of his smile in every pore, making her heart beat too fast, her breath come too quickly.

"Hi, Patrick." Her voice was husky and breathless, and she cringed at the sound.

"What are you doing out there on the porch?" His eyes crinkled. "Come in, come in."

She walked into the warmth of the hall, and Patrick pushed the door shut. He took her coat, his strong hands brushing against her shoulders. Streamers of heat coursed through her body, heat that had nothing to do with being inside and everything to do with Patrick's touch.

Helen's heart thudded against her ribs. What was happening to her? If she wasn't careful—

Control.

She grasped for it, turning from Patrick to his mother. She handed Bridget the flowers in their bright cellophane wrapper. "I didn't know what to bring for dinner, so I brought you these."

Bridget took them with a delighted smile. "They're beautiful. Thank you." She turned to the little boy. "Tommy, will you come and help me put these in some water?"

"Sure, Grandma." He grabbed her hand and towed her off down the hallway, leaving Patrick and Helen alone.

Patrick turned back from the coat closet, his gaze sweeping over her. His eyes darkened to the color of smoke, and his mouth curled upward in a smile. She saw the muscles of his shoulder flex and shift as he reached up to plant his hand against the wall. He leaned close, and she caught his scent. He smelled of aftershave—spicy and warm—and of something else, something masculine and elusive and all too appealing.

"I'm glad you came," he said, his warm breath brushing her cheek.

"I—" She struggled to keep her voice steady. "I said I would."

"And you always keep your promises?"

She gulped. "Yes. I do."

Sudden heat flared in his eyes, and he dipped his head toward hers. He was so close she could see the faint shadow of a beard along his jaw, the flutter of a muscle in his cheek, every contour of his sculpted mouth.

Helen's mouth went dry, and she moistened her lips. She felt his breath stir her hair, and then the barest brush of his mouth across her cheek....

"Patrick?" a male voice bawled from the back of the house.

The moment was shattered. Patrick jerked upright, his eyes dark, his chest rising and falling rapidly. Helen fought for air.

"Patrick, you'd better get back in here if you want to get that salad done."

"Coming, Dad!" Patrick called.

He reached out and ran his thumb over her cheek and across the corner of her mouth. "Sorry, Helen." His voice lowered to a smoky texture that was a little rough around the edges. "Maybe we can finish this...conversation later."

His thumb slid across her lower lip, and she felt the breath being pulled from her lungs. She knew she should pull away, duck under his arm and flee for the kitchen, but somehow she could only stand there staring at the hard line of his lips, lips she knew could be soft, so soft—

"Patrick!" The shout sounded again.

He caught her hand. "Come on. Time to meet my family."

The kitchen was a big warm room at the back of the house. The walls and cupboards were painted bright yellow, and crayon drawings were taped to the refrigerator. A rocking chair in one corner had a knitting bag tossed on its seat, and an upside-down paperback graced the windowsill between two lush, green plants.

The big pine table held eleven people, adults and children. To

Helen, it seemed like all the Monaghans were laughing and talking at once as they devoured steaks and home-baked rolls, a huge salad and corn on the cob.

"Do you all get together like this very often?" Helen whispered as she passed Patrick the salad for the third time.

He grinned. "This isn't all of us. Moira lives in Seattle, and Rand, his wife Zoe, and their kids live in California."

Sean, Patrick's father, winked at Helen from the foot of the table. He was a tall man with faded red hair and a kind, weatherworn face. "You think it's noisy now, but you should hear it at Christmas."

"You all get together at Christmas?" Helen asked curiously.

"Every year," Deirdre, Patrick's oldest sister, chimed in. "We rotate whose house we go to. We all take a turn—at least, all of us who are married." She shot Patrick a meaningful look.

Helen swallowed and slid a sideways glance at Patrick. Deirdre was Tommy's mother. Was there more than a hint in her words?

"Hoping to marry me off so you can get out of your turn, DeeDee?" Patrick drawled.

She bristled. "Of course not! You know I love having Christmas at our house. But I just think—"

"You think you have a duty to get your brothers married," Adam said from the other side of the table. He turned to Helen. "DeeDee's a teacher, and she's tried to fix Patrick or me up with every unmarried teacher in her school."

"That's not true," Deirdre said indignantly.

"Right," Patrick said. "You haven't tried to fix us up with any of the men."

"I just want you to be happy!" she protested. Then she relented, a giggle escaping her lips. "Okay, okay, I'm a terrible meddler. I admit it. So sue me."

Patrick waved his fork at Helen. "Do you have to put up with this from your brothers and sisters?"

She stiffened. The last thing she wanted to talk about was her own family. "I'm an only child."

Deirdre regarded her with sympathy. "That must have been

lonely. There's six of us. I can't even imagine what it would be like to grow up without brothers and sisters.''

Helen looked down at her plate. ''It was...all right.''

''Where do your parents live now?'' Deirdre asked. ''You're not from Evergreen, are you?''

''No. I'm, um, from Seattle.'' She felt a dull flush begin to spread across her cheeks, and she prayed it would go away before it made Deirdre even more curious.

Deirdre looked at her speculatively. ''And do—''

''Give it a rest, Deirdre.'' Patrick put his hand on the back of Helen's chair. ''She came for dinner, not the third degree.''

Helen gave him a grateful look. She didn't want to talk about her family. Not here. Not in front of these happy, loving people. Right now, she wanted to forget about her mother. To pretend, just for a few minutes, that she had a real family. A family like this one.

Bridget broke the awkward silence by standing. ''Well, if everyone's done, I think I'll start cleaning up.''

Helen pushed back her chair and began gathering plates.

Bridget smiled and took the plates out of her hands. ''I know you and Patrick have business to discuss. Go on.''

''But—''

''The men cooked. Deirdre and I'll clean up with the children.'' Bridget bustled off to the sink. ''I've got plenty of help, dear.''

Patrick came up behind Helen and took her hand. She pulled away hastily, but he leaned close, and she saw the laughter in his eyes. ''So are you still in one piece?''

''Why wouldn't I be?''

He tipped his head toward the other end of the kitchen. ''That mob can be a lot to deal with all at once. Not to mention my sister and her insatiable curiosity. And you're not used to big families, are you?''

''No.'' She looked away. ''I'm not.''

''Well, you're great with the kids. A natural.'' Patrick paused. ''Do you want to have your own someday?''

Helen sucked in her breath. Suddenly the air seemed to be filled with a shimmering tension and heat. Against her will, she felt her gaze being pulled back to Patrick. This time she saw hunger in his silver eyes, hunger and desire, and her mind spun from children to the way they were created, to the memory of making love with him that night.…

A slow liquid heat slid through her belly, and she dragged her gaze away from his dangerous eyes. "No," she said tightly. "I don't want kids. All my energy goes into my career. I don't have any left over for anything else."

"Oh." There was a moment of silence, and then Patrick shrugged. "Come on, darlin'. Dad's waiting in the living room."

Fighting to regain her composure, Helen followed him into the other room. Sean was sitting in a worn leather chair by the window, and Patrick sat on the plaid couch. Helen glanced around, but there was nowhere else to sit. Biting her lip, she sat beside Patrick.

Sean cleared his throat. "I guess we might as well cut to the chase. Helen, Patrick tells me you don't believe he killed Marty Fletcher."

"No, I don't." She forced her mind onto the case, trying not to think about how close she was sitting to Patrick. "But I need more information before I can convince my boss to forget about arresting your son."

Sean nodded slowly. "I see."

"Dad agrees with you, by the way," Patrick said. "He thinks the stolen files must have something to do with why Marty was killed."

"It's too much of a coincidence otherwise," Sean said. "Don't you think, Helen?"

"Probably. But I'd like to know more about the Turner case before I jump to any conclusions. Patrick, will you tell us about it?"

Beside her, Patrick stretched out his long legs. From her peripheral vision, Helen could see the way his jeans stretched over his muscular thighs, see the way the denim cupped his—

She jerked her gaze away and tried to concentrate on what he was saying.

"There's not really that much to tell," he said. "Turner was twenty-five, and she'd been a prostitute since she was a teenager. A chambermaid found her early Sunday morning in a room at the Lucky Seven Motel. The autopsy confirmed she'd been strangled, but we guessed that just by looking at her.''

"Any witnesses?" Her voice sounded a little strange, but nobody else seemed to notice.

"Nope. Turner rented the room on a monthly basis, so she didn't have to check in with the night clerk. And the people on either side of her didn't hear anything.''

"Are you sure she was killed there?" Sean asked.

"Yeah. Probably by a john. So Marty and I split forces. I interviewed her pimp and her friends, and Marty went down to the strip to find anyone who'd seen her that night.''

Helen looked at Patrick. "Did you get anywhere?"

"We only had the case for a day and a half before Marty was shot. I was slogging through interviews, but Marty hit pay dirt. He had an informant who saw Jamie Lee with some guy in a car, heading toward the Lucky Seven. We were on our way to see the informant when Marty was shot.''

"The two cases have to be connected." Sean's face was reflective. "And the break-in at Helen's office confirms it.''

"But what's the connection?" Patrick shoved his hand through his black hair. "I think we should—''

Warning bells went off in Helen's mind. "We?" she interrupted. "Patrick, I already told you. You aren't going to be involved in my investigation. I came to you for information and nothing else.''

"Nothing else?" A smile played around the corners of his mouth, and his silver eyes caught hers and held. Electricity crackled in the air, hot and compelling and dangerous.

She forced herself to look away from him. "Nothing.''

"Are you sure that's wise?" Sean asked quietly.

"What do you mean?"

"Patrick told me that you don't trust the police, that you plan to investigate on your own." He paused. "It could be dangerous.''

"I can take care of myself." Helen lifted her chin. "I'm a prosecutor. I'm used to dealing with criminals. Informants."

Patrick made a frustrated sound. "Dad and I both know that, Helen. But what if you run into trouble? Whoever we're looking for has already killed twice."

"That doesn't mean—"

He cut her off. "I don't want you to get hurt because of this." He paused, and his voice deepened to a low rasp. "Because of *me*."

Helen's heartbeat skidded out of control. What was that emotion she heard in his voice? She had the dangerous urge to turn to him, to look into his pewter eyes and….

Oh, God, she was a fool.

She kept her neck rigid, her gaze fixed straight ahead. "I'm not going to get hurt."

Sean nodded slowly. "You're young. You think you're invincible. I used to think so, too." He pointed to his leg. "How do you think this happened?"

"I…I don't know." She'd noticed his limp earlier but hadn't thought anything of it. Sean had to be well over sixty. People that age often had arthritis.

Sean looked her straight in the eye. "I was shot in the knee during a drug raid. My partner—his name was Ted Wright, and we'd known each other since we were boys—was killed."

The sound of plates clattering and cheerful laughter drifted out from the kitchen. But the living room was silent, the air thrumming with grief.

Helen spoke gently. "I'm very sorry."

Sean's face was drawn. "So am I. But we were both young and reckless. We went in separately, instead of together. We figured we could cover more ground that way, but instead…."

Helen bit her lip. "What are you saying?"

"You're a very brave young woman. But you're not invincible. None of us is. To think so isn't courage, it's foolishness."

"Okay," she said. "I admit there's danger. But I don't see how working with Patrick will make things any safer."

"I'm a police officer," Patrick said. "I have experience dealing with dangerous situations, with violence."

"Are you saying I need protection?"

"Yes," Sean said bluntly. "Someone you can trust absolutely. Someone you can rely on. More than a bodyguard. A *partner*."

Helen's gaze went involuntarily to Patrick. For once he wasn't smiling. His gray eyes were serious, his jaw hard. "You don't have to like me. But you can trust me. I promise I'll protect you." His voice turned slightly ironic. "Whatever you may think of me as a person, I'm a damn good cop."

"I know," she said. "But—"

"I know the case. I know the players. You need me, Helen." His eyes never left her face. "If you really want to win this case, you need me."

Helen looked down at her clenched hands. The case. She had to remember that the important thing was the case. This case could make her career. She couldn't let her emotions—her fear of losing control, of giving in to the feelings that swept through her each time they touched—make her lose sight of her goal.

She took a deep breath. "Okay. We'll work together on this." Patrick's face split into a grin, and she gave him a hard stare. "But I have to be in charge."

He saluted her with two fingers. "Aye-aye, Captain."

She folded her arms across her chest. "I'm serious. You mess things up, and I could get tossed off this case. Or even out of the prosecutor's office. And you could end up in jail."

"I know. Don't worry, we'll work together."

Together. The word was seductive. Dangerous. A shiver of anticipation raced down her spine.

Patrick's mouth curved in a smile as tempting as sin. "Together," he repeated softly.

Her mouth went dry. Memories flooded through her. Memories of Patrick whispering against her throat, his breath, his lips, setting her skin alight. Memories of collapsing onto his bed—*together*—legs tangled, skin fused. Wanting. Needing. Taking.

Helen squeezed her eyes shut. She flattened her palms against the rough wool of the couch, fighting for control. What was she doing? How could she let Patrick make her remember, make her feel those same things again?

He'd exploded through her life like a blazing meteor once, but she wouldn't let it happen again. This time, they would *work* together. That was all.

This time, she'd keep control.

Gritting her teeth, she forced her eyes open.

Patrick was watching her with a hint of something like amusement lurking around his lips. "So what's our first move, Cap'n?"

She cleared her throat, trying to sound competent. Businesslike. "I'm going to reinterview the eyewitness tonight."

"I'll go with you."

"You can't. She's identified you as a murderer—she'd hardly welcome you into her home."

"So I'll just come along for the ride and wait outside."

She wanted desperately to refuse, but she'd already agreed to work with him. She knew she'd better start getting used to having him around. And it was only a car ride, after all. Surely she could handle that.

Grudgingly she nodded.

"What next?" Sean asked.

"I want to head down to the strip," Patrick said. "Marty's informant is out there somewhere."

Helen drummed her fingers against the couch. "Patrick, I've been thinking about the informant. I know Marty didn't tell you who it was. But you didn't get along, did you?"

"That's the understatement of the century."

"Could he have told someone else? Maybe his wife?"

Patrick rubbed his hand over his jaw. "I guess it's possible. Let's go talk to her tomorrow."

"I'll go," she said. "You'd better not come."

"Why?"

"Why?" She stared at him. "She probably thinks you murdered her husband!"

"Angel?" Patrick threw back his head and laughed, long and deep. "No way."

Helen's eyes narrowed. "Angel?"

"That's her name. At least, that's what her friends call her."

"You know her...well?"

"Well enough. I know she doesn't think I killed Marty. In fact, she called me the day after the murder and invited me over."

"Why didn't you tell me this before?" she demanded.

"I didn't think it was important. She wasn't asking me over to talk about the case."

"No?" An unexpected spurt of anger squeezed in her chest. "Then why was she inviting you over? For comfort?"

He grinned wickedly. "You could call it that."

"Patrick!" Sean barked. "You didn't—"

"No, Dad, I didn't go. I had enough on my mind. I'd just gotten back from the lineup, and I was expecting to be arrested in the morning."

"And I suppose if it wasn't for that, you would have been over there like a shot?" Helen asked.

Patrick tucked his hand under her chin, tilting it up so he could look into her eyes. Humor glimmered in his gaze. "What's this? Jealousy?"

She scowled and jerked her head away from his strong hand, trying to pretend his touch didn't affect her. "No, of course not. I just wish you'd told me before."

He shrugged. "I'll call her tonight and tell her we're coming over in the morning."

"You do that." She looked at her watch and stood. "We'd better get going."

Sean got to his feet and shook her hand. His palm was calloused and hard, his handshake firm. "Thank you for helping my son. You're a good woman, Helen Stewart."

Warmth curled through her at his words. She sensed that Sean Monaghan's approval wasn't something he gave lightly.

"Thank you," she said quietly.

Sean put his other hand on top of their clasped ones. "Please. Come and see me and Bridget any time you like. If you're in the area, stop by and say hello. We'd love to see you."

She smiled. "I'll be sure to stop by sometime."

After they said their goodbyes, Helen and Patrick walked out to her car. It had stopped raining and the darkened street smelled clean and fresh. Helen unlocked the passenger door and walked around to the driver's side.

She climbed into her car and started the engine, sliding a sideways look at Patrick. "I enjoyed meeting your parents. And the rest of your family. They're lovely people."

He flashed her a smile. "They liked you, too."

"Your family seems really close," she said, unable to keep a hint of wistfulness from her tone.

"Yeah, I guess we are. My parents—when we were kids, they taught us that family is the most important thing. More important than anything else." He glanced at her, his gaze oddly intense. "I think all of us grew up to agree with them."

"I can see that."

He was silent for a moment, and when he spoke again, his voice was casual. Almost too casual. "By the way, don't feel like you have to take my dad's invitation too seriously."

"Why?" she asked curiously. "Does he ask every woman you bring for dinner to come back and visit?"

"No." Patrick cleared his throat. "Other than my ex-wife, I've never brought a woman here for dinner. Except you."

She stared at him. Other than his ex-wife, she was the only one? But why—

The answer occurred to her even before the question had fully formed in her mind. The only reason he'd brought her there was to discuss the case with his father. It was business, not personal.

And that was all she wanted it to be, she reminded herself as she pulled out onto the street. Business. The fact that she'd let Patrick kiss her in the hallway before dinner meant absolutely nothing.

Nothing at all.

Chapter 6

Helen drove toward Tammy's apartment. She was intensely aware of Patrick, who lounged in the passenger seat, staring out the window. The air between them was charged, but neither of them spoke. The only sounds were the rhythmic shush of the wipers, the patter of the rain on the roof.

In silence, Helen turned onto Salish Avenue.

Patrick shifted restlessly. "Where does the witness live?"

"Out at the other end of Salish."

"On Salish?" He jerked upright and smacked his fist into his palm. "That's it! We've got her!"

"What are you talking about?"

"Didn't you say she was on her way home from her shift at the hospital when she witnessed the shooting?"

"That's what she said in her statement."

"She was lying."

Helen shook her head. "I don't get it."

"Don't you? Think about it. Where's the hospital?"

"It's downtown by the harbor, of course."

Patrick grinned. "And Tammy lives on Salish."

Suddenly, Helen saw what he was getting at. The fastest way to get to Tammy's apartment from the hospital was straight up Salish. The old highway, where the shooting had occurred, was south of town, in completely the wrong direction.

Helen raised her hand to her cheek. It felt hot. "I can't believe I didn't think of that."

He reached over and rubbed the back of her neck. Warmth radiated from his fingers as he massaged the tight muscles. "Don't worry about it. You can't think of everything."

She knew she should bat his hand away, but it felt good. Very good. The tension loosened as he dug in a little harder, and she had to stifle an instinctive groan of pleasure. "I—I overlooked a pretty major detail there," she managed to finally say.

"So you're not perfect. None of us is."

"But you caught it right away."

"I've lived in Evergreen all my life. Probably know the roads a lot better than you do." His hand slid down to her shoulder, and he rubbed deeply. "You've got to relax. Your muscles are way too tight."

She felt his touch all the way to her toes. Each of her senses was perfectly attuned to him—to the smell of his leather jacket and the weight of his hand, to the fit of his jeans and the black hair that spilled over his forehead. And to the way her tension melted beneath his touch, the instinctive loosening of her muscles, the shimmers of heat that slid through her, pooling in the pit of her stomach. Little by little, she felt her control slipping away....

She couldn't let this happen!

Abruptly she jerked away from his hand. "We're almost there," she said, trying to sound stern.

He gave her a lopsided grin that made her heart flip over. "Good. The sooner you talk to her, the sooner we can prove she was lying." His grin faded. "I wish I could be there."

Helen frowned. "You don't think I can handle it?"

"That's not what I meant. I just want to *do* something."

She shot him a look. "You were the one who wanted to come."

"Yeah, I know." He shrugged and lapsed into silence.

Tammy's pink stucco condo loomed up on the right. Helen turned into the private parking lot and pulled into a spot across from the building. She glanced at Patrick as she dumped her keys into her purse. "I shouldn't be more than half an hour or so."

"Take your time."

Her eyes narrowed. "What are you up to?"

"Nothing." His expression was innocent—too innocent.

"You're planning something, aren't you?"

His lips quirked, and she saw the wicked gleam in his eyes. "I might go for a little walk. Or something."

She stared at him for a long moment, and then she sighed in resignation. "Just make sure no one sees you." She slid out of the car, and then paused. "Patrick?"

"Yeah?"

"The flashlight's in the glove compartment."

Helen buzzed Tammy's number, and the front door clicked open. Resisting the urge to glance back at Patrick, she walked inside. She took the stairs to the second floor and knocked on Tammy's door.

A second later Tammy pulled it open. She'd touched up her hair since yesterday; the dark roots were gone, and the rest of her hair was a brassy red. Instead of her white nurse's uniform, she wore tight jeans and a purple satin blouse.

She glared at Helen. "You're late."

Helen's chest tightened. She was only five minutes late, but even that much was uncharacteristic of her. She was never late for anything.

Why was it that since Patrick had come back into her life, everything had turned upside down?

She forced a smile to her lips. "I'm sorry. I hope I haven't inconvenienced you."

Scowling, Tammy opened the door a little wider. "Come in. But this better not take long. I've got a date in half an hour."

"On a Wednesday night?" Helen asked, surprised.

"I'm a nurse. I don't get weekends off like you lawyers. Not that it's any of your business." Tammy spun on her heel.

Helen followed her into the apartment and down a short hall-way filled with the cloying scent of an air freshener. The hall opened into a living room, and she glanced around.

The room was cluttered with furniture, all flashy and new. There was a matching blue plush sofa and love seat, and several black-lacquered coffee tables with gold accents were scattered around. In one corner stood an enormous television set. On the screen, a blond woman dripping diamonds sobbed in the arms of a tuxedo-clad older man.

Tammy picked up a remote control and muted the sound, leaving the picture on. She sat on the sofa and planted her feet squarely in front of her as though she was preparing to do battle. "So what do you want this time?"

"I want to talk to you about your statement."

Tammy scowled. "So talk."

Helen sat on the love seat. Something sharp dug into her thigh. She shifted uncomfortably and reached down to move whatever was poking her. A handful of papers had slipped down between the cushions, and she pulled them out. As she leaned forward to put them on the coffee table, she noticed there were several glossy travel brochures among them.

A thread of excitement twisted through her. It couldn't be a coincidence that Tammy was planning to leave town.

Keeping her face cool and calm, she looked up and met the other woman's eyes. "Going on a vacation?"

Tammy stiffened. "So what? I work hard. I'm entitled."

Helen picked up one of the brochures. "'Cruise the Mediter-ranean in Luxury,'" she read out loud. "Sounds pretty nice. Just the kind of vacation I need, too." She kept her voice light.

Tammy relaxed slightly. "Yeah. It'll be fun. I've never—" She stopped short.

Been on a cruise before, Helen mentally completed Tammy's statement. She flipped open the brochure and glanced at the prices. For a one-week cruise, they started at five thousand dollars. Luxury indeed. A very expensive luxury for a young nurse who was probably still paying off her furniture, not to mention her mortgage and her car payments.

Helen leaned forward. "Come into some money recently?"

"Maybe I did," Tammy said belligerently.

"Where from?"

"That's none of your business."

Anger flooded through Helen's chest. Tammy's lies had just about landed Patrick in jail. She wasn't going to sit here and listen to any more of them.

"I can make it my business." She slapped the brochure down on the table. "You're a witness in a major felony case. If you've been paid to lie, you're in serious trouble."

"Nobody's paid me!"

"We can subpoena your bank records. See if there are any major deposits in the last few weeks."

Tammy smirked. "You go right ahead."

"We can look at every financial transaction you've made for years. And not just your bank accounts, but your mortgage. Your credit record. *Everything*. You'd be better off telling the truth right now."

Tammy twisted her hands in her lap. "I *have* told the truth!"

There was a heartbeat's pause, and then Helen spoke. "Let's cut the crap. Why don't you tell me the real reason you were out on the old highway Monday night?"

"I already told you. I was on my way home from work."

"Via the highway? That's in the wrong direction."

"Maybe I wanted to visit a girlfriend on my way home."

"At one o'clock in the morning?" Helen demanded.

"She keeps late hours."

"What's her name? Where does she live?"

Tammy shifted uneasily. "I don't have to tell you that."

Helen pressed on. "Tell me again what you saw."

"I was driving down the road. I saw a car off to one side."

"Facing you? Or facing the other way?"

"Facing the other way."

"Then what?" Helen prompted.

"I slowed down. And I saw two men in front of the car."

"If they were in front of the car, how did you see them? You were behind the car, right?"

"I just did," Tammy mumbled.

"Where were they standing? Be precise."

Tammy moistened her lips. "Uh, the shorter one was standing in front of the car with his back to me. The taller one—the guy I saw at the police station—was standing by the passenger door, facing the shorter guy. And—"

Helen leaned forward. "And what?"

"Nothing."

It was a lie. Helen saw it in Tammy's eyes.

"Who else was there?" Her voice was as hard and cold as ice.

Tammy jerked her head up with a violent movement. "Nobody!"

Helen stood. "Do you realize that if you lie in court, you'll be committing perjury? And believe me, I'll make it my personal mission in life to see that you go to jail."

"But I'm telling the truth! There was no one else there. There were only the thr—" She stumbled to a halt. "I mean, the two of them."

Three. She'd been about to say three.

Helen's heart pounded. Patrick had been right. There had been someone else out there that night. And it looked like Tammy knew exactly who it was.

Trying to hide her elation, she took a card from her pocket and dropped it onto the coffee table. "Think carefully about your story. When you decide to tell the truth, call my pager. Day or night."

"I have told you the tr—"

Helen cut her off. "Is it worth any amount of money to protect a murderer? What if he decides to come after you next?"

"Get out!" Tammy's voice rose. "Get out of my house!"

Helen walked down the hall. "I'm going. But I'll be back to see you again. And next time, I'll have that subpoena."

Tammy slammed the door in her face.

Patrick glanced at the glowing dial of his watch. Twenty-five after nine. Helen had been inside for almost half an hour. He'd better head back to meet her.

He shone the flashlight through the window of Tammy's Trans Am for one last look, making a mental note of the box of condoms that peeked out from under the passenger seat. Tammy was sleeping with someone—he'd just love to find out who.

He switched off the flashlight and headed back around to the other side of the building. As he rounded the corner, he caught sight of Helen. She was striding down the front walk, her face alight. She stepped off the paved curb and into the parking lot, heading toward her car.

Patrick jogged across the wet grass. "Hey," he called. "What hap—"

The squeal of tires on wet pavement interrupted his words. A car hurtled out of nowhere, its headlights blinding. A thousand pounds of steel raced straight at Helen.

"Look out!" Patrick shouted. He sprinted across the lawn. "Helen!"

The car gained on her. The engine roared as the driver pushed it ever faster. Helen half turned, her mouth opening in a silent scream, and then the car was on her.

"Helen! No!" Patrick's bellow hung in the air. Tires screeching, the car pulled out onto Salish and disappeared. Patrick didn't even spare it a glance as he charged across the pavement to Helen.

She lay facedown between two parked cars. Patrick threw himself down on his knees beside her still form and grabbed her hand. It was limp—limp and lifeless—and hot, searing agony speared his chest.

She was dead. *Dead.* Just like....

The memories he'd tried so hard to bury three years ago spilled over into his heart, and a fresh wave of anguish burst through him. Moisture burned the backs of his eyes and he bowed his head.

Oh, God, Helen was dead, and it was his fault. Not an hour ago he'd promised he would protect her, and he'd failed. Failed to protect an innocent life...again. And this time he couldn't blame Jessica, couldn't blame anyone but himself.

"I'm so sorry," he whispered hoarsely. He knew Helen couldn't hear him, but he had to say the words, had to say them not just for her, but for the precious life he'd lost three long years ago. "So sorry."

"P-Patrick?" Helen whispered.

His breath froze in his throat. Surely he must have imagined her voice. Surely—

She stirred beneath his hands, and then her eyelids fluttered open.

Relief exploded through his body, sending a fierce rush of dizziness to his head. Thank God. She was alive.

"I'm here, sweetheart." His heart thudded against his ribs, and he fought to keep his voice calm. He stroked his hand across her hair. "Tell me where it hurts."

She started to push herself upright, and he put his arms around her, holding her securely against his chest. Her damp hair brushed his cheek, and he closed his eyes, his heart still pounding. He could feel her shaking, and he smoothed his hand up and down her back, murmuring low words of comfort as he would to a wounded child.

After a minute she pulled away. Opening his eyes, he saw that her cheek was scraped where she'd hit the pavement, and her elegant navy suit was wet and torn.

She raised the heel of her palm to her forehead. "I'm—I think I'm okay. The car…it didn't hit me." Her voice shook. "I heard you yell, and I jumped just in time."

He held her close. "It's okay, sweetheart. Don't think about it. Let's just get you home."

She gave a shaky laugh as she pulled away from him and got awkwardly to her feet. "Second time in two days someone's nearly run me over. I'm starting to think I'm jinxed."

Her words were light, but her face was pale and her legs unsteady. A fresh bolt of concern splintered through him, and he wrapped his arm around her waist. "Take it slow, Helen."

"I'm okay." She glanced up at him. "Really."

Patrick didn't loosen his grip. "Humor me."

She leaned against him just a little as they walked back to her car. He opened the passenger door and gently eased her inside. "Give me the keys."

"I can drive."

"No way."

"I'm fine. Really." She pushed herself unsteadily to her feet.

Patrick caught her arm and steadied her. "Don't be so stubborn. You were just about run over—that's enough to give anyone a shock. Now give me the keys."

She glared at him. "Don't order me around."

"Order you around?" He raked his hand through his hair. "I'm only trying to protect you."

Her eyes narrowed. "Protect me from what?"

The tangled mass of emotions that had boiled inside him since he'd seen the car racing toward her suddenly spilled over into anger. He grabbed her by the shoulders and glared down into her face. "Someone tried to kill you not five minutes ago. What the hell do you think I want to protect you from?"

"You think—" She moistened her lips. "You don't think it was an accident?"

"If that was an accident, I'm Ronald Reagan. That car was headed straight at you. If you hadn't dived out of the way, you'd be dead."

Her face went white, and she swayed dangerously. Patrick threw his arms around her, feeling the quivers of tension and fear that ran through her slender body. She put her arms around his neck, burying her face against his shoulder.

They stood that way for a long time. Gradually, Patrick's anger and fear edged away, melting into something else. Something else altogether. He became all too aware of Helen's slender body, her hips cradled against his, her breasts pressed against his chest. Her warm breath whispered against his neck. She shifted slightly, and his body stirred to life.

Patrick clenched his teeth, trying to suppress his reaction. This was definitely not the time or the place—but his body didn't care. He tried changing the angle of his hips, but Helen moved with him. His groin tightened even more, and he swore silently. Dammit, what was *wrong* with him?

Putting his hands on her shoulders, he eased himself away from her. "Okay, now?"

She gave him a faint smile. "I'm okay. But I think maybe you'd better drive after all."

"Good."

She lowered herself into the passenger seat and handed him the keys. He took them and curled his fingers around the back of her neck in a brief caress. Closing her door, he walked around to the driver's side.

The engine fired up with a smooth purr that was completely unlike the rattle and roar of his own car. Putting it in gear, he pulled out onto the road. Through narrowed eyes, he scanned the streets for any sign of a brown sedan.

Nothing.

After a few minutes Helen spoke. "Tammy—the witness—has been paid off."

Patrick frowned. In his concern for Helen, he'd forgotten all about the witness. "She has?"

"I'm pretty sure. There was someone else out there on Monday night with you and Marty. She let that much slip. Whoever it was must have paid her to lie."

He slammed his palm against the steering wheel. "So there *was* somebody else there." Somebody who'd probably just tried to kill Helen. His stomach twisted with something unpleasantly like guilt. If he could remember who it was—if he'd tried harder, done something different—would this even have happened?

If he'd tried harder, would it have happened before?

He clamped down on that thought. He wouldn't—couldn't—think about that. Not now.

He forced his mind away from his past and back to the night Marty was killed. There was nothing there, nothing but a dark empty space, and he gritted his teeth in frustration. "Dammit, why can't I remember?"

"It's not your fault," Helen said quietly.

"Yeah. Right."

She slid him a sideways glance, but said nothing.

He took a deep breath. "Did Tammy give any hint of who it was?"

"No. But I think...." Her voice lowered. "You were probably right last night. Whoever it was probably meant to kill you, too."

"Why do you say that?"

"Because even though she's obviously been paid to lie, Tammy didn't want to talk to me. And yesterday she didn't want to identify anyone. She said she didn't think she'd have to. Why?"

He bit back a curse. "If Marty and I were both dead, she wouldn't have had to ID anyone. She would've told her story to the cops, and that's it."

"Exactly." Helen paused. "Patrick? You'll be...careful?"

The concern in her voice sent strange tingles dancing through his body, and he brushed his fingers across her cheek. "You're the one who has to be careful. You almost got run over tonight. Not me."

"Did you get a look at the car? See who was driving?"

"Not really. It was a brown sedan, a late-seventies model. An American make. But I didn't see the driver." All he'd seen was Helen, caught in the headlights like a startled deer, with the car hurtling toward her. He hadn't seen the driver. He hadn't even looked at the tags.

Hell. Some cop he was.

Her brow wrinkled. "A brown sedan? Why does that seem familiar?"

"Do you know anyone who drives one?"

"No, not a seventies model. Franklin has a brown Mercedes, but it's pretty new." She bit her lip. "But I think I've seen an older brown car lately. I just can't think where."

"Try to think. Did you see it by your house? Or by your work? Maybe following you?"

Her eyes widened. "Wait a minute. I think—I think there was an old brown car outside my apartment last night while you were there. I saw it when I went into the kitchen."

"Are you sure about that?"

"Pretty sure. Do you think someone's following you?" Her face paled. "Or do you think they're following *me?*"

"I don't know." He tightened his hands on the steering wheel. "I wish I did."

Helen sighed. "It's hard to believe someone would want to kill me."

A fresh blade of guilt stabbed through him, mingling with remembered anger and pain. "The only reason someone would want to kill you is because of me."

"Because of the case, you mean."

Patrick drummed his fingers on the steering wheel as he turned onto Ocean Drive. "Maybe you'd better drop the case."

She jerked around and stared at him. In the faint glow of the streetlights, he saw the dark scrape across her cheek. The knife of guilt twisted a little deeper.

"Drop the case?" she demanded. "Have you lost your mind?"

"It's too dangerous."

"Then you're going to drop it, too?"

"No."

She scowled. "So it's too dangerous for me, but not for you? Why, Monaghan? Because I'm a woman?"

"No. Because it's not your problem."

"Not my problem? I'm the prosecutor, dammit." Her hands curled into fists. "I have to win this case."

He didn't miss the urgency in her voice. "Why is this case so important?"

"It could make my career. If I win, Franklin's offered to make me the executive deputy prosecutor. It's the best job in the office."

"And if you lose?"

"You said it last night." Her expression was tight, but he sensed the fear beneath it. "He'll throw me to the dogs without a thought."

Helen's building appeared on his right, and Patrick turned into her driveway. He pressed the door opener clipped to her visor, and the garage door rumbled upward.

He swept into the garage, parked in the space she pointed out, and came around to open her door. As he helped her to her feet, he chose his words carefully. "Is your career worth risking your life for? You almost died back there. And whoever did this will probably try again.''

Her eyes were bleak, bleak and empty. ''You don't understand. My career *is* my life. If I throw it away, what have I got left?''

''Everything you already have. Intelligence. Courage.'' His gaze dropped from her eyes to her mouth. ''Beauty.''

She snorted. ''Beauty. Right.'' She pulled away from him and started walking toward the elevator, her gait unsteady. ''Give me a break, Monaghan. Your charm is getting pretty tired.''

''Charm?'' He caught up with her and slid his arm around her waist. ''That wasn't charm. That was the simple truth.''

She tossed him a skeptical look. ''And how many women have you said that to in the past year?''

He didn't take his eyes from hers. ''Not one, Helen. Not a single one.''

Helen sucked in her breath. A bell dinged and the elevator doors slid open, but she didn't move. ''I'm not giving up this case. And nothing you say will change that. Nothing.''

Patrick stared at her. Her eyes were determined—as determined as those of any cop—and her jaw was set. Her slender hands were squeezed into fists, and he could tell by the set of her lips that she meant every word she said.

He nodded slowly, acknowledging defeat.

When they got to Helen's door, Patrick unlocked it quietly. ''Stay here,'' he whispered.

''Why?'' she rasped.

He tossed her an exasperated look. ''Do you even have to ask? What if someone's waiting inside?''

''I'm coming in with you.''

''No, you're—''

She pushed past him, marched into the hallway, and flipped on the lights. ''See? There's nobody here.'' Before he could stop her, she stalked down the hall, turning on every light. Swearing under his breath, he followed her.

Kitchen. Living room. Bathroom. All clear.

While she inspected the hall closet, he opened the last door. It was her bedroom. The cathedral ceiling was paneled in cedar, and her window was open, letting in the scent of the rain and the sea. Patrick scanned the room and checked the closet. There was nothing inside but rows of suits and blouses.

Turning from the closet, he looked around curiously. The room was every bit as classy as the rest of her apartment. A wrought-iron antique bedstead was covered with a fluffy midnight-blue duvet. On the oak bedside table stood a brass clock and a heavy leather-bound book. Patrick glanced at the title, and his mouth twisted. *Current Developments in Legal Philosophy.* Fascinating.

He walked over to the dresser. A heavy silver frame stood in one corner, holding a formal graduation photo of Helen looking serious and beautiful. A crystal dish held a few pairs of simple gold earrings. There was nothing else.

He frowned, glancing around the room again. There were no pictures. No letters. No cards. Nothing to indicate that she had friends and family back in Seattle—or here in Evergreen, for that matter.

My career is my life, she'd said downstairs. And earlier she'd told him she didn't have enough energy left over for anything else. His frown deepened. Did that include even friends and family?

"What the hell are you doing in here?"

Patrick spun around. Helen stood in the doorway, her fists jammed onto her hips. A tiny splinter of anger stabbed at his heart. Tightening his jaw, he tried to ignore it. What did he care if Helen was glaring at him as though he were an intruder?

Okay, so he wanted her. Wanted her badly. And she wanted him, too—he was sure of it. But that was just sex.

It shouldn't come as a big surprise that she didn't welcome his presence here amid her antiques and her crystal and her designer suits.

He didn't belong here, in her world. He never had. And he never would.

Not that he even wanted to. He'd tried that life with Jessica—tried and failed. And he'd ended up with nothing, nothing but shattered dreams and an emptiness deep inside where he'd once had love and hope.

He wasn't crazy enough to want to try it all over again. Not with Helen. Not with anyone.

Dragging in a breath, he looked up.

Helen was still glaring at him. "Well?" she demanded. "What are you doing?"

He gave a casual shrug. "Calm down, darlin'. I was just checking to make sure there was nobody in here."

"You thought someone might be hiding under the bed?"

"Anything's possible. You probably would have laughed earlier if I'd said someone might try to run you over."

"I suppose you're right. But we've checked the whole apartment, and it's secure." Helen picked up the phone beside the bed. "I'll call you a cab."

"A cab? What for?"

"Seeing as you don't want me to drive, you'll have to take a cab home. Unless you want to walk."

He shook his head. "I'm not going anywhere tonight."

She gasped. "You arrogant son of a—"

He grinned. "Is that an invitation?"

"What?"

"Well, I was thinking I'd sleep on your couch. You seem to be under the impression I'd be in your bed. Of course, if you'd prefer it that way...." He waggled his eyebrows.

She threw up her hands. "You are the most impossible man. What am I going to do with you?"

"I could make a few suggestions," he drawled.

"I just bet you could." She folded her arms across her breasts. "But you can forget it. You're not staying here tonight."

"It's up to you. But I don't know how old Gary across the hall will like having me outside your door in a sleeping bag."

"You wouldn't!"

He gave her a charming smile. "I would."

"Why, dammit?"

His smile faded. "Because you're in danger, Helen. Even if you don't want to admit it. And if you won't drop the case, you're stuck with me.'' He paused, and his voice roughened. ''I'm going to protect you—whether you like it or not.''

''I don't need your protection,'' she said, but the words were soft.

''Yeah, you do. Somebody's already tried to kill you once. You don't know if and when he'll try again.''

''And you think you can stop him?''

He clenched his fists. ''He'll have to kill me to get to you.''

Her blue eyes widened and a faint pink tinged her cheeks. ''You really mean that, don't you?''

''Yeah,'' he said. ''I do.''

She looked into his eyes. The color on her cheeks deepened, and her chest rose and fell a little faster. Patrick's heart began to thump—a slow, steady rhythm that he could feel throughout his body….

And then she turned away.

''Sheets and blankets are in the linen closet.'' She picked up a pillow from the bed and tossed it to him. ''Good night, Patrick.''

He hesitated for only a moment before he turned and walked out of her room. He closed the door behind him and leaned against the wall, his heart still thumping.

''Sweet dreams, Helen,'' he said softly.

Chapter 7

*H*elen sat in the front seat of the car, her heart thumping with excitement. She could hardly believe she was here—here, in Joe Wallace's jacked-up Duster, with Joe's arm draped around her shoulders.

She'd idolized him for months, but she'd never thought he'd actually ask her out. After all, he was the captain of the basketball team, one of the most popular guys in their high school, and she was just a lowly sophomore—and one with a notorious mother, to boot.

But here she was, in the brand-new turquoise miniskirt she'd bought with her own meager savings. Dangling earrings brushed at her neck, and she'd carefully applied a layer of Plum Passion lipstick to her mouth.

Joe parked the car in the alley behind a rickety house. The thump of a bass boomed through the night, punctuated by loud laughter. It sounded like the party was well under way.

Helen reached for the door, but Joe caught her hand. He grinned at her with the crooked smile that always made her stomach feel as if it was doing cartwheels.

"Let's not go in yet, babe." He reached under the seat and pulled out a thermos. *"Come on, have a drink first."*

He uncapped the thermos and handed it to her. It smelled sweet, like cola, but underneath the sugar she could smell the sharp tang of alcohol. She hesitated, but she didn't want Joe to think she was a baby. Drawing a breath, she lifted the thermos to her lips and drank.

After that, the whole night was a blur. Only pieces remained: Joe kissing her, handing her the thermos for another drink. Swallowing more of the alcohol that burned through her. Giggling wildly, kissing him back….

She woke up the next morning with a pounding headache and little memory of what had happened. She got up and stumbled into the bathroom to look in the mirror. When she saw her bloodshot eyes and stained, crumpled miniskirt, felt the hickey on her neck and the soreness between her legs, she knew.

The catcalls and whistles that followed her at school confirmed her suspicion. As did the sneers and whispers of the other girls.

"Tramp. Whore. Drunk. She's just like her mother."

Just like her mother….

Helen jerked awake, bathed in sweat, the sheets twisted damply around her body. Oh, God, she'd had the dream. Again.

It had been thirteen long years since that terrible night.

And twelve years since Joe Wallace had been killed, driving drunk in his precious Duster. But she kept reliving the nightmare, over and over again. Kept hearing the voices, as clear as if it had all happened yesterday.

Just like her mother, just like her mother….

Violently, Helen threw back the covers. Climbing out of bed, she paced over to the window. She pulled up the wooden blinds and gazed sightlessly out at the ocean. She heard the faint, steady roar of the water as it foamed over the rocks below, but for once, it didn't soothe her.

"I'm not like her," she whispered fiercely. She leaned her forehead against the chilly windowpane, her eyes blurred with tears. She squeezed them back. "I'm not."

Even as she spoke the words, she knew they were a lie. She knew it. She'd always known it. Everybody had.

Like mother, like daughter. All her life, she'd heard the taunt. All her life.

She'd been sixteen when that terrible night with Joe had shown her it was true. Deep down, she really was like her mother. But she'd fought it. Fought her nature. Struggled to keep perfect control. And she'd been winning.

At least, until the night she'd met Patrick.

Helen's throat tightened as the boom of the surf drifted to her ears, mocking her, making her remember....

She hadn't even wanted to go to the annual policemen's charity ball. She'd only gone because Franklin had bought tickets for everyone. She couldn't refuse; attending such functions was part of her job. But she certainly hadn't expected to enjoy it.

She went to the ball and sat in a corner sipping white wine and thinking about the assault case she was prosecuting. As often as she could, she discreetly checked her watch. She figured she could leave at eleven, late enough not to offend anyone but still early enough to get some work done at home.

Everything changed when she glanced up and saw Patrick Monaghan looking right at her.

He was leaning against the bar, a bottle of beer dangling from his hand. He wasn't wearing a tuxedo, but a black jacket and straight-legged jeans that emphasized the breadth of his shoulders and his lean hips. Against the stark white of his shirt, his face looked darkly handsome. Even from across the room, there was something dangerously compelling about him.

He smiled at her and lifted his beer in an impromptu toast. Helen dragged her gaze away. For some reason her cheeks were burning. Something low in her belly fluttered oddly.

She looked back toward the bar out of the corner of her eye, but he was gone. A faint feeling of disappointment filtered through her.

"Dance with me?"

The voice was deep and warm and smooth, gliding over her

like smoke. She jerked around and saw Patrick standing there. He smiled at her, and she swallowed hard. His smile was as attractive as sin and twice as persuasive.

He held out his hand to her, and before she quite knew what she was doing, she had taken it.

They danced several times. To Helen's amazement, she started to have fun. Patrick spun her around the dance floor, trying outrageous moves and making her laugh. He flirted with her so extravagantly that she laughed even more. He was funny and charming and definitely a little crazy, and she realized as the evening wore on that she liked him. Liked him a lot.

But she didn't mean for it to go any further. She didn't date much anyway—only men she knew she could keep at arm's length—and even if she had, she would never have gotten involved with a cop, someone who was practically a co-worker. And definitely not one with a reputation like Patrick's.

At eleven, just as she'd planned, she left.

She walked out to the parking lot, her high heels crunching against gravel. For some reason she half wished she'd stayed a little longer. Danced a few more dances with Patrick. The thought of going home and working just wasn't so appealing anymore.

The wind picked up, and she clutched her coat close to her body, shivering a little as she rounded the corner of the building. When she caught sight of her car, she stopped short.

Patrick was leaning against the hood, whistling softly. The wind ruffled his black hair. In the moonlight he looked mysterious, a little wicked—and irresistibly handsome.

Looking at him, she felt strangely light-headed. It was just the wine, she told herself. She must have drunk a little more than she'd thought.

He looked up and saw her standing there, and his pewter eyes crinkled in a smile. "Hello, darlin'."

"What are you doing on my car?" Helen flushed as soon as the words were out of her mouth. What a stupid question.

But the answer wasn't what she'd expected.

"Thought you might like to head out to the beach." Patrick

raised his voice over the rattle of the wind in the trees. "You said you like to go there when it's stormy. How about right now?"

Helen hesitated, and he grinned. "Don't worry, darlin'. I'm not going to attack you."

"I know," she blurted. She'd heard plenty of gossip about him, but never that he was dangerous. And there was something about his laughing gray eyes that made her feel sure he would never hurt her.

"So how 'bout it?" He held out his hand.

Helen stared at his outstretched hand. Maybe it was the wine, but suddenly she felt reckless. When was the last time she'd done anything spontaneous? Before tonight, how long had it been since she'd really had any fun? And it was just a walk on the beach, after all....

"Okay." She reached out and took Patrick's hand. His palm was warm, and their skin fused, sending tingles of awareness racing through her.

He tugged her toward the car. "Let's go."

Helen drove to the beach. She parked the car, and Patrick leaped out, flinging his arms wide.

"I love it out here!" he shouted above the wind.

His exuberance was catching. Helen kicked off her shoes and ran with him along the beach, reveling in the shriek of the wind and the pounding surf. It started to rain and she raised her face to the cool, stinging drops, drinking in the rain's magic.

They twirled like children, spinning around in circles until they collapsed, dizzy and laughing, onto the wet sand.

Patrick grabbed her hand, still laughing. "Aren't you glad you came, darlin'?"

The rain pelted down. She was covered in sand, her dress was ruined, and she was on a beach at midnight with a madman. And it was wonderful. She felt free, really free, for almost the first time in her life.

"Yes!" Laughter bubbled from her lips. "Yes!"

And he kissed her.

Nothing in her limited experience of men had prepared her for that kiss. It was as potent as the strongest whiskey—hot, fierce, dangerous. Desire sang through her veins like fire, and she felt the last icy remnants of control melt away.

The next morning she woke in Patrick's bed.

She sat up, clutching the sheet to her breasts, and looked down at Patrick's sleeping form. Naked, he was magnificent, sprawling across the tangled sheets like some pagan god. In the air, she could still smell the musky scent of sex.

Waves of utter shame broke over her. What had she done? She'd only had a few glasses of wine—surely that wasn't enough to make her lose control. But how could she have gone to bed with a man she'd only known for one night? And a man with a reputation like Patrick's? Everyone knew his wife had divorced him. Gossip had it he'd been playing around behind her back. Since then, he hadn't stayed with one woman for more than a few weeks.

And she had gone to bed with him. She'd lost control. Completely. Utterly. Oh, God, if anyone found out....

She's just like her mother. The ugly words from all those years ago echoed back to her.

She gathered her things and fled.

As she stared out the window, Helen's chest tightened. Ever since that night, she'd kept control. Tried to forget Patrick, forget the things he'd made her feel. But now he was back in her life, making her remember...making her *want*.

Helen's gaze flickered to the bedroom door. Patrick was just on the other side of that wall. Only a few feet away.

For a long moment she stared at the door, and then she balled her hands into fists and marched back over to her bed. She climbed under the covers and yanked them up to her chin.

"I'm not like my mother." Her voice cracked. "I'm in control."

The rich, warm smell of coffee tickled Helen's nose as she drifted awake. She yawned and stretched, wincing slightly at the soreness in her muscles, and flipped over to look at her clock.

A china cup and saucer blocked it from her view. Steam curled up from the top of the cup, and she frowned. What the—

She bolted upright and saw the bedroom door silently closing. "Patrick?"

He pushed the door back open and smiled at her. "Morning."

Helen stared at him. He looked sleepy, beautiful, and wholly, undeniably male. Dark stubble covered his jaw, and he was wearing nothing but his jeans. She gulped at the sight of his sculpted chest muscles and flat washboard stomach, dusted with finely curling black hair. Something deep inside her jolted to awareness, making warmth bloom through her belly.

She fought back the feeling and struggled to keep her gaze on Patrick's face. "What were you doing in here?"

"Bringing you coffee."

"But—" She glanced at the china cup and shoved her hands through her hair. "What time is it, anyway?"

"Almost six."

"I never would have taken you for an early riser."

"I'm not. But I know you are. And after last night, I figured you could use a good strong cup of coffee first thing."

Helen's mind spun. "You dragged yourself out of bed at the crack of dawn just so you could make me coffee?"

He shrugged. "You would have woken me when you got up anyway."

The warmth in her stomach spread through her limbs. She felt a smile tug at the corners of her mouth. "Thank you."

He looked into her eyes, and his voice deepened to the texture of gravel—rough, caressing. "Anytime."

Helen's heart hammered. With an effort she tore her eyes from his and cleared her throat. "But I don't actually drink coffee until I'm back from my morning run."

"You want to run this morning?"

"I run every morning."

Patrick's eyes darkened with concern. "You sure you want to go today? How are you feeling?"

"Fine." Helen climbed out of bed, grimacing as her feet hit

the floor. "Maybe a little stiff. But I'm sure I want to run today. I always do my best thinking on my morning run."

"Then I'll come with you."

She walked over to her dresser and opened one of her drawers. "Think you can keep up with me, Monaghan?"

He grinned. "Sure I can."

"Five miles?"

"Okay." He slid his hand absently over his stomach. "But we'll have to go to my place first so I can change."

She froze. The thought of going to his apartment—of returning to a place so filled with dangerous memories—sent a touch of panic racing through her body.

"No," she said. "No, we can't go there."

He raised his eyebrows. "You want me to run in my jeans?"

"You go change. I'll meet you at Centennial Park."

"My car's still out on South Commercial."

"I'll drop you off," she said. "You can pick up your car, go home and change, and meet me at the park."

"We already talked about this last night. For now, we'd better stick together."

Helen jammed her hands onto her hips. "I think I can handle being on my own for half an hour. I don't need a keeper."

Patrick pushed himself away from the door and looked at her closely. His eyes narrowed. "What's wrong?"

"Nothing," she snapped.

Patrick took a step toward her. His eyes didn't look sleepy anymore, and the teasing light was gone. Helen had the terrible feeling that he saw past her defenses, past her walls, and right into the most secret parts of her mind...and her heart.

"You don't want to go to my apartment," he said.

Helen shrugged and looked away.

"Why?" he asked softly.

"I just don't." She tossed her clothes onto her rumpled bed and folded her arms across her chest.

Patrick took another step closer. "It's because of what happened between us last year, isn't it? You're afraid."

She snorted. "Afraid of what?"

"Maybe you're afraid to remember that the ice you surround yourself with can be melted."

"No!" Her voice was a little too loud, and she hoped Patrick didn't hear the panic in it. "No, I'm not afraid."

"You're not? Prove it."

She was trapped. Clenching her fists, she dug her fingernails into her palms. "Fine. We'll go to your apartment. Now get the hell out of my room so I can change."

"Sure thing." He turned and headed out of her room. "I'll meet you in the hall in ten minutes."

Helen banged the door shut behind him.

The first fingers of dawn were just streaking over the eastern horizon. Helen's heart pounded as she strode up the steps to Patrick's building. Patrick unlocked the front door and held it open. Dragging in a breath, she plunged inside.

The entrance hall was clean but a little shabby, just as she remembered. Her feet echoed against worn linoleum as she followed Patrick down the hall to his door.

He unlocked three dead bolts and pushed it open. "Come on in."

Helen's throat tightened, but she forced herself to follow him inside. Patrick closed the door and shrugged out of his jacket, tossing it carelessly across an old leather armchair.

He turned back to her, and her breath caught. Memory flashed through her like lightning, trailing streamers of desire. This was exactly what had happened before. He'd turned and braced his arm against the wall, and then he'd—

"Helen?" Patrick's deep voice brought her crashing back to the present. "Are you all right?"

She gulped. "No, I...." Her voice trailed off as she stared into his eyes.

The concern in his eyes faded into heat, heat and some emotion she couldn't identify. Helen moistened her lips, her heartbeat suddenly racing out of control.

Patrick stepped slowly toward her. He planted his hand against the door, bracing himself as he lowered his head. Her lips parted, her stomach turning to liquid heat. She felt his warm breath on her face, saw his eyes darken to the color of smoke.

She knew she should open her mouth to say no, should push him away, but she couldn't speak, couldn't move, could only stand there, her bones melting, waiting….

And then his lips were on hers, testing, teasing, claiming her with a kiss of quicksilver fire. Heat exploded deep in the pit of her stomach, skidding through her body.

Helen wrapped her arms around his neck. She plowed her fingers into his hair, tangling them in the black, silky depths. Patrick slowly pushed her back against the door. He deepened the kiss, his tongue sliding past her lips to twine with hers.

She made a sound of pleasure deep in her throat at the taste of him—it was like wind and rain and fire. Patrick wrapped his arm around her hips and pulled her even closer. His strength was magnetic, compelling. She pressed herself against him, wanting to feel every contour of his hard, muscular body.

Her head fell back as he traced a line of kisses across her jaw and down her throat. The rasp of his unshaven jaw against her skin was erotic. She shuddered with pleasure, her hands clenching in his hair as he traced her collarbone with his tongue.

Patrick lifted his head and looked into her eyes, his lips less than an inch from hers. He was breathing hard, his chest rising and falling rapidly. His gaze fell to her mouth, and his eyes darkened.

She tightened her arms around his neck, pulling his head back down to hers. This time the gentleness was gone from his kiss. His mouth slanted across hers, hard and demanding. He kissed her with a fierce, possessive passion that told her unmistakably that she was his. She moved her hips instinctively against his, and a groan exploded from his lips, a groan of pure masculine frustration and need.

Suddenly the telephone rang. The sound pierced through the haze that clouded Helen's thoughts, dragging her up from the smoky depths of desire.

Patrick lifted his head from hers, his eyes almost black. "Ignore it," he rasped. "They'll call back."

For one wild moment she almost listened to him, but then the telephone rang again. The sound was like a knife, slicing away the last clinging remnants of whatever insanity had gripped her. She pushed away from Patrick with a little cry, wrenched open the door, and fled.

Adrenaline pumped through her body as she ran into the lobby, slammed her way through the door, and charged out into the chill morning rain. Ignoring her car, she raced down the street, her heart pounding with shame and fury and the tattered remains of desire, trying to outrun the knowledge of her own weakness.

"Helen!" Patrick shouted.

She didn't look over her shoulder, just kept running.

"Helen, stop!"

She put on a burst of speed. Her lungs burned, and she gulped for air. She wasn't a sprinter, but she prayed she could outrun him.

Footsteps pounded behind her. A hand closed over her arm, yanking her to a halt. Patrick. Desperately, she tried to wrench her arm out of his grasp, but he held on. To her horror, she found that the warmth of his fingers was almost welcome against her wet, chilled skin.

Hot tears of shame clogged her eyes. "Let me go," she insisted. "Just let me go."

"I can't." Patrick's voice was flat. "It's not safe for you to be out here alone, darlin'."

"Darling? Is that what I am?" She raised her hand to dash away a wet strand of hair that was stuck to her cheek. "Me and how many other women?"

His eyes narrowed. "Is that what this is about? Other women? Okay, I admit I haven't lived like a monk. But—"

She suppressed the urge to stamp her foot like a child. "I don't care how many other women you've slept with, Monaghan. But I'm not going to be one of them. You can't just sleep with me and toss me away."

"Toss you away? What the hell are you talking about? You're the one who crawled out of my bed and took off without a word."

She gasped in fury. "Are you telling me that if I'd stayed, you would have been happy to have me there in the morning? That you wanted more than just—''

"You never bothered to find out what I wanted," he said harshly. "You didn't even give me a chance."

"A chance?" She glared at him. "I knew too much about you, Monaghan. Love 'em and leave 'em, that's your specialty."

"I never made anyone any promises."

"No?" Helen balled her cold, wet hands into fists and jammed them onto her hips. "Not even to your wife?"

Pure, cold rage slid over his face, turning his eyes to ice. "Leave her out of this."

"Why? You said you never made anyone any promises. What would you call a marriage vow? Just how many times did you break that vow before she threw you out?"

"I never broke it! Not once!"

Helen tossed her head, her wet hair slapping against her neck. "You expect me to believe that? Knowing your reputation?"

"I don't give a damn what you believe."

"Then why did you get divorced? Tell me!"

He turned away, his arms folded across his chest, a muscle working in his jaw.

"I thought so," she said contemptuously.

He lifted his head to look at her, his eyes dark and dangerously turbulent. "Then you thought wrong," he said roughly. "You thought wrong."

Helen stared at him as cold rain trickled down her neck. He was telling the truth. She heard it in the rasp of his voice, the raw, aching anger in his eyes.

She took a deep breath. "Then why?"

"Why?" he asked bitterly. "Because she wanted me to be somebody else. The kind of man she grew up with, the kind of man she worked with. A man with power, money, class. She was a lawyer, and after she left me, she married a guy from her firm. I guess that's what she wanted all along."

"That's why she divorced you?" Helen asked in disbelief. "Because you're a cop instead of a lawyer?"

"It wasn't just that." He dragged his hand over his eyes, and suddenly he sounded very tired. "I wanted kids—lots of them—and she...."

Helen waited for him to finish, but he said nothing, just stood there in the rain, his eyes shadowed and distant.

"She didn't want kids?" Helen asked finally.

Slowly his eyes focused again, and he looked at her, his jaw tight and hard. "No. At least, not with me."

She took another deep breath. "If you wanted such different things, why did you get married in the first place?"

"Why does anyone get married? We were young. We thought we were in love. Hell, I'd been in love with Jessica since we were kids. Even though our first meeting wasn't exactly the greatest."

"How did you meet?"

"I'd just broken her big brother's nose."

"Her brother was—"

"Yeah. The kid who called my sister names." He shook his head. "Five years later, Jessica was the Homecoming Queen at her school, and I was crazy about her. And she was crazy about me, too. Her parents said it would never work, but Jessica didn't care. Back then, she didn't care about success and money and social position...."

"So what happened?" Helen asked quietly.

"I don't know. I guess she started to care about those things once she was married to a guy who didn't have them. And when I started asking her about having kids, she realized she didn't want them to have a father like me."

"A cop."

"Not just a cop. But a cop who's never going to make captain. Or even lieutenant. A cop who's lousy at playing politics and following the rules. A *troublemaker*."

"So she didn't like the way you did your job?"

"It was more than my job. It was everything. She didn't like my family, my friends, my car, my clothes, the way I spent my time." His voice cracked suddenly. "It didn't matter what I did. I just couldn't be who she wanted me to be."

Helen's breath caught. Suddenly she thought she understood. "So now...you don't make anyone any promises."

"That's right." His eyes hardened, and she could almost see the walls going back up around him. "I don't."

"But why—"

Abruptly he crossed his arms over his chest. "Look, darlin', I'd rather not tell you my whole life story out here on the sidewalk, okay?"

"Okay," she said softly.

There was an awkward silence.

Patrick raked his hand through his dripping hair. "You still want to go for that run?"

She nodded.

"I still have to change."

Her cheeks heated. "You want to go back to your apartment?"

He looked her in the eye. "It'll only take five minutes."

"Okay." She bit her lip. "Let's go."

Patrick cursed himself silently as he peeled off his soaking jeans and threw on his sweatpants. On the other side of the screens that shielded his bed from the rest of his apartment, he heard Helen's shoes squeak as she paced up and down.

He pulled a clean T-shirt over his head. What was he *doing?* Why had he told Helen all those things about his marriage to Jessica? Sure, she'd asked, but so had lots of other women, and he'd never had any trouble keeping from spilling his guts before.

And, dammit, why had he kissed her like that? Her body might react to him like tinder to flame, but she'd made it clear time and again that she had no intention of getting involved.

He dug into his top drawer for some sweat socks, but there weren't any there. Swearing under his breath, he turned to his wicker laundry basket. It was full to overflowing, and he rooted through it until he found a pair of socks that didn't smell too much like his basketball shoes.

He yanked on the socks, mulling over what had happened. Deep down, he knew why he'd kissed her. It was because he wanted her. Wanted her too much for pride or caution or anything else to get in the way.

And she wanted him, too. Beneath her icy exterior, she was

burning with heat—a heat unlike any he'd ever experienced. It was explosive. Like lightning.

Patrick closed his eyes at the memory of their kiss. Need raced through him, hot and urgent, and his heart thudded against his ribs. Oh, God, she'd tasted so good—like mint and sweetness and rain, a taste all her own.

But then she'd pushed him away, he reminded himself grimly. And it shouldn't have come as a surprise. After all, he hadn't been good enough for her a year ago, and nothing had changed. He still wasn't her *type,* and there was nothing he could do—nothing he even wanted to do—to change that.

He'd been down that road before, and he wasn't about to set foot on it again.

The old pain and anger tangled through his body, even as he dragged out the well-worn arguments. It was just as well. He didn't need any complications in his life. Didn't want a serious relationship anyway.

Or did he?

The thought made him freeze. "Hell," he muttered savagely. "I really am losing it."

Because no matter how much he wanted Helen—no matter how hot was the attraction that flared between them—he just wasn't serious relationship material. Not anymore.

If he ever really had been....

"Your five minutes are just about up," Helen called.

"Coming!" Shoving the thought of her out of his mind, he stood. He grabbed his Beretta, checked the clip, and tucked it into the holster at his waist. Pulling out his T-shirt so the gun was covered, he stepped into the main room.

Helen turned from the window. "What have you got there?"

"My gun."

She frowned. "I thought they took your badge and your gun when you were suspended?"

"That was the department's gun. This one is mine."

Her blue eyes were steady, but her hands shook a little as she shoved back her damp hair. "I never thought I'd be jogging with someone who was carrying a gun."

"You probably never thought anyone would try to kill you, either."

"You're right. And I suppose it's better to be cautious."

Patrick nodded. Caution—yeah, that's all it was. Not instinct. Definitely not the primal instinct of a man who wanted to keep his woman safe.

He forced a casual smile to his face. "You ready, darlin'?"

She nodded.

He locked the door and followed her out into the waiting morning.

Chapter 8

The rain poured down, soaking Helen to the skin as she ran. Her muscles stretched and heated, keeping her warm as she pushed herself to the limit. No matter what the weather, running always calmed her body and cleared her mind.

She needed to clear her mind. *And* calm her body. After the shattering power of Patrick's kiss, the wildness of her own response, she needed it desperately. Needed to restore her balance, her control. Because she couldn't let it happen again.

Not ever.

"I'm not like my mother," she muttered between her teeth. "I'm *not*."

"What's that?" Patrick asked. He kept pace with her easily, his feet pounding, his legs moving with a rhythmic grace.

She flushed, realizing she'd spoken out loud. "Nothing."

"Nothing? It sounded like you said—"

"It was nothing," she said loudly. She fumbled for a way to change the subject. "Uh, how are you doing, anyway?"

He tossed her a grin. "Fine." He didn't even sound winded. "You?"

In response, she picked up the pace. A sodden pile of leaves lay on the ground, and she kicked her way through them. The pungent scent of rotting leaves floated up to her, mingling with the clean smell of the rain.

Patrick laughed as he caught up with her. "You're a lot tougher than you look."

"So are you."

He shot her a look of mock outrage. "You didn't think I'd be able to go the distance?"

"Okay, I admit it. I thought you'd collapse gasping after about five blocks. Evergreen isn't that big. I know pretty much all the serious runners, and you're not one of them."

"Nope," he said. "I'm not."

"So how did you know you could keep up with me?"

"I have a secret weapon. I play basketball."

"Basketball?"

"That's right. Me and some of the other guys from the P.D. play pickup a couple times a week." Patrick paused. "But that's not where I get the serious action. I volunteer at the Open Door, play basketball with the kids. Man, can some of them run."

Helen's jaw almost dropped. "The Open Door? You mean that drop-in center downtown for troubled kids?"

"Yeah." He shot her a look. "Why are you so surprised?"

"Because—" She broke off in confusion. "I just didn't know you did any volunteer work, that's all."

"You thought I spent all my free time drinking beer and going to orgies?"

"Of course not," she said hastily.

The corner of his mouth tipped up in a wry smile. "Sure you did. But there's lots you don't know about me."

Helen bit her lip. Patrick was right. There was definitely more to him than met the eye. Much more.

She sneaked a glance at him. Rain dripped down the side of his face and plastered his T-shirt to his hard chest. As she watched, he swiped his arm across his forehead, pushing back damp locks of black hair.

Helen's breath snagged in her throat. She could get used to

this, she realized. To having Patrick running beside her, matching his stride to hers. To the faint masculine smell that wafted to her through the rain. To the sound of his steady breathing, the sight of his long leg muscles bunching and shifting beneath his track pants.

"Like what you see?"

She jerked her gaze up and saw his wicked grin. Color flew to her cheeks. "I...I was, uh, noticing your shoes."

"They're just your basic ordinary running shoes. Got 'em at that new sports store downtown." There was a definite twinkle in his eyes. "You in the market for a new pair?"

She gulped. "Maybe. Mine are—are getting pretty old."

His gaze slid down her body, over her soaking T-shirt and down her legs to her feet. She felt his look as though it was a physical touch, as though his hands were running down her body. Gooseflesh rose in awareness, and to her horror, she felt her nipples harden into tight, aching peaks. It was just the cold, she told herself frantically, the cold and the rain....

Finally, he brought his gaze back up to her face. "I don't know," he said, his voice the texture of smoke. "They look pretty good to me."

She almost choked. He wasn't talking about her shoes, and she knew it. Just like he probably knew she hadn't been staring at his runners to begin with.

Oh, God, she was a fool.

Angrily, she jerked her gaze away from him. Staring straight ahead, she tried to concentrate on the feel of the ground beneath her feet, the drip of the rain off the cedars overhead.

She had to get hold of herself. Running was supposed to help her do that. She just had to concentrate on her timing, her pace, on the path that stretched through the trees. Not on Patrick.

Keeping her gaze rigidly ahead, she focused on the rhythm of her feet. One-two. One-two. One-two.

She was so preoccupied that she didn't see the other runner bursting off a side path—until he slammed right into her.

"Patrick!" she screamed.

She fell hard, landing in a puddle of oozing black mud. Her

teeth came down on her tongue. The salty tang of blood filled her mouth, and she let out a little cry of pain. Out of the corner of her eye, she saw a blurring rush of movement. Her feet slipping in the mud, she scrambled to her feet. Her heart thumped as she glanced around wildly.

Patrick held a runner pinned to a cedar tree. His arm was across the other man's throat, his knee against the man's groin. His face was a mask of cold fury. "Who the hell are you?"

The runner made a strangled sound, his eyes cutting to Helen in a silent, desperate plea.

Helen gasped as she recognized him. "Let him go, Patrick!"

Patrick shot her an incredulous look. "Are you out of—"

"It's George Hauser. He's a V.P. at Woodfiber Technology, and he always runs here. I see him almost every morning."

Patrick's eyes narrowed, but he dropped his arm from the other man's throat and stepped back. George doubled over, gasping for breath.

"Are you okay?" Helen asked.

Slowly, painfully, he straightened. "I don't think your boyfriend's done any permanent damage."

"He's not my boyfriend. He's a cop."

"A cop, huh?" George grinned weakly. "Next time I'll be sure to watch where I'm going."

Helen bit her lip. "No, it was my fault. I wasn't paying attention. I didn't even see you until we crashed into each other."

"I knocked you down, didn't I?" A concerned frown creased his forehead, and he touched her shoulder. "Are you okay?"

Behind her, Patrick made a low noise, almost a growl.

"I'm fine," she said quickly. "Really."

"Good." George glanced at Patrick and his face went a little pale. He jerked his hand away from her shoulder. "I'd better be going. I have an early meeting." After a quick goodbye, he limped off down the trail.

Helen swung around to face Patrick. He stood with his arms folded across his chest, his eyes hard.

She tightened her lips. "You didn't have to be so rude to George. He didn't mean to knock me down."

"What was I supposed to do? Ask him who he was and hope like hell he didn't pull a knife or a gun and kill you right there?"

"Of course not! But you could have apologized. He didn't mean to hurt me."

"No kidding. From the way he was looking at you, I bet *hurting* you was the last thing on his mind. You date that guy or something?"

"No. I don't. Not that it's any of your business."

His face closed. "No, I guess it isn't."

"Damn right."

They stared at each other, the silence tense and angry.

Finally, Patrick let out his breath. "Look, I'm sorry." He spread his hands. "I thought he was trying to hurt you, and it isn't easy to go from wanting to rip a guy's head off to friendly chat in the blink of an eye."

"You wanted to...rip his head off?"

"Yeah, of course." He shrugged. "I told you. I thought he was trying to hurt you."

Helen sucked in her breath. When was the last time anyone had cared enough to actually want to protect her? Had anyone, ever? Her mother never had, that was for sure.

She swallowed hard and looked up at Patrick. "Thank you for wanting to protect me."

"You don't have to thank me. I'm just doing my job."

"Your job? Is that all it is?" As soon as the words were out of her mouth, she wanted to snatch them back, but it was too late.

His silver eyes met hers with an almost audible clash. "No," he said, his voice rasping. "It's not. And you know it."

His words struck her with the force of a physical blow. Shock shuddered through her, shock and some other emotion she didn't want to identify.

It was dangerous. Too dangerous.

"We'd better get going," she whispered.

Patrick was silent. He stood still and looked at her, his eyes never leaving hers. Slowly he lifted one hand and stretched it toward her. Tension arced between them, crackling through the slow rain.

She wanted to take his hand. To let him pull her into his arms. Oh, how she wanted it. She wanted it with a deep, slow ache that was as frightening as it was powerful.

Stepping away from him was one of the hardest things she'd ever done. But she did it. Stepped backward, her feet squelching in the mud, and forced herself to keep her hands at her sides. "We don't want to be late to see Marty's widow."

Patrick's hand dropped back to his side, and he turned away. "No," he said, and the flat tone of his voice speared at her heart. "We wouldn't want that."

An hour later Helen pulled up in front of the Fletchers's unkempt bungalow. She checked her watch. She and Patrick had both gone home to change, but to her relief, it hadn't made them late.

She got out of the car and followed Patrick up the walk, her heels clicking against the cracked pavement. The sound made her smile. In her suit and heels, she felt far more confident. In control.

She could handle this thing with Patrick. She was sure of it. He already seemed to have forgotten the incident in the park, thank goodness. By the time they'd made it back to the car, he'd been his usual cocky self. And if she thought she saw a hint of pain lurking deep in his eyes, it was only her imagination. It had to be.

Patrick bounded up the stairs and knocked on the peeling front door. As Helen reached the top of the steps, Angel Fletcher pulled the door open.

At least, Helen thought the woman was Angel. But she didn't look like any grieving widow Helen had ever seen. She wore a filmy red peignoir over her lush curves, and her dark hair tumbled around her shoulders in mussed, sexy curls.

Suddenly, Helen remembered what Patrick had said about Angel inviting him over for "comfort." A tiny fist of anger squeezed in her chest. Gritting her teeth, she told herself to ignore it. Why should she care if Angel was pursuing Patrick? If they slept together?

She shouldn't. She *didn't*.

"Patrick." The woman put her hand on his arm. Her fingernails were long, sculpted, bloodred.

Patrick smiled. "Angel. Good to see you."

Angel's gaze flickered to Helen, and her smile turned to ice. "You never said anything about bringing someone else along."

Helen shot Patrick a glare. He winked at her and gave Angel a look as innocent as a choirboy's. "Didn't I?"

"No." She pouted. "I thought you were coming to...comfort me."

Helen broke in. "Mrs. Fletcher, I'm Helen Stewart from the county prosecutor's office. Patrick and I would like to ask you a few questions. Do you mind if we come in?"

Angel sighed dramatically and tossed her head. "No, I guess not."

She flounced back into the house, clouds of sweet perfume wafting behind her. Patrick shrugged and walked into the hall, and Helen followed.

"Why didn't you tell her I was coming?" she whispered angrily.

"Lots of witnesses hold things back if they have too much time to think about what they're going to say. So I always try to surprise them. You got a problem with that?"

"No," she said grudgingly. "I suppose not."

They left their coats in the hall and walked into the small living room where Angel lounged on a faded brocade couch.

Helen glanced around, trying to hide her distaste. Ashtrays were everywhere, and the room stank of stale cigarette smoke. Heavy, dark furniture crowded the room, and the curtains were still drawn, making it seem even more claustrophobic. A fat tabby cat was curled in Angel's lap, and a black cat weaved in and out around her ankles, purring loudly.

Patrick sat in an armchair, instead of on the couch next to Angel. Helen felt the tension in her neck muscles relax a little. Not that she cared where he sat, she told herself.

Stiffly, she sat on the couch. "Mrs. Fletcher, I'm sorry to intrude on your grief." To her own ears, her words sounded too formal and not quite sincere. What was wrong with her? Interviewing witnesses had always been one of her strengths.

"Yeah?" Angel demanded. "Then what're you doing here?"

Helen glanced at Patrick for help. There was a hint of a smile around his mouth—almost as if he was enjoying her predicament. She glared at him, and he shrugged and gestured for her to go ahead.

Taking a deep breath, she plunged right in. "I need to ask you a few questions about your husband's death."

"What about it?"

"Do you know anything about his last case?"

"No." Angel shot a look at Patrick. "You know how he was. He never told me nothing."

"Yeah," Patrick said quietly. "I know how he was."

Angel's face changed. Suddenly she looked very young, very vulnerable. Helen looked at her in surprise. She'd thought Angel was around Patrick's age, but now she realized that Angel was a good ten years younger. Maybe in her mid-twenties at most.

"Marty wasn't always an easy man to live with?" she asked.

"Easy?" Angel gave a bitter laugh. "What a joke."

"What made it difficult?"

She hesitated, and then she spoke abruptly. "He drank."

Helen swallowed hard. "A lot?"

"Oh, yeah." Angel laughed again, but this time Helen heard the sadness beneath the anger. "He'd go out late at night. I'd lie there, wondering if he was on a case. Or a bender."

Helen nodded slowly, compassion seeping through her. She knew what that was like. The terrible wondering, the uncertainty, the fear. "It must have been very hard for you. How long were you married?"

"Four years. He didn't drink so bad when we first met, but he was getting worse all the time. I tried to get him to stop, but..."

"But he didn't?"

Angel grimaced. "No way. He just drank more. And he started gambling, too. I inherited this house and all the furniture from my grandma when she died. It was all paid off, but Marty took out a mortgage on it. Gambling debts, he said."

"You must have been very worried."

"I was. I didn't know what was gonna happen to us, with him drinking and gambling away every penny. I'm a hairdresser, and I make good money, but Marty took it out of the bank as fast as it went in."

Helen shook her head sympathetically.

"Some marriage, huh?" Angel said. "Lately, I never saw him. And when he was home, he didn't talk to me. Said he had something on his mind. He wouldn't even touch me. We hadn't had sex in months."

"Oh, no," Helen said softly. "That must have been terrible." The last remnants of her earlier dislike slipped away, replaced by sympathy. No wonder the girl had flirted with Patrick. She had to be starved for affection.

Angel leaned over to the coffee table and shook a cigarette out of a package. She lit it with trembling hands and inhaled deeply. "Yeah, well, I probably should've left him. Plenty of other guys out there." She blew out a cloud of smoke. Even through the brown haze, Helen saw the tears in her eyes. "But I loved him, you know? He was a jerk, but I loved him anyway."

"I'm very sorry for your loss," Helen said gently.

Angel looked straight into her eyes. For an instant Helen felt an unspoken bond between them, a bond of suffering, of understanding.

"You really mean that, don't you?" Angel said. A rasp of pain threaded through her voice—the pain of a deep, aching loneliness, a loneliness Helen understood all too well.

Helen nodded. "I really do."

Angel held her gaze. "So, you gonna catch the guy that killed him? The police aren't doing nothing about it. Ed Carmel came around here with some other guy, and they tried to tell me Patrick killed him." She snorted. "As if."

"Don't worry. We'll catch the killer," Patrick said. "We already have a few leads. We're pretty sure Marty was killed because of the case he was working on."

"You were working on it, too, right?" Angel asked.

"Yeah. But Marty didn't tell me everything he was up to. We thought maybe he talked to you about it."

"Like I said, he never told me nothing."

"Did he keep a diary?" Helen asked. "Or a calendar? Somewhere he noted his appointments?"

"Marty? No way. Only thing he ever wrote down was the numbers of the horses he bet on."

"What about a hiding place? Somewhere he might have kept important papers?"

"Yeah, he had a place. A cubbyhole in the wall of the garage." Angel's lip curled. "He kept his girlie magazines out there. Thought I didn't know about it, but I did."

"Mind if we take a look?" Helen asked.

Angel stood. "Why not?"

Helen got up to follow her, and Patrick stood, as well. She started into the hall after Angel, but Patrick caught her hand and pulled her back.

"What is it?" she whispered.

He put his mouth beside her ear. "I had to tell you," he said softly. His warm breath tickled the side of her neck, sending shivers down her back. "You're doing great with her."

Warmth spread through her body. "You think so?"

"I do."

"Patrick…." She pulled back to look into his eyes. "I'm sorry I implied you were sleeping with Angel. Or intending to."

"Yeah, well, I'm not."

"I know that now. And I'm sorry for assuming you were."

"It's okay." He touched her cheek. "But next time, keep it in mind. I know there's been gossip about me. And women. But my reputation is pretty exaggerated. Believe me."

Her mouth went suddenly dry. "Patrick, I—"

The impatient sound of Angel's voice shattered the moment. "You guys coming or what?"

"Be right there!" Helen called. She pulled away from Patrick with a twinge of regret. As he turned away, she thought she saw a flash of the same regret in his eyes.

She put the thought out of her mind as she followed him down the hall.

Angel was waiting for them in the kitchen. They followed her through a door and into the garage. It was dark and cold, and it smelled like paint and engine oil. Angel pulled on a string that dangled down from the ceiling, and a dim bulb sprang on.

"There." She pointed at a panel in the back wall, above the freezer. "Right behind that board."

Patrick reached over the freezer. He shoved the board hard, and it scraped aside. Leaning forward, he peered into the small, dark space, and his shoulders stiffened. "Helen!" His voice was hoarse with excitement. "Take a look at this."

Helen planted her hands on the cold metal of the freezer and stood on tiptoe to see into the cubbyhole.

She gasped.

Sitting on top of Marty Fletcher's collection of porn magazines were piles of bills. Hundred-dollar bills. There were ten stacks of them, held together with elastic bands.

"That...that must be at least a hundred thousand dollars," she said.

Patrick's eyes met hers. "Looks like Marty had a little money after all."

"I don't understand," Angel said faintly. "Where did he get it?"

"From the mortgage?" Helen suggested.

"It was only for thirty thousand dollars—this house isn't worth that much." Angel raised her hand to her mouth. "I don't know where Marty could've gotten so much money."

A payoff. The thought flew into Helen's mind. It was the only place a cop on a cop's salary could get so much cash. The cynical light in Patrick's eyes told her he'd come to exactly the same conclusion.

He turned to Angel. "I'm sorry, but we're going to have to take the money."

She bit her lip. "Do you have to? With all Marty's debts, and the funeral to pay for—"

"I'm sorry, but the money is evidence," Helen said gently. "It may be the reason Marty was killed. But I promise you, if the money did legally belong to Marty, you'll get it back.''

"You promise?"

"I promise."

Angel let out a big sigh. "Okay."

"Do you have a bag we can use?" Patrick asked.

She nodded and went back into the kitchen. She emerged with a flowered pink shopping bag. "You can use this."

He swept the contents of the cubbyhole into the bag, and put his arm around her shoulders. "You trust me, don't you?"

"Yeah, of course."

"Good. Then don't tell anyone about the money. You'll be a whole lot safer if you forget you ever saw it."

Angel shivered. "Okay."

"Good girl." Patrick gave her shoulders a squeeze and released her.

"Do you have any relatives outside Evergreen?" Helen asked. "Or friends? Someone you could visit for a week or so?"

"Uh, yeah. My brother lives in Seattle. But he's been staying up here with me the last couple days."

"Where is your brother now?" Helen asked.

A faint color rose to Angel's cheeks. Her gaze flickered to Patrick and then to the ground. "I, uh, asked him to go out for a couple hours."

"When will he be back?"

"He has a cell phone. I told him I'd call him."

"You do that. Right away. And as soon as he gets back, the two of you should go down to his place, okay?"

"Okay." Angel bit her lip. "Marty was involved in something pretty bad, wasn't he?"

"We don't know what he was involved in," Helen said quietly. "But it may have been something dangerous. For now, you'll be safer in Seattle."

Angel twisted her hands together until her knuckles turned white. "I just wish I knew what was going on."

"So do I," Helen said. "Believe me, so do I."

Patrick followed Helen down her hall and into her living room. She walked ahead of him, her hips swaying slightly, and he grinned appreciatively. He liked the way she walked almost as much as the way she ran. Her walk was graceful, classy, strong. And to him, almost unbearably sexy.

She sat on her yellow couch, dropped the flowered shopping bag onto the floor, and peered down at her suit. "Yuck. I'm covered in cat hair."

Patrick sat beside her. "You really were great back there at Angel's, partner."

She smiled. "Thanks."

"I never would have gotten so much out of her—especially the thing about the hiding place. But you knew just what to say to her."

"Being a prosecutor, you learn how to read people's cues. How to get them to open up."

"It was more than that. You really seemed to understand where she was coming from."

Helen stiffened and turned away. "It was nothing," she said, her voice tight.

Patrick frowned. "Is something wrong?"

"No. Nothing." She grabbed her briefcase and stood abruptly. "Excuse me. I'm going to change before I get cat hair all over the place." She strode out of the room.

He stared after her. Something was definitely wrong. She'd gotten upset when he said she seemed to understand Angel. Why?

Suddenly it struck him. Maybe she really *had* understood Angel. Maybe she'd been married to an alcoholic herself. After all, he knew nothing about her past. He didn't even know how old she was. Twenty-eight? Thirty? Old enough to be divorced, anyway.

He glanced around the living room. Unlike his own apartment, there were no photos on the walls, no albums on her bookshelves that might give him a clue to her past. He walked over to her rolltop desk. Legal papers were stacked on top, and a couple of bills lay in a cubbyhole. The only letter was an appeal from a Christmas charity fund.

"What do you think you're doing?"

Patrick spun around.

Helen stood directly behind him, her hands on her hips. She had changed into a gray suit that skimmed her slender body, and a pair of black heels that made her legs go on forever. Beneath her sheer hose, he could see the smooth muscles of her calves. He still remembered running his hands up her legs, remembered the way her skin had felt, soft and supple beneath his palms.

He felt his body begin to stir—even though this was definitely *not* the time. He turned away to hide his reaction. "I was just looking around."

Helen banged down the top of her desk. "Stay away from my papers, Monaghan."

"Hey, I didn't mean to pry. I was just curious."

"What about?"

"About you."

Her eyes narrowed. "Why?"

"I just realized you know almost everything about me. You've even met most of my family. And I don't know the first thing about you."

"What do you want to know?"

Patrick looked into her angry blue eyes and shrugged. "Everything."

"There's not much to tell. I grew up in Seattle. Did a philosophy degree there. Then law. After that, I came here."

"Have you ever been married?"

"No."

"What about family?"

Her gaze slid away from his. "I already told you. I'm an only child."

"And your parents? Are they still living?"

Her face hardened, and she looked at her watch. "Patrick, I have to go to the office."

"What for?"

"I've got a meeting with Franklin." She paused. "I'm going to recommend that you no longer be considered a suspect."

Patrick's heart began to thump. This was what he'd been work-

PLAY

RUN

FOR THE

ROSES

and get

THREE FREE GIFTS!

HOW TO PLAY:

1. With a coin, carefully scratch off the silver box at the right. Then check the claim chart to see what we have for you — **FREE BOOKS** and a **FREE GIFT** — **ALL YOURS FREE!**

2. Send back the card and you'll receive two brand-new Silhouette Intimate Moments® novels. These books have a cover price of $4.25 each, but they are yours to keep absolutely free.

3. There's no catch. You're under no obligation to buy anything. We charge nothing — ZERO — for your first shipment. And you don't have to make any minimum number of purchases — not even one!

4. The fact is, thousands of readers enjoy receiving books by mail from the Silhouette Reader Service™. They like the convenience of home delivery...they like getting the best new novels months before they're available in stores...and they love our discount prices!

5. We hope that after receiving your free books you'll want to remain a subscriber. But the choice is yours — to continue or cancel, any time at all! So why not take us up on our invitation, with no risk of any kind. You'll be glad you did!

This surprise mystery gift
Will be yours **FREE** –
When you play
RUN for the ROSES

PLAY

RUN FOR THE ROSES

Scratch
Here
See Claim Chart

YES! I have scratched off the silver box. Please send me all the gifts
for which I qualify. I understand that I am under no obligation to
purchase any books, as explained on the back and opposite page.

RUN for the ROSES	Claim Chart
♚ ♚ ♚	**2 FREE BOOKS AND A MYSTERY GIFT!**
♚ ♚	**1 FREE BOOK!**
♚	**TRY AGAIN!**

Name _____
(PLEASE PRINT CLEARLY)

Address _____ Apt.#_____

City _____ State _____ Zip _____

(U-SIL-IM-10/98)   **245 SDL CJAN**

The Silhouette Reader Service™ — Here's how it works:

Accepting free books places you under no obligation to buy anything. You may keep the books and gift and return the shipping statement marked "cancel." If you do not cancel, about a month later we'll send you 6 additional novels and bill you just $3.57 each, plus 25¢ delivery per book and applicable sales tax, if any.* That's the complete price — and compared to cover prices of $4.25 each — quite a bargain! You may cancel at any time, but if you choose to continue, every month we'll send you 6 more books, which you may either purchase at the discount price...or return to us and cancel your subscription.

*Terms and prices subject to change without notice. Sales tax applicable in N.Y.

If offer card is missing write to: Silhouette Reader Service, 3010 Walden Ave., P.O. Box 1867, Buffalo NY 14240-1867

BUSINESS REPLY MAIL
FIRST-CLASS MAIL   PERMIT NO. 717   BUFFALO, NY

POSTAGE WILL BE PAID BY ADDRESSEE

SILHOUETTE READER SERVICE
3010 WALDEN AVE
PO BOX 1867
BUFFALO NY 14240-9952

NO POSTAGE
NECESSARY
IF MAILED
IN THE
UNITED STATES

ing for. Praying for. If Carmel didn't drag out the paperwork, he could be back on the force by this afternoon.

He knew he should be doing a victory dance around the living room, but for some crazy reason, all he could think of was that he wouldn't see Helen anymore.

He squeezed his hands tight. "You think you have enough to take to Franklin?"

Helen frowned. "Of course. I've shaken Tammy's testimony, and she was the only real witness." She nodded at the flowered shopping bag by the couch. "And the money shows that Marty was involved in something illegal. Probably a payoff. That means there's someone else out there with a strong motive for murder. Charging you doesn't make sense."

"I just don't see how it all fits together. If Marty was killed because of the money, then how does Carmel fit in? Why was your office broken into?"

Helen shook her head. "Maybe Carmel was paid off, too. Maybe it had something to do with Jamie Lee's murder."

"You think Marty knew who killed her?"

"I don't know. I suppose it's possible."

Patrick's jaw hardened. "Dammit, I wish I could remember what happened. I must have seen whoever was out on the highway that night. If I could—"

"But you can't," Helen said swiftly. "And there's no point in kicking yourself about it."

"Maybe if I kick myself, I'll remember."

"You don't have to remember. Once I've convinced Franklin you're not a suspect, we'll put a full team on the case. They'll dig into every angle. Put Tammy Weston under surveillance. Find out who paid off Marty and why."

Patrick digested her words in silence. She was right, of course. With half a dozen detectives on the case, with the full resources of the police department involved, the case would probably be solved in a matter of days.

Helen looked at her watch again. "I've got to go."

"Yeah. I know."

This was it. It was over.

Helen picked up the shopping bag and walked out into the hall. Patrick followed her. He grabbed his leather jacket and shrugged into it. As she pulled on her raincoat, he turned to face her. She stilled. Her golden lashes swept down, hiding her eyes, but then she looked up, into his face.

Patrick's heart slammed into his ribs. Her blue eyes were the color of the ocean in a winter storm, turbulent with emotion.

He opened his mouth to speak, but his throat had gone dry.

Helen moistened her lips. "Goodbye, Patrick."

Chapter 9

Patrick knew he should just open the door and walk away. It was over—Helen had made that crystal clear. Besides, walking away was what he did best.

Only this time, he couldn't do it.

He reached for Helen, his hands closing over her shoulders. Her eyes widened as she stared up at him. Her chest rose and fell rapidly, her breath coming in little sharp bursts. Tiny quivers of tension ran through her body.

Patrick stared into her eyes. They mirrored his own, filled with liquid heat and unmistakable desire.

He slid his hands down her back and pulled her into his arms. Her breasts bumped against his chest, and he felt her rapid heartbeat against his ribs.

Slowly, ever so slowly, he lowered his head. He brushed his mouth over hers in a feather-light kiss. Her lips were soft and giving, and she let out a tiny sigh.

Hot, sharp desire stabbed through him, shooting straight to his groin. He groaned and tightened his arm around her slender waist, hauling her against him. Helen flung her arms around his neck and molded herself to his body, tangling her hands in his hair. As he lowered his head to kiss her again, Patrick realized he was lost.

He took her lips with the pent-up need of days and months of wanting her. He slanted his mouth across hers, demanding a response. Helen moaned softly, straining even closer to him. Her curves fit perfectly against his body, almost as though she'd been made for him.

Only for him.

He wanted to claim her, to mark her as his own. Urgently he deepened the kiss, his tongue swirling into her mouth. God, she was sweet, he thought through the haze of fierce desire. She tasted like mint and rain. He wanted to taste all of her, to savor her every scent.

He tugged her even closer, breathing in the faint musky smell of her perfume. His heart thudded against his chest as she slid one of her hands under his jacket. With her palm, she stroked the muscles of his back. Heat flamed everywhere she touched.

Patrick shrugged out of his jacket without breaking the kiss, and Helen made a husky sound of approval. She tugged the hem of his T-shirt out of his jeans, and he felt her cool fingers glide over his skin. Emboldened, he pushed her raincoat off her shoulders. It whispered to the ground at their feet.

Sliding his hand over the silky fabric of her blouse, he cupped her breast. The warm, soft curve fit his palm perfectly, and his body tightened painfully in response. Slowly, gently, he stroked his thumb over her nipple. It hardened into a tight peak, thrusting against his palm. His breath hissed out from between his teeth. She was so beautiful—so passionate.

His touch light and teasing, he circled her nipple with his fingertips. Helen arched against him with a low, shuddering moan. Her fingers kneaded his shoulders as he slid his kiss over her jaw. He nipped delicately at the side of her throat, and her head fell back in abandon.

His own knees grew weak as he tasted the skin in the hollow of her throat. She tasted so good—better than he had remembered, better than anything he could have imagined. Her heat, her scent, her taste, filled his senses, until he was almost blind with need.

She leaned back against his arm, and he felt his muscles tremble. Slowly he backed her against the wall. She lifted her leg and wrapped it around his hips, pulling him even closer.

The world spun, and Patrick groaned. He wanted her worse than he'd ever wanted anything in his life. Hell, he wanted her so badly he thought he might die of it.

Helen dug her fingers into his hair, pulling his lips to hers. He kissed her deeply, his tongue plunging into her mouth. Her hips jerked against his, and his heartbeat almost exploded.

Patrick fought to contain the aching tide of need and desire. If they didn't slow down, they were going to make love standing up right here in the hallway. And as much as he wanted to claim her here and now, Helen deserved more than that. Far more.

He dragged his mouth from hers.

Helen's eyes fluttered open. They were dark blue—almost navy—and drugged with passion. Her lips were red and swollen, moist with his kiss.

Patrick smiled slowly, drinking in her beauty. "Helen," he said, savoring the taste of her name on his lips. "Let's take it to the bedroom."

She froze.

Something in her eyes went wild. Not with passion, not with heat, but with something more like fear. She jerked her hands away from his back and thrust them between their bodies to push at his chest.

Patrick stared at her, desire falling away from him in confusion. "What is it? Are you all right?"

She shoved at him again.

He let her go and backed up a few feet. "Tell me what's wrong."

She wrapped her arms around her waist, pressing herself back against the wall. The wild, trapped look in her eyes made his heart pound in fear.

"Talk to me," he said urgently.

"Get out."

An icicle pierced his heart. "What?"

"I said, get out!" Her voice rose. "Don't you hear me?"

He stared at her. "What's going on?"

Helen lifted her head to look into his eyes, and he realized to his horror that she was crying. Tears glittered in her eyes, on her lashes, and a single crystal drop slid down her cheek.

He'd never seen her cry before—not even when she'd almost been run over last night. And now, she was crying because of him. The knowledge twisted in his heart like a blade.

"Damn you, Patrick Monaghan." Her voice was as hard and cold as diamonds. "Get the hell out of my apartment. Now."

He tried one last time. "Helen, I'm sor—"

"Get out!"

He grabbed his jacket and went.

Helen checked her makeup in the rearview mirror one last time as she pulled into the parking lot behind her office. Her eyes were still a little red from crying, but with any luck, no one would notice. It would ruin her reputation if anyone realized she actually cried. Prosecutors—good ones—couldn't be weak.

And she was weak. So weak.

If Patrick hadn't pulled away from her, if he hadn't had the decency to try to take her into the bedroom, she would have let him make love to her. In the hallway. Standing up. She'd wanted him so badly that she wouldn't have cared if they'd had an audience looking on. Just like her mother had never cared. Lana had never given a damn, not even if her daughter was in the same room.

She'd lost control. Again. And it showed her what she was. Deep down, she was like her mother. It was true.

Fresh tears welled up in Helen's eyes, and she choked them back as she parked the car and turned off the ignition. Her throat burned with the effort of holding back her tears. As she climbed out of the car, into the rain, the cruel words of her classmates spun back to her.

She's just like her mother. Just like her mother.

A wave of anguish rose up inside her, threatening to snap the tenuous threads of control. But she wouldn't humiliate herself. She wouldn't cry, here in the parking lot, where anyone could see her.

She wouldn't lose control…again.

Helen planted her hand on the slick rainy glass of the car window. Steadying herself, she took a long, deep breath and tried to think clearly.

Maybe, deep down, she was like her mother. But she would fight it. Fight her real nature. After all, she never had to see Patrick again. And it was only with him that the madness took her. Only with him that she lost control….

"I won't ever see him again," she said out loud. "The case is over. I don't have to see him anymore."

For some reason, that only made her feel worse.

Grimly, she straightened. She wouldn't think about it now. Wouldn't think about *him*. She had her career to think about, to occupy her time. She wouldn't waste any more energy on Patrick Monaghan.

Squaring her shoulders, she marched across the parking lot and into the building. She went to her office, dumped her briefcase on her desk, and hung up her coat. Taking a deep breath, she picked up the flowered shopping bag of money and headed down the hall to Franklin's office. His door was half open, so she tapped briefly and walked inside.

Franklin sat tilted back in his huge leather chair, the telephone tucked against his shoulder. He frowned as he scribbled notes on a pad. "Uh-huh," he said into the phone. "Are you sure? Right." Looking up, he motioned Helen to a chair.

She sat with the pink shopping bag on her lap. Glancing over Franklin's shoulder, she looked out the window. A mist was rolling in from the sea, turning the world a drab, unrelieved gray. A few drops of rain slid down the windowpane.

"Okay, I'll call you back." Franklin hung up the phone and turned to Helen with a smile. "I'm glad you're here. Your timing is excellent, as usual."

"Thank you." She hesitated briefly, then plunged ahead. "Franklin, there's something I need to discuss with you."

He held up a hand. "Not now. That was Ed Carmel on the phone. There's been a new development in the Monaghan case."

"What kind of development?"

"The eyewitness. What's her name?" Franklin glanced down at his notes. "Tammy Weston. She's just been found murdered. Strangled."

Helen gasped. The room spun with a slow, sickening blur. "Wh-when?"

"Her neighbor found her this morning. The medical examiner can't pinpoint the time until after the autopsy, but she says the girl was killed sometime last night."

Helen almost choked. "Oh, my God."

"What is it?"

"I went and saw her last night." Her face felt frozen with horror. "She must—it must be why she was killed."

"Probably not. Looks like Monaghan weaseled her address out of someone in the department. He probably went over and killed her as soon as he found out where she lived."

"Patrick?" she whispered. For an instant the world dimmed. She grabbed Franklin's desk for support, the sharp edge of the wood biting into her palm. She pressed her hand against it even harder, almost welcoming the pain.

"A witness saw Monaghan outside her apartment last night," Franklin said. "Described him perfectly."

Bile rose in Helen's throat. "Of course he was there." She nearly choked. Desperately she struggled to sound calm. "But you don't understand. He didn't kill her. He had no reason to."

"What are you talking about? He had every reason. She was an eyewitness. She identified him as a murderer."

"But she was lying."

He frowned. "What?"

"Someone paid her to lie. I'm sure of it." Quickly she filled him in on the details of her discussion with Tammy, concluding, "So Patrick had no reason to kill her. It was probably whoever paid her to lie."

"Did you tape the conversation?" he asked sharply.

"No. I thought she might not talk if I was taping her."

"Too bad." He steepled his fingers. "But what if she was lying last night, instead of on Tuesday? Maybe Monaghan got to her, threatened her life if she didn't cast doubt on her statement. Then he changed his mind and killed her."

"No!" Helen blurted.

His eyes narrowed. "You seem very certain of that."

Her heart thumped, and she fought to keep her voice level. "I know he didn't kill her."

"And how can you be so sure?"

She bit her lip. This was it. "Because he spent the night at my apartment."

"What?" Franklin roared. He stood, shoving back his chair so hard it crashed to the floor. "He did *what?*"

"It's really not like it sounds—"

He struck the desk with his fist. His coffee cup jumped and clattered. "You spent the night with a murder suspect? Have you lost your mind?"

"I didn't spend the night with him. Not in the sense you're suggesting. Someone tried to run me over, and he was worried about me. He slept on the couch, not in my bed." She took a deep breath. "But that's not the point. He didn't kill Tammy. Or Marty. I'm sure of it."

"Is that right?" Franklin's voice was as thin and sharp as ice. "Why are you so convinced?"

Helen lifted the shopping bag off her lap and placed it on Franklin's desk. "This bag contains a large sum of cash, retrieved from Marty Fletcher's garage."

"And?" he said coldly.

She stared at him. "There's almost a hundred thousand dollars here. Somebody must have paid Marty off."

Franklin looked down at the bag, and then back up to meet her gaze. His eyes were like steel. "And if it is a payoff, how does that clear Monaghan? If he was the one who paid Fletcher off, that would give him a strong motive for murder. Maybe Fletcher had something on him and Monaghan was tired of paying him to keep quiet. So he decided to silence Fletcher permanently."

"No!" Helen's heart banged against her ribs. "Patrick didn't—"

He cut her off. "It's clear to me what's going on here." His face was a cold mask. "You've allowed your feelings for Monaghan to overcome your professional judgment."

"That's not true!"

"I trusted you with this case. I knew you'd had a fling with Monaghan, but I overlooked it because I thought it was over. And because I thought you were the woman for the job." He paused ominously. "Clearly, I was wrong."

Helen swallowed hard. "I know it looks bad that he spent the night at my apartment. But I am not having an affair with him. And I'm on top of the case. We have some solid leads. I'm sure the investigating team will find the real killer shortly, and when they do, I'll prosecute him. And win."

Franklin gave her a long, hard look. "No. You won't."

Her throat tightened painfully. "What are you saying?" She fought to keep her composure. "Are you taking me off the case?"

"That's right." His eyes bored into hers. "But that's not all."

"What?"

"Helen, you're fired."

Patrick sat on his couch, trying to concentrate. He held his clipboard in his lap as he wrote down everything he knew about Marty's murder. The case was out of his hands, but he wanted to give the new investigating team the best possible head start.

He jotted a note and frowned down at it. His scrawl was even more illegible than usual. He could hardly read what he'd written—no way anyone else would be able to decipher it.

"Hell," he muttered. He peeled the paper off the top of the pad, scrunched it into a ball, and tossed it into the wastepaper basket under the table. Involuntarily, his gaze slid to the telephone that sat on top of the table. His chest tightened, and he yanked his gaze away.

He should move the phone. Put it somewhere out of sight. That way, he wouldn't be so tempted to call Helen. *Helen.* He closed his eyes, picturing her: her graceful walk, the golden gleam of her hair, her beautiful mouth curving in a smile.

Dammit, even after everything that had happened this morning—after she'd pushed him away *again*—he still wanted her. Wanted her worse than he'd ever wanted any woman...even Jessica.

He didn't want to feel this way. As if he'd screwed up. Screwed up and lost something, something precious. It reminded him too much of what he'd lost three years before, and he'd sworn never to feel that way again. Never to let anything—or anyone—matter to him so much.

No, it was over. Finished. And he had to stop thinking about her....

The phone rang, and his heart leaped. He grabbed the receiver so fast he almost knocked over the phone. "Hello?"

"Patrick?" Adam barked.

A crazy feeling of disappointment skidded through him, but he suppressed it. Who had he expected, anyway? Not Helen. Not after the way she'd thrown him out of her apartment this morning.

"Dammit, Patrick, are you there?"

"Yeah." With an effort, he forced his mind away from Helen. "Have you got some good news for me?"

"Good news! What are you talking about, good news?"

Patrick frowned. "I thought—"

"I don't even want to know what you thought! I told you to keep out of trouble. I can't believe you were stupid enough to take Helen Stewart to bed."

"Take her to—what?"

"And now you're both in it up to your eyes. I hope you're happy with yourself, Patrick. Ruining her career because you're too damn randy to keep it in your pants!"

Patrick lifted the phone away from his ear and stared at it. Adam must have lost his mind. He waited until his brother's shouts subsided before he lifted the receiver back to his mouth. "Adam, what the hell are you talking about?"

"You don't know?" Adam paused. "Helen hasn't called you?"

"No, she hasn't. I'm not exactly her favorite person right now. And now the case is over, she doesn't have any reason to call me."

"Over?" Adam shouted. "*Over?* It's not anything like over. In fact, it just got a whole lot worse."

"Will you calm down and tell me what's going on?"

"Tammy Weston was murdered last night."

Patrick let out a long, slow whistle. "You're kidding."

"No, I'm not. I just got off the phone with Lieutenant Carmel. Patrick, you're unofficially a suspect."

A sick feeling of foreboding curled through Patrick's stomach. "There must be some mistake. This morning, Helen was going to tell Franklin Chambers that I should no longer be considered a suspect in Marty's murder. So why the hell would I kill Tammy Weston?"

"Chambers isn't about to listen to anything Helen says."

"Why not?"

"He fired her this morning."

Patrick shot off the couch. "No! There must be a mistake!"

"There's no mistake. Every lawyer in town is talking about it. Word has it Franklin sacked her for sleeping with you."

Pure, cold fury surged through Patrick's body. "I don't believe it. Why the hell didn't you call me right away?"

"I've been on the phone trying to find out what's going on. But let me give you a piece of advice. From now on, keep your nose clean. And stay away from Helen Stewart! Don't—"

Patrick banged down the phone. He threw on his jacket, yanked on his shoes, and charged out of the house.

Helen. He had to find Helen.

This whole thing was his fault. Dammit, if he hadn't pressured her in the first place, she never would have gotten involved in this mess. And if he hadn't practically blackmailed her, she wouldn't have let him stay the night at her place. The gossips wouldn't be saying they were having an affair. And Franklin Chambers wouldn't have fired her.

Patrick clenched his teeth as he sprinted through the rain. He really had screwed up this time. It was all his fault Helen had lost her job. The job she'd admitted was the most important thing in the world to her. More important than her safety.

More important than her life.

Fear tightened in his chest. Oh, God, he couldn't let his mistakes cause another death....

He had to find her. He had to make sure she was safe.

As he reached his car, he suddenly knew where she'd be. The place she loved the most, the place she always went when she was upset.

He leaped into his car, fired up the engine, and roared off to the beach.

Helen sat on the cold, damp log, staring into the water. Waves pounded against the shore, whipped to a frenzy by the sharp, biting wind. Rain slashed down, soaking her to the skin, but she didn't move.

It didn't matter. Nothing mattered.

The tide was coming in, and the water crept closer. A wave broke over her feet, soaking her Ferragamo pumps. They were her most expensive shoes—her favorites. She'd put them on that morning to give herself confidence for her meeting with Franklin.

The wave sucked one of the pumps back into the water, pulling it into the surging foam. Helen watched as it floated away, pitching and tossing in the waves. A second later a bigger wave broke over her feet. It soaked her ankles and calves, making her panty hose cling wetly to her skin.

Soon, the water would creep up higher.

Helen stared into the surging water. It didn't matter if she got soaked. It didn't matter if she ruined her best wool suit. Her career was over. She would never need the suit again.

Her mind felt slow and numb as she tried to think it through, to absorb what had happened. She could probably sue Franklin for wrongful dismissal, she thought dully. After all, he'd implied he was firing her for having an affair with Patrick, and she hadn't had one.

But there was really no point in suing. She knew the truth. Sure, she hadn't slept with Patrick. But she could have. Would have, if Patrick hadn't pulled away from her. She'd lost control, and she'd paid for it with her career.

It wasn't any more than she deserved.

"Helen!"

Patrick's deep voice pierced the ice that encased her mind. Fiercely, she pushed the voice away, willing herself not to hear it. She already had enough problems without indulging in aural hallucinations.

"Helen!"

She jerked up her head.

Patrick ran along the edge of the surf. His arms pumped, his feet kicking up sprays of water as he raced through the wind and the rain.

He careened to a halt in front of her, water eddying around his calves, his jeans plastered wetly to his strong thighs. "Helen. Thank God you're all right."

"All right?" A burst of hysterical laughter swelled up in her throat. She gave in to it, sucking air into lungs that burned with the effort of holding back tears. "Sure, I'm all right. I've just lost my job. Ruined my career. Lost the only thing in the world that meant anything to me."

Patrick winced and dragged his hands through his wet hair. "Helen, I can't tell you how sorry I am. This whole thing is my fault." His eyes were dark. "I wasn't meaning to make light of what's happened. I just…I was worried about you."

She looked away from him as the icy calm reclaimed her. "Don't," she said. "Don't worry about me. I'll be fine."

Another wave swirled toward her, rocking the log she sat on. Freezing salt water crept up almost to her knees, and a strand of dark green seaweed wound itself around her leg. Patrick stood in water up to his thighs.

Helen looked past him, out to the ocean as it boomed and crashed. The wind picked up, sending a crest of icy spray into her face. She didn't bother to wipe it away.

Patrick's voice floated to her as if from a great distance. "Helen, we've got to get out of here. The tide's coming in. You're going to catch pneumonia."

"You go. I'm staying here."

He reached for her, but she struck away his hand. "I said go!"

"I won't leave you here!" A wave hit him, and he staggered, almost falling into the water. He scrambled onto the log where she sat and stood on top of it, his arms folded across his chest. "You can't just give up like this, Stewart!"

She whipped up her head, her soaking hair flying forward to stick to her cheek. "Give up? It's not a matter of giving up. I've been thrown out of the game."

"Yeah, well, maybe it's time to start arguing with the ump."

"Franklin, you mean? Not a chance. He's so worried about how he'll look on television, he's not about to give me a second chance."

"What if you prove you were right?"

"Prove that you're innocent, you mean?" She gave a bitter laugh. "Franklin will never believe anything I say. And even if I did find the real killer, he would never rehire me. That would mean he'd have to admit in public that he was wrong, and he'll never do that."

"Then you're just going to give up." There was anger in Patrick's voice. "I never pegged you as a quitter, Stewart."

Quitter. She'd never been a quitter. She'd always fought, ever since she was a child. Refused to listen to all the people who said she'd never make it, said she'd end up like her mother. She'd fought her way out of the slums. Through university. Into the prosecutor's office.

Pain stabbed through her, and she squeezed her eyes shut. There was no point in fighting now. It was all over. She knew what she was. It was inside her. And there was no way she could fight her own soul.

Thunder boomed and a flash of lightning rent the sky. The storm had finally hit. Helen raised her face to the sky. This was what she'd been waiting for—this wildness, this display of nature that matched the despair in her heart.

Another wave crashed and broke. The freezing water hit her skin, and she gasped, welcoming the icy feel of it.

And then Patrick's strong arms closed around her, lifting her, cradling her like a child.

"Put me down!" she demanded.

"No," he said grimly. "I'm taking you home."

He held her against his soaking chest and began wading through the hip-deep water. The sky had gone dark, almost black. A streak of lightning flashed across it, electrifying the air.

Helen pounded against his chest. "Put me down, dammit! How dare you—" To her horror, she felt hot tears start to her eyes. They seeped out from under her lids as she pushed against him, struggling to get free of his arms.

Above the rushing roar of the water, she heard his deep voice. "That's right. Fight me, Helen. Feel the anger. Feel your strength."

The tears flooded down her cheeks. "I'm not strong," she said brokenly. "Not at all."

He tightened his arms around her. "Yes, you are. Helen, you're the strongest person I've ever met. You can't give up now. You can't just let Franklin take your career away from you."

"It's too late." A giant sob rose in her throat. "He already has taken it away."

"It's never too late. You're a fighter. I know you are. We can fight this thing together."

She lifted her blurry eyes to his face. "T-together?"

His expression was deadly serious, his jaw tight. "You lost your job because of me. The very least I owe you is to try and fix things."

"You don't owe me anything."

"Yeah, I do. I got you into this mess. But we can get you out of it. Together." He paused, his eyes boring into hers. "But you have to fight."

She wanted to tell him no. She wanted to tell him to put her back down in the water, to let her surround herself with the cold wind and the icy rain, to freeze what was left of her heart into a hard little nugget that couldn't be hurt.

But his arms were warm, so warm and so strong. And when

she looked into his eyes, she had the craziest feeling that everything was going to be all right....

She took a deep, shaky breath. "Okay, Monaghan. We'll fight."

His face broke into a huge grin, and he hugged her tight. "You got yourself a deal, Stewart."

Still cradling her in his arms, he strode on through the rain. Helen closed her eyes and laid her head against his rock-hard chest. Under her wet cheek, she could feel his heart thumping, and she felt herself almost smile.

She'd lost her job. Her career was in ruins. Ten minutes ago she'd felt as if the world was coming to an end. But somehow, with Patrick carrying her through the storm, the world didn't seem so bleak after all.

Opening her eyes, she lifted her head. "Patrick?"

"What is it?"

"Thank you for coming to get me."

He stopped, stopped with the rain pelting down and the water swirling around his muscular thighs, stopped and looked straight into her eyes.

"Anytime, Helen," he said softly. "Anytime."

Chapter 10

Patrick clenched the steering wheel as he drove back into town. The speedometer climbed as he raced past other drivers.

In the passenger seat beside him, Helen was shivering. He'd thrown his leather jacket around her shoulders when he put her in the car, but her teeth chattered so loudly they almost drowned out the patter of the rain on the convertible's roof.

Fear—as cold as the rain that slid down the windows—twisted through Patrick's chest. What if Helen had hypothermia? He didn't know how long she'd been sitting out there in the freezing wind and rain. And being in his car wasn't much better. The heater hadn't worked in months.

He had to get her somewhere warm and dry. Fast.

His apartment was closer than hers, so he took her there. He screeched to a halt right in front and went around to open her door. She swung her legs out of the car, and he took her hands. They were icy-cold, and as he pulled her to her feet, her body was racked by violent shivers.

A fresh shard of fear stabbed through him. Swiftly he wrapped his arm around her and led her inside.

"You need a hot bath and a warm drink," he said as he closed the door behind them.

She gave him a shaky smile. "Sounds good to me."

Patrick strode into the bathroom. His tub was old-fashioned—the deep, porcelain, claw-footed kind—and he cranked on the hot water tap full-blast. He dug out some bath salts Deirdre had given him two Christmases ago and dumped a healthy amount into the steaming water. All his towels were faded and worn, but he pulled out the best of them and left them on the counter.

He grabbed his terry robe off the back of the door and went back out to the main room. Helen was in the kitchen, filling the kettle. She put it on the stove and turned on the gas.

Relief expanded in Patrick's chest. Helen looked better already. Her cheeks had a little color, and she wasn't shivering anymore.

For a moment he just stood and watched her. Having her here—in his apartment, in his kitchen—gave him a feeling of deep satisfaction. It was strange. Since his divorce, he hadn't wanted any other woman here. This was his own space, his private sanctuary, a place where he didn't ever have to apologize for who he was.

But somehow, having Helen here felt perfectly right. Just like it had last year. Almost as though this was exactly where she belonged....

The thought made his jaw harden. Helen didn't belong here. She never had—and never would. She was only here now because he'd gotten her into trouble and he owed it to her to get her back out.

That fact didn't change anything personal between them. And he'd better not let himself forget it.

Abruptly, he walked into the kitchen and handed her the robe. "Here. You can put this on when you're done in the bath. I put out some towels, and soap and shampoo are by the sink."

"Thank you for going to all this trouble," she said quietly.

He resisted the urge to reach out and brush her wet hair off her cheek. "It's no trouble. Go on. You'd better get in the water before it turns cold."

Helen disappeared into the bathroom. Patrick stripped off his own wet clothes and threw on jeans and a sweatshirt. As he walked back into the kitchen, he heard faint splashing noises, and then the sound of water draining out of the tub.

Suddenly he had the crazy urge to charge into the bathroom and haul her into his arms. To make love to her so thoroughly she'd never even think about going to the beach and letting the water rise around her, about giving up the fight.

"Give it a rest, Monaghan," he muttered. He poured boiling water into two stoneware mugs and rummaged in a cupboard for the container of instant hot chocolate. "She doesn't need any more trouble in her life."

And he was trouble, he told himself grimly. Just like Jessica had always said. She'd screamed it at him, that last terrible night. Screamed it when he'd confronted her with the medical bill, the evidence of what she'd done.

"You think I'd actually go through with it? You think I'm going to let you ruin my life?" Her face had been distorted with fury. *"Forget it, Patrick. I've had enough trouble from you. I'm leaving you. Tonight."*

He hadn't wanted to believe her then, hadn't wanted to believe that what she'd done had anything to do with him. Sure, some part of him had blamed himself, but mostly he'd told himself it was Jessica's fault, Jessica's selfishness, Jessica who was really to blame.

But now…now, looking at the wreck he'd made of Helen's life, he couldn't help wondering if Jessica had been right.…

"Is that hot chocolate?" Helen's husky voice came from right behind him.

He started, spilling hot chocolate across the counter. How long had she been standing there? Had his thoughts shown on his face? His throat tight, he grabbed a rag and started mopping up the spill.

"Yeah, it is," he said, trying to sound normal. "Your mug's over there." He nodded toward the end of the counter.

"Thanks."

Patrick finished wiping the counter and tossed the rag into the sink. Picking up his own mug, he turned to walk over to the table.

He froze.

Helen stood beside the table, looking out the window. She wore his old blue robe, the belt knotted around her waist. The sun had come out, and light filtered through the raindrops on the window, casting a spiderweb of gold over her hair.

She was so beautiful it almost took his breath away.

He struggled to think of something to say. "Feeling better?"

"Thanks. I am." She turned away from the window and sat, curling her feet beneath her. She lifted the mug of hot chocolate and took a delicate sip. "Mmm. This is good."

Patrick sat across from her. "Thought we could both stand to warm up a little."

She put down her mug and looked straight at him. "Patrick, I feel like a fool for what happened back there. But when Franklin fired me, it was like the sky had fallen. All I could think of was getting away." Her brow wrinkled. "How did you find me?"

He shrugged. "Lucky guess."

"No, seriously."

Patrick shifted in his chair. "Last year, you told me you always went to the beach when you were upset."

"I can't believe you remember that." She gave a little laugh. "I don't even remember saying it."

"Well, you did." He remembered it vividly. He remembered everything about that night with a perfect, crystal clarity. He remembered the exact feel of her lips beneath his when he'd kissed her, the little catch of her breath when she'd touched him for the first time. He remembered her low, husky moan when he'd thrust inside her, remembered the taste of the sweat at the base of her throat.

Oh, yes, he remembered everything.

"I'm glad you remembered," she said softly.

He looked into her eyes. "I wasn't sure you'd be happy to see me. Especially after what happened this morning."

A wave of color flooded across her face. "You mean, in my hall?"

"Yeah," he said, his voice rasping. Memory speared through him, memory of the explosive heat of that kiss, and his groin tightened in an immediate response. Gritting his teeth, he tried to get his body under control. She hadn't wanted it to happen, he reminded himself. He'd actually made her *cry*.

The thought of hurting her dashed a bucket of ice water over the banked embers of his desire.

He set down his mug. "Helen, I can't tell you how sorry I am."

"You are?"

"I never wanted to hurt you." He laid his palms flat on the table for emphasis. "And I promise you. It won't happen again." No matter how much—how badly—he wanted it to.

Helen's golden lashes swept down, hiding her eyes.

Guilt twisted through him, and he curled his hands into fists. "I know you don't have any reason to believe me. Or to trust me. Not after the way I've already messed up your life. But I mean this, Helen. From now on, it'll be all business."

She looked up. "Business?"

"We have to prove to Franklin that he was wrong." Patrick paused. "Adam said Franklin fired you because he thinks you're having an affair with me."

"There's no way we can prove we aren't sleeping together."

"I know. But if I wasn't a murder suspect, it wouldn't matter if we were or not."

Helen bit her lip. "So if we find Marty's killer—"

"Franklin would have to admit he was wrong to fire you."

"I told you before. He'll never admit he's wrong. He's too concerned about how he looks on television to admit publicly that he made a mistake."

"We can make him admit it. If he knows he'll look worse by holding back, we can make him."

Hope flared in her eyes. "Maybe…maybe you're right."

Patrick let out a breath he hadn't even realized he was holding. "We can do it. I know we can."

"I hope so." Helen paused. "But I don't have the faintest idea where to start."

He smiled at her. "You've already taken the first step. Deciding that your career is worth fighting for."

She tipped her head to one side, an answering smile curving her lips. "Thanks to you."

Her words sent a vicious punch of guilt to his gut. "I don't deserve any thanks. If it wasn't for me, you never would have lost your job to begin with." He squeezed his mug tight, his knuckles whitening. "I owe you, Helen."

"You don't owe me anything."

"No?"

She looked away. "No."

Patrick frowned. Why wouldn't she admit that he owed her? Surely she couldn't think it was her own fault she'd lost her job. Or did she? Was that why she'd been out on the beach—because she blamed herself?

He wanted to pull her into his arms and soothe her, to tell her it wasn't her fault, but he knew he didn't have that right. Especially after he'd promised not to touch her.

Grimly, he forced his mind back to the case. If he was going to help her at all, he had to concentrate.

He cleared his throat. "Helen, we need to come up with a plan. Decide on our next move."

"Do you have any ideas?"

"I've been doing some thinking. Marty's murder is definitely connected to Tammy's. Most likely the killer paid Tammy to lie, then got nervous and killed her. But Marty's murder is also connected to Jamie Lee's. He was working on her case when he was killed, and the missing files prove something was up. The question is, how are the three cases connected?"

Helen's eyes widened. "Wait a minute. Didn't you tell me that Jamie Lee was strangled?"

"Yeah, why?"

"That's how Tammy was murdered, too."

Patrick slapped his palm on the table. "It has to be the same guy who killed all three of them. It just has to be."

"Carmel?"

"Carmel's probably involved somehow, but I can't see him as a killer. Like we said this morning, maybe whoever paid off Marty also paid off Carmel."

"If it isn't Carmel, then who?"

"That's the question. But whoever it is, we'll find him. He's killed three times in less than a week. He must be getting worried. Probably careless."

"And more dangerous," Helen said.

Ice trickled down Patrick's spine. She was right, of course. Looking at her, he couldn't stop his chest from tightening with worry.

He sucked in a deep breath. "Helen, you're going to have to be very careful."

She looked into his eyes. "You, too."

"Don't worry about me. I can take care of myself."

"I know." She smiled faintly. "But that's not going to keep me from worrying."

Something warm, something altogether too welcome, curled through Patrick's stomach. So she was worried about him. That meant she cared...at least a little.

He dragged his mind back to the case. "So, we've got three murders to choose from. Where do you want to start?"

"I think we should try and find Marty's informant. Somebody out there knows who the killer is, and I think we should try and find that somebody."

"The question is how. Marty didn't tell me or Angel who it was, and I doubt he told anyone else."

She gazed at him thoughtfully. "Last night, you mentioned heading down to the strip. You think we might find the informant down there?"

"Yeah. Marty was working the strip when the informant contacted him."

"So let's head down to the strip tonight and see if we can find him."

"Not you." The thought of Helen down there—possibly in danger—made Patrick clench his teeth. "I'll go alone."

"If you're going, I'm going."

"No way." He spoke harshly. "It wouldn't be safe for you."

She folded her arms across her chest. "You were the one who

wanted to work together. *Together.* You can't back out on me now."

"When I said we'd work together, I didn't mean I wanted to drag you into dangerous situations."

"I'm a big girl. I can make my own decisions."

He shook his head. "Even if it was safe, you'd stick out like a sore thumb. You'd make it harder to get information out of people."

Helen glared at him. "I could blend in if I tried."

He almost laughed, but he caught it just in time. "No way," he said. "You're way too classy. You know the strip—it's filled with drunks and prostitutes and bikers. One look at you and everyone would know you didn't belong."

"I said, I could blend in." Her voice was low and determined. "My career is at stake here. My life."

He dragged his hand through his hair. "Trust me. It's better if you don't come. Especially because of your career."

"Why?"

"Because things have gone too far for me to play by the rules. When I go down there, anything could happen. And I don't want to get you into any more trouble."

Helen stood up abruptly. "I've played by the rules all my life. *All my life.* And look where it's gotten me. I'm ready to break a few rules myself."

"You don't really mean that."

"No? My career is already history. What have I got to lose?" She stalked away from the table and disappeared behind the screens that surrounded his bed. He heard wood scrape on wood, and then a thud. He frowned as he heard the distinctive squeak of his second dresser drawer being opened.

"What are you doing?" he called.

"Borrowing a T-shirt and some sweatpants. My own clothes are ruined, and I have to go shopping to get ready for tonight." She reappeared, wearing baggy sweatpants rolled up around the ankle, and one of his T-shirts. It was so big it hit her mid-thigh.

She looked adorable. And determined.

He could feel a headache already starting. Hell. He wanted to protect her, but Helen was one stubborn woman. Stubborn, and brave, and more determined than any woman he'd ever met.

"Okay." He shook his head in defeat. "Okay, I'll let you come with me."

She tossed her head. "You'll *let* me? It was never a question of what you would or wouldn't let me do. The only question was whether we're going to do it separately—or together."

Patrick glanced at the bathroom door for what had to be the tenth time that evening. Helen had been in there for half an hour, at least. He'd never been able to figure out why it took women so long to get ready to go out. What was she doing in there, anyway?

That afternoon, they'd gone shopping at the big mall out on the interstate so Helen could buy what she needed. Clothes? Makeup? He wasn't sure. He'd tried to peek into her bags, but she'd just laughed and snatched them away.

Impatiently, he glanced at the bathroom door again—just as it opened and a woman walked out.

His jaw dropped. "Helen?"

It had to be her. She'd gone into the bathroom and locked the door half an hour ago, so unless some other woman had climbed in the window, it was her.

But he never would have recognized her.

This woman was wearing a sleek, bright red miniskirt and a low-necked black top that fit her like a second skin. Her hair was curled and a little mussed, as though she'd just gotten out of bed, and her mouth was fire-engine red. Long, long legs stretched out beneath the hem of her skirt, and her feet were encased in black spike heels.

She looked tough. Dangerous. And unbelievably sexy. Just looking at her made him as hard as a rock. He wanted to fling her down on the bed right now and—

Stifling a groan, he forced his mind away from that thought. But his body didn't cooperate, and his tight jeans did nothing to hide it. Grabbing a pillow, he yanked it onto his lap.

Helen stuck out her hip and splayed her fingers across it. "Hey there, big boy," she said, her voice husky.

"Helen." Her name stuck in his throat. "I can't believe it's you."

She grinned. "Think I'll fit in?"

"Fit in?" He eyed her. No way she'd fit in anywhere, not looking like that. She'd stand out as the sexiest woman for blocks. And judging by his own reaction, she wouldn't be the only thing standing out, either. He bit back another groan. "Hell, I'll have to beat the men off with a stick."

"Don't worry, Monaghan. I can take care of myself."

His gaze dipped down her body and back up again. "I'm starting to believe you can."

"At least they'll never guess I'm a prosecutor." Her face fell. "Or that I *was* a prosecutor."

He almost reached over and gave her hand a reassuring squeeze, but at the last minute he stopped himself. If he touched her, he didn't think he'd be responsible for his actions. Just being in the same room as her was driving him out of his mind.

"You'll be a prosecutor again." His voice was hoarse—almost a rasp—but she seemed not to notice.

"You really think so?"

He managed what he hoped was a casual grin. "If it's a matter of getting information out of a guy? You bet. No red-blooded American male under eighty is going to be able to resist you in that outfit." Including himself.

"I just hope we find Marty's informant. We *have* to find him." She sounded grim and determined—determined enough to take on a dozen crazed killers, if necessary.

A fierce burst of protectiveness shot through him. Why the hell had he agreed to this, anyway?

But it was too late to stop it now.

Patrick stood. "I want you to be very careful." His voice cracked suddenly. "I don't want anything to happen to you." Turning away so she wouldn't see his face, he picked up his keys and grabbed the old leather motorcycle jacket he'd dug out of the back of his closet.

Her heels tapped against the floor as she came up behind him. The light scent of her perfume filled his senses, and then she touched his shoulder. Heat raced through him as her fingers lightly brushed the skin of his neck.

"You be careful, too, Patrick. I—" She paused, and her voice lowered. "Just be careful."

Music boomed from the speakers overhead, filling the smoky, crowded space with a relentless beat. Onstage, exotic dancers gyrated their hips, coming just close enough to the edge of the stage for men to slip folded bills into their sequined G-strings.

It was the sixth or seventh bar they'd been to that evening— Helen had already lost count. They'd started at State and Third, working their way systematically down the strip. Somewhere out here in the sleazy mass of strip bars and cheap beer joints was Marty's informant.

So far, they hadn't had any luck finding him, but maybe this bar would be the one. If they were lucky.

Helen glanced at Patrick. He leaned one hip against a bar stool, talking to the man on his other side. In his black leather jacket and tight jeans, his jaw unshaven, Patrick looked as dangerous as any of the other patrons in the bar. Dangerous—and dangerously handsome. Just looking at him was enough to make her pulse speed up. Way, way up.

Suddenly he half turned toward her. Their eyes met, and he grinned. For an instant she saw a flash of heat in his silver eyes. Low in her belly, she felt that slow, familiar curl of desire.

She dragged her gaze away. Hadn't she already gotten into enough trouble by letting her feelings for Patrick run wild? Well, no more. Okay, he'd been good to her that afternoon. Too good. But that didn't mean she should stand around staring at him like a lovesick calf.

They were partners. Working together to solve the case. And that was all.

Leaning over, she tapped Patrick on the shoulder. "I'm going to the ladies' room," she shouted above the booming music.

"You want me to come with you?"

"No, I'll be fine." Resolutely, she turned away and struggled through the noisy, sweaty crowd. The washroom was a good place to strike up conversations with other women. Something about sinks and mirrors and the absence of men always seemed to encourage confidences. Besides, it would give her a few minutes away from Patrick—a chance to get her feelings firmly under control.

She pushed open the door to the ladies' room and walked inside. It was tiny, filthy, and very hot—the only window was nailed shut and covered with iron bars. The stench of cigarette smoke, vomit, and stale beer almost made her gag.

Swiftly, she glanced around. The room was empty, but she didn't want to go back out and face Patrick right away. Not until she was sure she was back in control. And she might as well fix her makeup while she was here.

As she stepped over to the tiny, cracked mirror, a muffled sob drifted out from one of the stalls. Helen's heart skipped. So she wasn't alone after all.

She walked over to the stall and tapped on the pitted wooden door, reminding herself to speak in the relaxed slang of her childhood. "Hey, you okay in there?"

The only response was a strangled sob.

"Hon?" Helen said. "Open the door, okay?"

She heard the scrape of the lock, and then the door swung open. A young woman with a tangled mane of dark, permed hair sat on the toilet, her face stained with tears.

She looked up at Helen through bleary eyes and snuffled. "Do I know you?"

"I don't think so. My name's, uh, Tiffany."

"I'm Sue." The young woman offered her a shaky smile. "I probably look like hell, don't I?"

"Yeah, you do." Helen gave her a wry smile. "You want to talk about it, hon? Probably some guy, right?"

Sue shook her head, fresh tears spilling over her cheeks. "M-my best friend was murdered a couple days ago."

Excitement shot through Helen's body, but she kept her face neutral. "You mean, Jamie Lee?"

Sue looked up. "Yeah, that's right. Did you know her?"

"Knew her a couple years back, down in Seattle," Helen lied.

"Seattle? She was glad to get outta there. Candy—you know her sister?—she stayed down there, but Jamie thought it was safer workin' up here." Her face crumpled. "But it wasn't."

"Cops haven't caught the guy, have they?"

"No way. They sent some fat pig down here. The guy was a loser. I *told* him I saw Jamie take off with some guy, but he didn't even listen to me."

Helen's eyes widened. "You saw Jamie the night she was killed?"

"Yeah. Saw her gettin' into a brown car in the alley out back."

Helen's heart banged against her ribs. A brown car—it had to be the killer. "Did you get a look at the guy?"

"Nah, it was too dark back there." Sue looked at her curiously. "Why?"

Helen shrugged. "Can't be too careful. If there's some guy out there killin' girls, I want to know who it is."

"For sure." Sue grimaced. "I didn't see him, but I think it was one of Jamie Lee's regulars. She said somethin' earlier about meeting him at midnight."

"She had regulars?"

Sue nodded. "Couple older guys."

"Did you know who they were?"

"No way. She said they'd kill her if she told anyone. Guess they were real scared of havin' it get around."

"Is there anyone else who might know?"

Sue shrugged. "Maybe Candy, Jamie's sister. She was closer to Jamie than anyone."

"She still living in Seattle?"

"Yeah. She don't hook no more, though. She dances at some club down on Second." Sue bit her lip and pushed herself off the toilet. "Speaking of dancin', I'd better get going. I'm on in a couple minutes."

"Hey, be careful out there," Helen said.

"Yeah." Sue flashed her a smile. "You, too."

Helen waited until she was sure the other woman was gone,

and then she grabbed her purse and hurried back into the bar to find Patrick. She stopped short.

He wasn't there.

The bar stool where he'd been sitting was empty, and she couldn't see him at any of the other tables. Helen's mouth went dry. Where was he? Had something happened to him? He wouldn't have just gone off and left her, she was sure of it....

A touch of panic spun through her body, but she clamped down on it. She would find him. She had to.

Dragging in a breath, she flagged the bartender, a tough-looking woman with shaggy hair and big, blunt-nailed hands.

"What can I get ya?" the bartender asked.

"I'm looking for a man."

The woman threw back her head and let out a throaty laugh. "Ain't we all?"

"No, I mean I'm looking for a particular man. He was standing right here about ten minutes ago. Tall. Dark hair. Black leather jacket."

"Look around ya, babe. I got too many customers to keep tabs on 'em all."

Helen dug into her purse for a twenty-dollar bill. She put it on the counter. "This help you remember?"

The bartender smiled, revealing a gold tooth. "Yeah, maybe. Cute guy, right? Great shoulders."

"Where'd he go?"

"You wanna know? You better be a bit more generous."

Helen gritted her teeth and fished out another twenty. "Here. Now where did he go?"

"He left with another guy. They went out through the fire exit." The bartender nodded at a door to one side of the stage.

Helen spun on her heel. Her heart thumped as she pushed her way through the crowd to the door. Why had Patrick left? It must have been something important—he wouldn't have left without telling her unless he'd had to. Had the other man had information, something he'd wanted to say in private? Or was Patrick in trouble?

The thought sent a sharp pang of fear through her body, and

she quickened her pace. Shoving open the heavy steel fire door, she plunged into the narrow alley behind the bar.

It was dark. Very dark. There were no streetlights back here, and when the door clanged shut behind her, the only source of light was abruptly cut off.

"Patrick?" she called.

No reply. She listened, but she couldn't hear the sound of any voices. Where was he? Farther down the alley?

Squaring her shoulders, she walked around an overflowing garbage bin and headed down the alley. The tap of her heels echoed loudly, magnified by the cement walls on either side.

In the distance, she could still hear the thumping bass of the strip club, and the faint roar of an engine reminded her she was in the heart of the city. But the darkness in the alley was absolute. It enveloped her, and the panic flooded back, stronger this time. Oh, God, if something had happened to him….

She fought back the fear, fought to keep her voice strong and clear. "Patrick? Are you here?"

Silence.

She kept walking. A few yards farther along, a second alley opened up, running perpendicular to the first. She paused and peered down it.

A single, naked bulb over a doorway at the other end of the alley provided a small splash of light. A dark-haired man stood under the light with his back to the door, surrounded by four or five other men.

It was Patrick.

Relief raced through her at the sight of him, relief so fierce and strong that it sent a wave of dizziness to her head. Putting her hand against the wall, she steadied herself and took a deep breath.

Suddenly she heard a jumble of raised voices. She jerked up her head just as one of the men punched Patrick in the stomach. In a blur of movement, Patrick hit him back.

The man stumbled backward with a noisy grunt, his hands covering his face. "You broke my nose!"

Patrick hit him again.

All the other men converged on him in a rush.

Chapter 11

"**P**atrick!" Helen screamed.

She sprinted toward him. Her spike heels made her slip and stumble, but she didn't want to waste precious seconds kicking them off. From the end of the alley, she heard grunts and shouts and the sickening crunch of bone against bone. Patrick disappeared into a heaving mass of flying fists and legs, and her heart thudded with panic.

Patrick had to be all right—he just had to!

As she neared the end of the alley, she glanced around wildly. Two men with bloody faces were sprawled across the ground, out cold. Patrick stood with his back to the wall, his arms pinned by a couple of thugs. A short man wearing a clingy silk shirt and a tangle of gold chains deliberately drew back his fist and punched him in the face.

With a shriek of pure outrage, Helen charged the stranger.

He half turned. "What the—"

She slammed into him full-force. He stumbled backward, away from Patrick. Her momentum carried her with him, and he struck out at her. His fist crashed into her stomach, and pain exploded through her body. She fell back against the alley wall, gasping for breath.

Through a haze of pain and panic, she saw the man raise his fist again. She ducked and fumbled for her shoe. Her heart hammered as her fingers closed around it. She dodged another blow and sprang up with the shoe in her hand. Turning out the metal spike on the end of the heel, she smashed the man in the face.

Blood gushed down his cheek. He staggered back, clutching his forehead. "I can't see! You bitch, you've blinded me!"

Helen hit him again. The metal spike sank into his flesh, and he fell to the ground with a hoarse scream. She whirled around, her shoe still raised, ready to fight off the other two men.

Patrick had already dealt with them. They were running away down the alley, their footsteps clattering against the concrete as they disappeared into the darkness.

"Good work, sweetheart," Patrick said. He was leaning against the wooden door. In the ring of light cast by the naked bulb, Helen saw that his face was covered with blood.

Her mouth dry with fear, she flew across the alley. "Patrick! Are you all right?"

"Fine." He gave her a crooked grin. "Just fine."

She threw her arms around him just as he closed his eyes and slid down the wall to the ground.

Helen dragged Patrick's arm around her shoulders as he climbed out of the car. He tried to pull away, but she kept her arm firmly around his waist as she led him up the stairs and into his building.

"I can walk on my own," he muttered.

"I'm not taking any chances," she said grimly. "You're too heavy for me to carry if you pass out."

"I'm not going to pass out!"

"You already did once. It scared the hell out of me, Monaghan. I thought I was going to have to leave you in that alley while I went for the car. What if those guys had come back?"

Patrick cracked a lopsided smile, and then winced and touched his broken lip. "I could've handled it."

"No, you couldn't. You're not Rambo, Patrick. As much as I'm sure you'd like to be."

"Rambo? Nope, I never wanted to be him. Too many guns. When I was a kid, I always wanted to be Bruce Lee."

"You've got to be kidding."

"Okay, maybe Clint Eastwood."

She sighed. "You're impossible, you know that?"

"Yeah." The corner of his mouth twitched up.

Helen stared at him. Even beaten and bruised, Patrick kept his sense of humor—and his pride. Just at the moment, his pride made her want to strangle him, but a part of her responded to his arrogance. His strength. And that same treacherous part wanted to kiss his swollen lips, to soothe his battered body with her own.

Part of her, she told herself sternly, was a fool.

She jerked her gaze away from him and fumbled through his keys. Finding the right ones, she unlocked the series of dead bolts and pushed the door open. Blindly, she groped for the light switch and flicked it on.

She turned to look at Patrick, who was propped up against the doorjamb. His lower lip was broken and swollen, and blood stained his face and neck. His hands were bloody, too, and his knuckles scraped. But instead of repelling her, seeing his injuries made her want to kiss him even more.

She covered her instinctive reaction with a frown. "You look awful," she said flatly.

"Yeah, well, I don't feel so hot, either." Patrick pushed himself away from the door. He let out a muffled groan and wrapped his arm around his ribs. "Somehow I don't remember Dirty Harry ever feeling like this."

"Ribs hurt pretty badly?"

"They hurt a little, yeah."

"They're probably cracked." She kicked the door shut and tugged Patrick's arm around her shoulders once again. "You're going to bed."

"I'm not gonna argue with you there."

Slowly, Helen led him across the room. This time, he didn't pull away. His breathing came in harsh rasps, and he leaned on her just a little. Helen tightened her lips and tried to concentrate on getting him to the bed. Not on the hard beauty of his chest or the weight of his hand on her shoulder. Definitely not on the feel of his denim-clad thigh rubbing intimately against hers.

Finally, they made it to the bed. Heaving a mental sigh of relief, Helen let go of Patrick.

He collapsed onto the bed with a groan. "Hell. I feel like I just got run over by a truck."

"You pretty much did. Five of them."

"Five, huh? No wonder my ribs hurt."

She sat on the edge of the bed, careful to keep several inches of space between them. "Who were they, anyway?"

"You remember the guy with the gold chains? The one you jumped on? He was Jamie Lee's pimp. Name's Rocky."

"What were you doing out there with him?"

"One of the other guys came up to me in the bar and said he had some information about Jamie Lee. When I went outside with him, Rocky and his friends were waiting. Rocky said he'd heard I was asking questions about him, and he wanted me to know he didn't appreciate it."

Helen stared at him in exasperation. "Why did you go outside in the first place? Didn't you realize it could be a setup?"

Patrick shrugged. "I figured it was worth the risk."

"You just never give up, do you, Monaghan?"

"Nope." His eyes turned dark and serious. "Helen, listen to me. The situation wasn't that dangerous. They might have broken a few bones, but it was only a warning. They weren't going to kill me."

"What are you saying?"

"I'm saying you shouldn't have come charging down that alley."

A spark of anger ignited in her chest. "So I should have just left you there? And walked away?"

"That's right."

She glared at him. "I thought we were partners."

"We are, but—"

"But only when it's not dangerous."

Patrick's jaw hardened. "I've already put you in enough danger. I don't want you in any more. You could have been badly injured or even killed back there." He clenched his hands into fists. "Do you have any idea how that makes me feel?"

"You're not my keeper!"

"No, I'm not! I just care enough about you that I don't want to see you bleeding to death in some back alley!"

Helen gasped, and Patrick dragged his hand over his eyes. "Dammit, I'm sorry. I shouldn't have said that. It's just—the idea of you getting hurt makes me crazy."

"Well, I didn't get hurt."

"No, but you could have." He grabbed her hand. "Why did you do it? There isn't another woman in the state who would have run screaming *toward* those guys instead of away from them."

The feel of his warm palm against hers sent ribbons of heat racing up her arm. Suddenly she felt light-headed, almost dizzy.

"Helen?"

She gulped, struggling to concentrate on his question. "Why did I do it? I don't—don't know. I didn't even stop to think. When I saw that man hit you, I just knew I had to stop him. I had to protect you—any way I could."

"I'm not worth risking your life for." His jaw tightened. "Do you hear me? *I'm not worth it.*"

She looked straight into his silver eyes. "No?"

"No." Patrick jerked his hand out of her grasp and sat up. His face contorted with pain as he swung his legs over the side of the bed.

"What are you doing?" Helen demanded.

"I'm going to the bathroom to clean up."

"No, you're not. Get back into bed. I'll get everything you need and bring it here."

"You don't have to do that."

"I know I don't have to, but I'm going to." Helen got to her feet. "I'll be back in a minute."

Helen boiled a kettle of water and gathered all the first-aid supplies she could find. Balancing a bowl of steaming water on her arm, she made her way around the screens to Patrick's bed.

She almost dropped everything on the floor.

Patrick stood with his back to her—his naked back. Broad, defined shoulders tapered down to a narrow waist. There were several dark red bruises around his ribs, but they didn't detract from the sleek beauty of his golden skin, from the aura of power and strength that radiated from his muscular body.

Helen stood transfixed by his beauty as he peeled off his jeans and dumped them on a chair. His hips were lean, sexy, perfectly proportioned. His legs rippled with thickly corded muscles. Even his feet—long and just a little flat—looked beautiful to her.

Patrick turned to get into bed. His eyes met hers, and he froze. A dark red flush started around the base of his neck and swept up his bruised face in a tide of color. Helen's eyes widened. He was blushing. Patrick Monaghan was actually blushing because she'd seen him naked. She could hardly believe it.

"Helen." He dove into bed and yanked the covers up to his chest. "I didn't know you were there."

Suddenly she realized she'd been staring. Staring shamelessly. No wonder the poor man had blushed. Her own cheeks heating with embarrassment, she put the bowl of water and her other supplies down on the wooden dresser by his bed.

"Looks like you've probably got some bruised ribs." She tried to sound cool and casual, as though all she'd been doing was checking out his injuries. Not his body.

It didn't work. Her voice came out husky and breathless—the voice of a lover, not a nurse—and she felt herself go an even darker red. Fortunately, Patrick didn't seem to notice.

"I guess," he muttered. He leaned over and reached for a washcloth.

Helen snatched it out of his reach. "No way. You're going to lie there and behave yourself while I clean you up."

His eyes hardened. "I'll be fine. Just leave the stuff there. I'll deal with it myself."

Helen crossed her arms over her chest and glared at him. She understood his pride, but this was ridiculous. "You are not going

to deal with it yourself. You are going to lie there quietly while
I disinfect your cuts and bruises and check your ribs.''

''But—''

''No buts.''

He heaved an exaggerated sigh. ''Okay, Nurse Stewart. I see
who's in charge here—and it isn't me.''

''Damn right.''

Patrick lay back and closed his eyes. Helen soaked a washcloth
in the hot water and gently sponged away the blood on his face.
She bit her lip when she saw the extent of his injuries. He had a
nasty cut high on one cheek, and his lower lip was split and puffy.
One of his eyes was badly swollen already, but his nose wasn't
broken and all his teeth were still there.

Looking at his bruised and battered face, she felt a dangerous
tenderness swell up in her chest. Ruthlessly she suppressed it.
She'd looked after injured men before, she reminded herself. Why
should this be any different?

''So what's the damage?'' he asked.

''I think you're going to live, Monaghan.'' She uncapped the
bottle of antiseptic and sloshed some onto a cotton ball. She
pressed the cotton onto the cut on his cheek, and he flinched.

''Sure doesn't feel like it.'' He winced as she sponged the cut.
''Ouch. That stings.''

''It's antiseptic. I know it stings, but you don't want these cuts
to get infected.'' Helen tossed out the cotton ball and soaked a
fresh one. When she was done cleaning the cut, she put a small
bandage over it and moved on to his split lip.

His lower lip was badly swollen and obviously sore. As gently
as she could, she stroked the cotton over the cut. Slowly, she
traced the outline of his lip. Her heart began to beat a little faster.
Touching him like this, she couldn't help remembering the way
his mouth had felt on hers that morning. Soft—and then hard—
and then soft again, and oh, so warm. When he'd kissed his way
down her throat, the feel of his mouth on her skin had sent fire
coursing through her body....

Her fingers gentled, lingering on his mouth. Patrick's breathing
shallowed. She brushed the cotton across the soft inside of

his lip, and he made a strangled sound.

She jerked her hand away. "Did I hurt you?"

"No. No, you didn't." Patrick's expression was pained, his eyes squeezed shut.

Helen frowned. "Are you sure?"

His breath hissed out from between his teeth, and she thought she heard him swear under his breath. "Just get on with it, okay?"

"Sure," she said stiffly.

She took his right hand and started cleaning his scraped knuckles. His thumb rubbed against the back of her hand, rasping faintly on her skin. Heat whispered through her at his touch. She looked down at his strong, tanned fingers, at the wisps of black hair that swirled across the back of his hand, and she remembered the way he'd touched her last year, remembered his hands gliding across her naked skin.

Suddenly she wanted to touch him—and not with the touch of a nurse. Tentatively she slid her thumb over his palm.

Patrick flinched.

Helen bit her lip and picked up the bottle of antiseptic. Patrick was in pain, she told herself sternly. She should be concentrating on cleaning his cuts and bruises, not wondering whether his strong hands would still feel so good against her skin....

Hastily, she finished cleaning and bandaging his knuckles. When she was done, she reached for the blankets that covered his chest.

Patrick grabbed her wrists. "What are you doing?"

"What do you think I'm doing?" She wrenched her hands out of his grasp. "I'm going to look at your ribs."

"No."

"What's the problem, Monaghan?" She gave him a sarcastic smile. "You have a sudden attack of modesty? No need. I've seen your chest before, if you remember."

Something flickered deep in his eyes. "I remember," he rasped. "Don't ever doubt that."

Her heart began to thump. "I'm not going to ravish you," she said, praying he wouldn't notice the way her voice cracked. "I just want to see if your ribs are broken."

"How are you going to tell? You used to be a doctor?"

"No. I was the industrial first-aid attendant in a factory. That's how I put myself through college."

He closed his eyes. "Okay. Go ahead."

Leaning forward, Helen pulled the blankets down to his waist. Her gaze slid across his chest, and she sucked in her breath. Somehow she'd managed to forget exactly what his naked, powerful torso looked like.

Now, she stared at his broad chest, at the thick, well-defined muscles. His stomach was flat and hard, a ripple of ridged muscles marching downward. Fine black hair covered his chest, tapering as it ran across his belly and under the blankets that covered his hips....

With an effort, she forced her gaze back up to Patrick's ribs. There was some ugly bruising, mostly on his left side. Trying to concentrate, she ran her hand over his ribs. The feel of warm skin and crisp, soft hair beneath her hand made her heart thump even harder, and she struggled to keep her mind on her job. Checking each rib, she slid her fingers higher, across the bulge of his muscle, over the little nub of his nipple.

Patrick swore.

Helen jerked up her head. "Did that hurt?" She applied more pressure. "Was it there, or—"

Patrick grabbed her hand, his fingers closing over it like a vise. Roughly, he dragged it away from his chest. His eyes were still squeezed shut, his mouth a flat, hard line.

Helen twisted her hand out of his grasp. "I know you don't like this, but I have to do it. If your ribs are broken, you have to go to the hospital."

"They're not broken."

"You seem to be having a lot of pain if it's just bruises."

"It's not pain," he said from between his teeth.

"What do you mean?"

Slowly, Patrick opened his eyes. They were smoky, turbulent, dark. "I mean, you're not hurting me."

"You mean—"

He yanked his gaze away from hers. "Just go away, Helen."

"Why?" she asked, suddenly breathless.

"Because if you don't, I'm going to do something I'll regret."

"Like what?"

Silence.

Helen sucked in her breath. An electric charge leaped between them like a flame, drawing her, pulling her in. Her insides melted, turning to liquid warmth. With a sharp, crystal clarity, she realized that she wanted him. Wanted him badly. Wanted him so much, it actually hurt.

The ache low in her belly throbbed, and suddenly she felt reckless. To hell with tomorrow. To hell with the consequences. Her life—her career—was already in ruins. What did she have left to lose?

Slowly she reached out and laid her palm against his unshaven cheek. His stubble rasped against her hand, and she felt a tiny shiver race through her body. "Like what?" she asked again.

"Nothing," Patrick muttered.

Deliberately she put her other hand on the pillow, beside his head. Leaning down, she brushed a feather-light kiss across his lips. "Did you mean something like that?" she whispered against his mouth.

"No," he growled.

"Then what?" Delicately she ran her tongue over his swollen lower lip.

"I meant something more like this." Patrick clamped his arms around her waist and hauled her against him. Helen gasped as his mouth came down on hers. His kiss was hard and demanding, his lips slanting across hers with a fiery passion that sent waves of heat racing to her core. Their tongues tangled as he plundered her mouth with an urgency, a desperation, that tore at her heart.

He tasted of heat and whiskey, desire and smoke—a heady mixture that was all his own. He filled her senses. The world, the case, the ruin of her career, everything was lost. There was only the feel of his strong arms around her waist, his hands roving over her back. Only the scent of him, the wild sensation of his tongue plunging rhythmically into her mouth.

Helen moaned deep in her throat as Patrick tugged her fully onto the bed. She lay flush against him, her legs tangling with his, her breasts brushing against the muscular wall of his chest. She twisted even closer to him, wanting to feel his strength. It felt right, so right, to wrap her arms around him, to kiss him with all the longing in her soul.

Patrick's lips slid from her mouth, across her hair. His teeth grated gently against her earlobe, and she shivered in shock and pleasure. He kissed the delicate underside of her jaw, leaving a trail of fire as his mouth slid down her throat and came back up to claim her lips once more.

She'd waited so long for this, Helen realized. To be back here with him, in his arms, in his bed. This was what she'd wanted ever since she'd fled that morning last year, but she'd been too afraid. Too wrapped up in her career and her rules, too frightened of losing everything.

Too afraid of what he made her feel, of the fire that raged inside her when he was near.

He was so beautiful. She ran one of her hands across his chest and up to his shoulder. She kneaded the thickly corded muscles, reveling in his strength, his power, his warmth. Curling her palm around the back of his neck, she buried her fingers in the rough silk of his hair, pulling him even closer, losing herself in his kiss.

Patrick slid his hand across her back and up her side, testing the curve of her waist. He stroked upward, cupping her breast. The heat of his hand burned through the thin fabric of her top. Helen gasped as hot, liquid desire twisted through her. Her nipples hardened with a rush, aching for his intimate touch. When he teasingly circled her nipple with his finger, she arched her back, thrusting against his palm.

"Please," she whispered brokenly against his mouth. "More."

Patrick pulled back and lifted his head to look straight at her. His eyes were dark, glittering with heat and desire. But there was more than desire. Deep in his eyes, Helen saw tenderness. She felt it in his touch as he raised his hand to her cheek and dragged his knuckle over her jaw in a rough caress.

"Are you sure?" he said. "I don't want to do anything you'll regret."

His sensitivity shook her, making her want him—need him— even more. "I'm sure," she whispered, her voice shaky. "But are you sure you won't regret it?"

He didn't take his eyes from hers. "Never."

She slid her hand over his hip. "Then what are we waiting for?"

Patrick's mouth descended on hers once again. This time his kiss was an unmistakable brand of possession. Helen dug her fingers into his hair, responding with all the reckless passion she'd denied herself for so long. She arched against him, loving the feel of his hard body pressed against hers, the sound of his harsh breathing, his urgent touch.

Patrick broke the kiss and slid his lips down her body. Helen shivered with a delicious heat as he kissed the hollow of her shoulder, then the soft swell of her breast. He took her nipple into his mouth and sucked gently, tasting her through the thin layer of fabric. Helen twisted upward, desire cresting hard and fast. But she wanted more. She wanted to feel her bare skin against his. To feel the heat of his mouth, the texture of his hands, with no barriers between them.

As if he could sense her thoughts, Patrick hooked his hands in the hem of her top and yanked it over her head, sending it flying across the room. The wisp of satin and lace beneath it followed, and then his lips and tongue were on her body and the world spun out of control.

Sensation swirled through her. Heat. Wanting. Desire—blazing and urgent, unlike anything she'd ever felt. She heard herself moan as she dug her fingernails into his back, and Patrick made a harsh sound of need.

He ran his hand under her skirt and between her thighs, cupping her, even as his lips tugged at her breast. Helen almost came off the bed. She arched upward against his hand, her heart thudding out of control. Patrick slid his fingers into her panties, slowly, surely, teasing her slick folds. The coil of aching longing within her almost exploded.

"Patrick...please...I can't...."

She cried out in instinctive protest as he withdrew his hand, but he found the zipper to her skirt and dragged it down over her hips, taking her panties with it. Tossing them aside, he leaned over and grabbed something out of a drawer.

A second later, he came to her in a rush of heat and strength. Her hips surged upward, seeking his strength, but he paused and lifted his head to look into her eyes.

She couldn't wait any longer. She wanted him too badly to wait.

She grabbed his shoulders and dragged him down to her, even as she pushed herself up to meet him, opening for him. A groan exploded from his lips as he plunged into her with one long, deep thrust, and then he kissed her, his tongue delving rhythmically into her mouth.

Patrick was steel and wildfire and heat within her, blazing with a reckless passion. His dark, pagan beauty thrilled her. Through the haze of her own desire, Helen watched as he flung back his head, his neck cording with tension. She wrapped her legs about his hips, pulling him deeper, farther, closer.

And then the coil of desire within her burst into a thousand pieces, and she fell over the edge. With one final thrust, Patrick joined her. He called her name hoarsely and buried his face against her neck as he shuddered with a release that shattered them both.

Patrick tightened his arm around Helen's waist, pulling her a little closer. She curled against him, one of her legs thrown over his thighs. Her breasts pressed against his chest, and her silky hair brushed his shoulder. He felt the sweat cooling against his skin as his heartbeat gradually slowed and his breathing came back to normal.

Making love with Helen had been every bit as incredible, as explosive, as he remembered—and more. She was so passionate.

So beautiful. So completely unlike any other woman he'd ever been with.

She was his. Finally. And he never wanted to let her go.

He ran a possessive hand over the curve of her waist and across her hip. His fingers slipped into the nest of dark blond curls at the junction of her thighs.

Helen gave a breathless laugh and tilted back her head to look into his eyes. "Better be careful what you're doing there."

Her husky voice sent a bolt of need straight to his groin, and he leaned over to kiss her thoroughly, exploring her beautiful mouth. She made a soft noise of satisfaction, and he pulled back just a little. "Careful?" he asked. "Why?"

Helen smiled against his mouth. "Because if you don't stop, I might end up taking advantage of an injured man—again."

"Injured? Who's injured? I feel better than I have in years."

Helen looked at him from under her lashes, her blue eyes sparkling. "You do, do you?"

"Yeah."

"Then maybe you should start hiring guys to beat you up more often."

He grinned. "You think that's why I'm feeling so good?"

She shrugged, a smile tugging at her lips. "What else could it be?"

He pretended to think about it, and she punched him lightly in the ribs. He groaned. "Hey!"

"That's for being ungallant," she teased.

"Ungallant?" He tried to look innocent. "Who, me?"

Laughter bubbled from Helen's lips, a sound of pure, undiluted happiness. Patrick felt his heart expand. Seeing her smile, hearing her laugh, made him realize how badly he wanted her to be happy—with him.

He wanted her to stay in his arms. In his bed. Wanted her to stay...in his life.

Abruptly, his muscles tensed. In his *life?* What was he thinking? He hadn't wanted that from any woman—hadn't allowed himself to want it—since his divorce.

And he shouldn't be thinking about that now, of all times. Not now, when he finally had Helen in his arms. For now he should concentrate on enjoying the moment. After all, who knew how long it would last?

Last year Helen hadn't even hung around the next morning. It wasn't too likely that now he was a murder suspect and had gotten her fired from her job, she was suddenly going to want to stick around.

Helen pushed herself up on one elbow and leaned over to cup his cheek. Her eyes were serious, her laughter gone. "What's wrong?"

He managed a smile. "Nothing."

"Is it the case?"

"Yeah," he lied.

"Shh." She laid her hand over his lips, and he saw anguish in her eyes. "Don't. Let's not think about it. Not tonight."

He kissed her fingers. "Okay."

Helen replaced her hand with her lips, kissing him with a hopeless passion that sent desire racing through him once again. She twined her arms around his neck, whispering against his mouth. "Just make love to me, Patrick. Make me forget."

A helpless groan escaped his lips as she found him with her hands, stroking and caressing him until he knew he had to bury himself inside her or die. As she straddled his thighs and guided him into her tight, moist depths, he closed his eyes with a pleasure so intense it was almost pain.

When it was over, Helen collapsed against him, her body still shaking with the force of her release. Patrick held her tight, cradling her against his chest. Her breathing slowed and deepened, her muscles relaxed, as she drifted into sleep.

Patrick stared down at her peacefully sleeping face. No matter what happened tomorrow, he was glad she was here with him now. Here, curled up in his arms, as warm and trusting as a child....

The thought made his throat tighten, and he pulled her even closer. As if holding her now, tonight, could somehow make up for what he'd lost, for the dream that Jessica had destroyed. He knew it couldn't—not really—but he wouldn't think about that. Not tonight. For tonight, he'd think only about the woman in his arms.

For tonight, he'd let himself pretend he still believed in dreams.

Chapter 12

Golden light filtered across Helen's face as she blinked her eyes open. It was morning—and she was in Patrick's bed. Warmth flooded through her, and a secret smile slid across her lips.

Behind her, she heard the steady rasp of Patrick's breathing. He was curled around her, one heavy arm flung across her hip. His hand rested possessively on her stomach. In the air, on the sheets, she smelled the musky scent of their lovemaking.

A shiver of pleasure ran through her body, and she pressed herself a little closer to Patrick's warm chest. Last night had been wonderful. It had been good between them—so good that the memory made her heart beat faster, her breath come quick and shallow.

Last night, she'd been reckless and wild. For the first time in her life, she was following her emotions, her intuition, rather than her logic. She was breaking the rules she'd followed all her life—and it was wonderful.

She felt free. Free to dress in clothes she wouldn't have been caught dead in a week ago. Free to attack a thug with her shoe instead of dutifully calling the police to report an assault. Free to take control of her life instead of being ruled by fear.

And she was free to make sweet love with Patrick Monaghan— even though she knew whatever was between them couldn't last forever. Even though she knew Patrick wasn't looking for a real relationship, only something temporary, something where he didn't have to make any promises.

She's just like her mother....

The faint echo of memory floated through her mind. Helen pushed it fiercely away. She wouldn't think about her mother. She wouldn't think about her past or her future. Her carefully constructed life, her career, everything was in ruins.

For now, she would just concentrate on getting through one day at a time.

Just like her mother. Just like her mother.

The whisper was louder this time. Helen shook her head, trying to block it out, but the words chased themselves around and around in her mind, twisting through her until her heart was pounding and her palms were slick with sweat.

She knew from long experience that there was almost no way to stop it. No way, except to go running...or to bury herself in her work. In a career she no longer had.

Black despair flooded up inside her, but she forced it back. She wasn't going to give up yet. Not while she still had any fight left in her body.

But if she had any hope of winning, she'd better get moving. She couldn't lie around in bed all day.

Biting her lip, she pushed at Patrick's arm. He mumbled something and tugged her closer, pulling her back against his broad chest. For a moment she was tempted—more than tempted—to give in to him, but the whisper deep in her mind stopped her before she could.

Gritting her teeth, she rolled away from Patrick and slid out of bed. After the warmth of Patrick's body, of the bed, the air felt cold against her skin. Temptation struck again, temptation to dive back under the covers, but resolutely she turned away.

On tiptoe, she headed into the shower and turned on the tap

full-blast. The hot water sluiced over her body, stinging her tender skin. The sensation reminded her of just why her skin was tender, of Patrick's hands and mouth on her body, of the incredible feel of him moving inside her. She closed her eyes, letting the water rain down on her. Why was it that making love with him hadn't cured the ache of need deep inside her? How was it possible that this morning, the ache was even worse?

Fiercely, she shook her head, spattering droplets of water against the shower curtain. She should be thinking about the case, not about Patrick. Forcing her mind away from him, she picked up the bar of soap. The case, she told herself firmly. She had to think about the case.

As she scrubbed herself clean, she ran over the information Sue had given her last night at the bar. About the man with the brown car. About Jamie Lee's sister—who lived in Seattle.

Her stomach lurched with the knowledge of what she had to do.

Seattle.

Today—whether she liked it or not—she'd be going home.

Patrick came awake slowly, conscious of a feeling of deep satisfaction. His ribs throbbed and the pain nagged at him, but the bed was warm and Helen's elusive scent lingered on the pillow. He breathed in deeply, and a smile slid across his bruised face. He reached for her—wanting to tug her into his arms and kiss her awake—but she wasn't there.

Patrick stretched his arm out a little farther. Instead of touching her warm, soft skin, his hand slid over sheets that were cold and empty. He opened his eyes and jerked upright.

She was gone.

"Helen?" he shouted.

Silence.

He leaped out of bed and strode naked out from behind the screens. The bathroom door was open, and the light was off. She wasn't in the kitchen or the main living area.

And she hadn't left a note.

Fear and anger pounded through his body, and he squeezed

his hands into fists. Dammit, where was she? Had something happened to her? Or had she just walked out on him *again?*

He was stalking toward the bed to grab his clothes when he heard the rasp of a key in his front door. The series of dead bolts clicked.

He dove for his gun. Shielding himself behind the couch, he aimed the gun at the door.

The door swung open, and Helen walked in.

Patrick let out his breath and lowered the gun as he stood up. "Helen."

She turned toward him, looking cool and beautiful and untouchable in a simple ivory blouse and a pencil-slim skirt. In one hand, she carried a small leather suitcase, and in the other, she held a white paper sack. "Patrick." Her gaze dropped to his gun. "What on earth are you doing?"

His relief at the sight of her dissolved into sudden anger. Dropping his gun onto the couch, he folded his arms over his bare chest. "What does it look like? I didn't know who was coming through that door." He scowled. "Where have you been?"

"I went to my apartment to get a few things."

"What?" His voice rose. "Why didn't you wake me?"

"I'm perfectly capable of driving to my own apartment." She dropped his key ring onto the coffee table, set down the paper sack, and straightened to face him. "Unless you're objecting to me borrowing your car."

"No. I'm objecting to you putting yourself in danger. Not to mention taking off without a word. How the hell do you think it feels to wake up and find you gone like that?"

She looked at him coolly. "You didn't have to worry. I can take care of myself just fine. I don't need a twenty-four-hour bodyguard."

The fist of anger tightened in his gut. Was that her way of saying she didn't need—or want—him? He'd figured it would happen sooner or later, but this was a whole lot sooner than he'd expected.

He narrowed his eyes. "So why did you have to go back to your place?"

"To get the things I need for Seattle. I wanted us to get an early start. We've got a lot to do."

"In Seattle? What are you talking about?"

"I talked to a stripper at the bar last night. She was Jamie Lee's best friend, and she saw Jamie getting into a car the night she was murdered. A brown car."

Patrick froze. "The killer. It must have been him. Driving the same car he used to try and kill you."

"My thoughts exactly."

"Did the girl see who was driving?"

Helen shook her head. "No, but she thinks it might have been one of Jamie Lee's regular customers. Apparently Jamie Lee had a few regulars."

"Does this girl know who they were? Know anything about them?"

"No. Jamie told her they'd kill her if she breathed a word about them to anyone. Apparently the only person she might have told is her sister Candy, who lives in Seattle."

"Then we'd better get down to Seattle right away."

"Exactly."

Patrick shoved his hands through his hair. He knew he should be excited about the new lead. Even ecstatic.

But instead he felt tense and angry. After last night, that incredible night, he'd imagined waking up slowly this morning. With Helen curled in his arms. He'd envisioned laughing with her, maybe eating breakfast in bed. Making sweet, hot love— again. And again.

He sure as hell hadn't imagined standing naked in his living room while Helen—looking altogether too damn cool and calm and lawyerly—informed him that they had to go to Seattle.

A splinter of hurt stabbed through the anger. Hadn't last night affected her at all?

"Why didn't you tell me this last night?" he asked abruptly.

"I was on my way to tell you when you disappeared from the bar. And then you were attacked by those thugs, and—"

"You could have told me when we got back here."

Helen glared at him. "Well, I forgot, okay? I'm not perfect. I was thinking about other things. Like whether you were going to die on me. I was worried sick about you, Monaghan.''

His anger drained away as swiftly as it had come. Suddenly he felt like a jerk. Who did he think he was? He'd known last night what he was getting himself into. He had no right to snarl at her now.

"Hell," he said roughly. "I'm sorry for barking at you like that. When I woke up and found you gone all over again, I guess I went a little crazy."

Helen looked at him, and her eyes softened. "Oh, Patrick, I'm sorry. I should have woken you." She gave him an apologetic smile. "I thought you could use the extra sleep, and I was sure I'd be back before you woke up."

Warmth burst through his chest. So that's why she'd sneaked out like that. She'd been concerned about him—not trying to reject him. That meant...that meant....

He reached for her, curling his hand around the back of her neck and burying his fingers in her hair. She came to him willingly and put her arms around his waist, resting her cheek against his naked shoulder.

He closed his eyes, savoring the feel of her in his arms. Breathing in deeply, he smelled the fresh shampoo—*his* shampoo—fragrance of her hair, the faint womanly scent that clung to her skin, and he felt the last remnants of his tension and anger melt away.

He kissed the top of her golden head. "Next time, wake me up, all right? It's dangerous out there."

She pulled away from him a little, raising a hand to trace his swollen lip. "Dangerous for who?" she said, her voice husky. "Looks to me like you're the one in danger."

The whisper of her fingers against his skin sent a surge of heat to his groin. He wrapped his arm around her hips and pulled her against him. "In danger? Maybe. From you, Helen. Maybe from you."

A smile curved her lips as she looked up into his eyes. "How're you feeling this morning?"

He pulled her a little closer and dipped his head down to kiss her. It was a long, slow kiss—a kiss as leisurely as the ones last night had been urgent. He explored her mouth thoroughly, loving the taste of her, the feel of her. Beneath her fragile silk blouse, he could feel the supple warmth of her skin, feel the rapid thump of her heart against his chest.

Finally, he broke the kiss. Helen was breathless, her lips swollen, her cheeks flushed. He surveyed her, drinking in her beauty, before he finally spoke. "I'm feeling just fine." He ran his thumb over her jaw. "What about you?"

"I'm fine, too." Her voice was husky. "Better than fine."

"Good." Regretfully, he lifted his hand away from her face. "There's nothing I'd like better than to invite you back to bed, but I guess we'd better get ready to go."

They stared at each other for a long moment, and then Helen pulled away and walked over to the coffee table. She opened the white paper sack she'd dropped on the table and pulled out a foam cup bearing the distinctive green logo of a gourmet coffee company.

"Here," she said. "I brought you some coffee."

Patrick took the cup. Her fingers brushed against his, sending a tingle racing up his arm.

"Thanks." He popped off the lid. Steam curled into the air, bringing with it the warm, bitter scent of coffee. He took a long swallow and set the cup back on the table. "I'm going to jump in the shower. I'll be ready to go in half an hour."

"Good. The sooner we find Candy Turner, the better."

Two hours later they were on the outskirts of Seattle. Helen clenched the steering wheel and stared out into the rain. Six solid lanes of congested traffic inched their way toward the downtown core. Concrete walls topped with metal fences rose up on either side of the interstate, which sliced through residential neighborhoods like a scar. Horns blared unceasingly. From the other side of the freeway, Helen heard the wail of a siren.

The closer they got to the city, the tighter the knot in her stomach wound.

"You doing okay with this traffic?" Patrick asked.

Helen gripped the steering wheel even tighter. "I don't know where it's coming from. It's too late in the morning for rush hour. And we're nowhere near downtown. We still have to cross the ship canal."

"It's just life in the big city, I guess. Aren't you glad you don't live here anymore?"

She tensed. "How did you know I used to live here?"

"You told me so the other day, remember?"

"Right." She let out her breath, relieved he hadn't heard it through the grapevine. She'd told very few people in Evergreen even that much about her past—and she hadn't told a soul about her mother. When she'd left Seattle, she'd wanted to leave the past behind....

She looked out at the city. Memory tangled through her mind, dragging the old, rusty pain with it. Memories of wandering through downtown streets, looking for her mother. Of seeing Lana stumble out of an endless stream of different bars with different men. Of days and months and years crawling by in a blur of shame and misery.

Oh, yes, she was glad she didn't still live in Seattle. It was bad enough coming here twice a year to visit her mother. Bad enough that the memories of her childhood here would haunt her for the rest of her life.

"Hey," Patrick said softly. "What's wrong?"

The sound of his deep voice wrenched her thoughts away from the past. "Nothing. It's just a pain sitting in traffic."

"Are you sure that's all?"

Helen glanced over at him. His handsome face was concerned, his silver eyes serious. Suddenly, irrationally, she felt the urge to tell him. To tell him about her childhood. About her mother's drinking, her endless parade of men. To confess all the shameful secrets of her past.

But she couldn't tell him. She couldn't bear to see the concern in his eyes turn to disgust and revulsion. Patrick would never understand—not with a happy, loving family like his.

She forced a smile to her lips. "Really. It's just the traffic."

Patrick tapped his fingers against the dashboard. "Where are we headed?"

She didn't hesitate; there was no way she'd take Patrick to her mother's apartment. "I thought we could get set up in a hotel and start phoning around to find Candy."

"If you want, we could go to my sister's place."

"I thought Deirdre lived in Evergreen."

"Not Deirdre. My other sister, Moira. You haven't met her."

Helen hesitated. "I wouldn't want to impose."

"It wouldn't be an imposition. Moira's family. Besides, she loves having company. She's single, and she's got this big old house, so there's lots of room."

"Are you sure?"

"You bet. And the best part of it is, she lives out by Lake Washington, so we can take the next exit."

Helen glanced at the traffic as they crawled forward. At this rate, it would probably take them at least an hour just to get downtown. And the University of Washington exit was just coming up on their right.

"Okay," she said. "But only if you're sure your sister won't mind."

Patrick took her hand and squeezed. "Trust me. She won't mind."

Twenty minutes later they pulled up outside a rambling older house. The white clapboard siding was weather-beaten and needed a coat of paint, and the huge porch in front sagged more than a little. But the house had a welcoming, lived-in feel that reminded Helen of the older Monaghans's home.

A row of wind chimes hung from the porch roof, making music as Patrick and Helen walked down the front path. A giant maple guarded the front yard. Someone had raked its bright, fallen leaves into a pile by its trunk, and the damp, pungent scent filled the air.

Helen followed Patrick up the wide stairs that led to the porch. She glanced around curiously. Two huge wicker chairs stood on the porch with a table between them. A colorful woven mat sat beneath the front door. Beside it stood a pair of muddy boots.

Patrick twisted the old-fashioned doorbell. It rasped with a faintly musical sound. A moment later a woman pulled open the door. She was tall and slender and unmistakably a Monaghan. Her hair was red, like her father's, but she had Patrick's sculpted mouth and Adam's light green eyes.

She threw her arms around Patrick's neck and gave him a fierce hug. "Patrick! I wasn't expecting you!"

Patrick hugged her back. "Long time no see, stranger."

Helen watched them, a faint pang in her heart. What would it be like to have a sister or a brother? A family that actually cared?

Moira pulled away from Patrick, and her smile faded as she looked at his face. Lifting her hand to his bruised cheek, she touched it lightly. "What in God's name happened to you?"

"It's a long story."

"I'll bet. Well, you'd better come in and tell me everything." She turned to Helen and held out her hand with a welcoming smile. "I'm Moira Monaghan. You must be Helen Stewart."

Helen shook the other woman's hand. "Hi, Moira. I'm Helen." She hesitated. "How did you know who I was?"

Moira grinned. "Oh, I've heard all about you from Dad."

A whirl of confused emotions slid through Helen. So Sean had been talking about her—she didn't know what to make of that. She cast a sideways glance at Patrick, and he smiled back at her. The tension in her stomach unfurled a little at the warmth in his eyes.

Patrick turned back to Moira. "When did you talk to Dad?"

"Just last night." She pulled them both into the hallway and shut the door. "You know how he is. He calls me every couple days just to make sure I haven't crashed."

"Crashed?" Helen asked. "Are you a pilot?"

"I fly the news helicopter for Channel Seven." Moira smiled wryly. "And my parents just love it, believe me. Especially my father."

Patrick slung his arm around her shoulders. "You should've become a teacher, like DeeDee."

Moira elbowed him in the ribs, and he groaned. "You're one to talk," she said. "Showing up on my doorstep with a face like a rainbow. You look as if someone jumped up and down on your head.''

"You're not too far wrong there," Patrick said.

"You always were a magnet for trouble." She turned to Helen with a grin. "How do you put up with him, anyway?"

"I, uh...." Helen's cheeks flamed.

Moira's grin widened. "I see." She glanced at Patrick. "Well, I think I'll go put on a fresh pot of coffee."

"I'm just going to grab our bags," Patrick said. "You mind if we stay for a few days?"

"Mind? Of course not. You're family. Treat it like your own house." She turned and disappeared into the kitchen.

Patrick slid his arm around Helen's shoulders. "See? I told you she wouldn't mind."

Helen shook her head, still a little dazed by the force of Moira's personality. "She's so...friendly."

"That's our Moira. As easygoing as they come." He touched her cheek. "I'm going to get our stuff out of the car. I'll be back in a couple minutes."

"Do you need a hand?"

"No, that's okay." He tossed the keys into the air and caught them with a flourish. "Go on and talk to Moira."

Helen walked back to the kitchen and poked her head in the door. The room was large and bright, with red countertops and a brilliant yellow-tiled floor. Coils of garlic hung from the ceiling, and a heaping basket of fruit stood on the counter. The whole room smelled of cinnamon and nutmeg.

Moira stood by the sink, measuring coffee into an automatic coffeemaker. She looked up and smiled as Helen walked in. "Have a seat. Coffee'll be ready in a few minutes."

"Thanks." Helen sat at the kitchen table.

Moira turned on the coffeepot and strode over to the table to join her. Tossing her mane of hair over her shoulder, she gave Helen a sympathetic smile. "I was sorry to hear about your job."

Helen took a sharp breath at the reminder. Her throat tightened, and she felt tears sting the back of her eyes. "It's okay," she mumbled, embarrassed.

Moira propped her chin on her hands. "I'm sorry. I didn't mean to embarrass you by mentioning it. But, honey, you should know—there's no secrets in this family."

Helen flushed. No secrets. Did that mean that everyone in the Monaghan family knew about her and Patrick? Knew they'd slept together a year ago...and last night?

Moira flashed her a reassuring grin. "At least," she amended, "there aren't very many. Don't worry, I'm not going to broadcast it to my parents that you and Patrick are lovers."

If she went any redder, Helen figured she'd set off the smoke alarm in Moira's kitchen. "How did you know?"

"That you're lovers? It's written all over your faces. Besides, Patrick never would have brought you here—or to my parents' house—if he didn't have pretty strong feelings for you."

"Strong feelings?" Helen bit her lip. She couldn't stay here, in Patrick's sister's house, knowing that Moira believed a lie. Opening her mouth, she forced herself to speak. "I—I don't think you understand."

"Understand what?"

"Patrick and I—it's not like that."

"No?" Moira's green eyes were frank and understanding. "Then what is it like?"

Helen bit her lip. "He doesn't have those kinds of feelings for me."

"How do you know?"

"I just know." She took another deep breath. She'd gone this far—she might as well tell the whole truth. "He told me himself. Ever since he got divorced, he hasn't made anyone any promises. And he doesn't want to."

"And?"

Helen stared at her. "Don't you understand? All his relationships are strictly temporary. Including this one."

Moira just smiled and shook her head. "Honey, I think you're underestimating yourself."

"I don't think so."

"You want to bet?" Her smile turned into a wicked grin—a

grin so much like her brother's that Helen couldn't help responding to it with a faint smile of her own.

"Besides," Moira said. Her eyes crinkled. "You have the whole family on your side. And believe me, we Monaghans can be very persuasive when we want something badly enough."

"Don't I know it," Helen muttered.

"Are you telling Helen all the family secrets, Moira?"

Helen's gaze snapped to the doorway. Patrick lounged against the door frame, a grin tugging at his lips. She wanted to sink under the table. How long had he been there? How much had he heard?

Moira gave her a conspiratorial wink and turned to Patrick. "I didn't tell her the half of it," she said easily. "Didn't even mention the time you and Jake Rafferty—"

"Stop, Moira, stop!" He slid Helen a laughing look, and she breathed a sigh of relief. Surely he couldn't have heard what they'd been saying and still look so unconcerned. "Any story about me and Jake ends the same way—with both of us having our hides tanned by our fathers for one crime or another."

"Damn right." Moira tilted back her chair and looked over at Helen, her eyes dancing with humor. "I swear, this brother of mine got into more mischief than the rest of us put together."

"I don't know about that, Moira. I remember a few times you got into some pretty spectacular trouble yourself." He sat next to Helen and put his arm over the back of her chair, curling his hand around her shoulder.

The feel of his warm hand on her shoulder sent pleasure twisting through her body. It felt so natural, so good, having him touch her in this casual way. Almost as if theirs was a real relationship....

Helen bit her lip. Just why was he so casual about touching her in front of his sister? Was it possible that Moira was right? That he really did have feelings for her, that somewhere deep down, he wanted more than a temporary fling?

Helen pushed the thought away. She wouldn't think about the future. About what might happen. Right now, she was here with Patrick. And that was enough.

She forced her attention back to Patrick and Moira. They were laughing and talking about someone named Brian, and then Moira glanced over at the coffeepot. "Coffee's done. How do you take it, Helen?"

"Black, please."

"A woman after my own heart," Patrick said.

Helen caught her breath. For a moment the kitchen was still and utterly silent. She almost imagined she could hear the rapid beating of her own heart—and Patrick's.

A smile lurked around Moira's mouth. "Black, it is. Hope you don't mind it pretty strong."

"Uh, no," Helen said, her voice suddenly low and husky. "Strong is—is good." Her gaze slid involuntarily to Patrick.

He smiled, a slow beautiful smile that sent warmth racing through her blood. "Good."

Her lips twitching, Moira walked over to the counter. Taking down three mugs, she poured the coffee and carried it back to the table. She handed them each a mug and sat down, curling her fingers around her own. "So, what brings you to Seattle? Is it the case?"

Patrick nodded. "We're trying to track down the sister of a murder victim—the victim in the case Marty and I were working on when he was killed. Helen found a source who said the sister might be able to identify the killer."

"The sister lives in Seattle?"

"Yeah—we think so, anyway."

"Then you don't know where to find her," Moira said.

Helen shook her head. "No. We know her name and that she's a stripper in a club down on Second. But that's it."

Moira gave a long, slow whistle. "You've got your work cut out for you."

Patrick lifted his mug to his lips. "Sure do. And we have to get started pretty quick. Mind if we tie up your phone?"

Moira's gaze swept from Patrick to Helen, including Helen in the warmth of her smile. "Like I said before, you're family. Treat it like your own house. I have to work tonight, but if there's anything I can do to help, let me know."

Family. The word shivered through Helen like a promise. For a fleeting instant she wondered again what it would be like to have a real family. But there was no point in dreaming about it. It was something she'd never had—and never would have. Even the Monaghans's welcoming warmth wouldn't last forever. It would be gone as soon as her relationship with Patrick ended.

Her mother was all the family she'd ever have.

Helen's stomach tightened. She swallowed the last of her coffee and set her cup back on the table. "Thanks, Moira." She glanced at Patrick and shoved back her chair. "I guess we'd better get to work."

Chapter 13

Patrick hung up the phone in frustration. It was past seven, and he, Helen, and Moira had been on the phone all afternoon, trying to track down Candy Turner. Moira had finally left for work, but he and Helen were still hard at it. After calling every C. Turner in the phone book—and striking out completely—they'd started on the strip bars.

It was tedious, frustrating work.

Helen walked into the living room carrying fresh cups of coffee. "No luck?" she asked quietly.

Patrick heard the ragged edge of exhaustion in her voice and managed a smile. "Not yet. But we'll find her."

Helen set the cups down on the table. She looked tired and fragile, and Patrick's heart panged. How much more of this could she take?

She turned back to him. "Have you finished the strip clubs on Second?"

"Just about." He dragged both hands through his hair. "None of them would admit she worked there."

"Don't worry." Helen sat and slid her arm around his shoulders. "We'll just head down there and find her."

The determination in her voice, the feel of her arm wrapped firmly around him, made his worry melt away. He'd almost forgotten about that core of steel inside her. No matter how tired or how defeated she felt, she would keep on fighting to the last.

He leaned forward to grab the Yellow Pages. "I've still got two more bars to call."

Helen put her hand on his chest and gently pushed him back onto the couch. "Why don't I take another turn?" Her fingertips trailed down his shirt. "Looks like you could use a break."

Patrick let her push him onto the couch, his lips curling in a smile. The touch of her fingers against his chest made his skin come alive with sensation, and goose bumps rose everywhere she touched. Even after she turned away to reach for the phone, his skin still tingled with an electric warmth.

He watched as she checked the phone book and picked up the phone. She was so beautiful, her movements smooth and graceful. Cradling the receiver against her shoulder, she twirled the dial with long, elegant fingers.

Simply watching her dial the telephone made Patrick want her so badly that he had the wild urge to fling her down on Moira's couch and make love to her right here, right now.

He jerked his gaze away from her. This was definitely not the time, he told himself sternly. They had a job to do, a very serious job. One on which both their careers, and even their lives, might depend. And if he didn't want to screw up—again—he'd better concentrate on that job. Not on Helen.

Unfortunately, his body didn't agree with his brain. Patrick took a gulp of scalding coffee. It burned its way down his throat and into his stomach. Concentrating hard, he took another long swallow.

"Ms. Turner?" Helen said into the phone. "My name's Helen Stewart."

Patrick started. Boiling coffee spilled over his hand and splashed across his thigh. Had Helen found Candy?

"Yes, I'm sorry to bother you at work." Helen's voice was

tight with excitement. "But it's very important. It's about your sister, Jamie Lee."

A surge of elation raced through Patrick's body. She'd definitely found Candy. He had to restrain the urge to leap off the couch and do a victory dance around the living room.

"Could we possibly meet tonight? It really is very important, and I'd rather not discuss it over the phone." Helen made a noise of agreement. "That would be fine. Certainly. We'll see you at one. Thank you very much, Ms. Turner."

She hung up the phone with a whoop of victory. "We did it! Patrick, we did it!" She leaped off the couch and flung her arms in the air, fists clenched.

"She'll talk to us?"

A huge grin spread over Helen's face. "We have to meet her at an all-night coffee shop down by the Pike Place Market after she gets off her shift."

Patrick jumped off the couch and grabbed Helen's hand. "You did it!"

Helen threw her arms around his neck. He wrapped his arms around her waist, holding her close.

"We're going to get the killer." Her voice was muffled against his shoulder, but he heard the thread of steel in it. "We're getting closer all the time. I can feel it."

Patrick grinned and curled his hand around the back of her neck, burying his fingers in her silky hair. "You can feel it, can you?" he teased. "Is this the woman who said just a few days ago that she didn't have any feelings when it came to her work— just logic and reason?"

She tilted back her head, her blue eyes darkening to the color of the sea in a storm. "And look where that got me," she said, her voice tinged with bitterness. "Logic and reason didn't help me keep my job."

"And now?"

Her eyes softened, and her mouth curved in a smile. She stood on tiptoe, reaching up to him, her lips stopping only inches from his. "Now, I'm finally following my instincts. For the first time in my life, I'm doing what I want."

Her breath was warm and sweet on his face, and his body responded instantly. He fought against the hard rush of desire, needing to be sure that this was really what she wanted.

"And what do you want?" he asked, his voice husky and low with need.

She swallowed. "I want...you."

Her words exploded in his mind, and he hauled her against him, claiming her mouth in a fiery kiss. Her head fell back, her lips parting with a tiny, breathless moan. Patrick took advantage of it, deepening the kiss, sliding his tongue past her sweet lips to tangle with hers in an intricate dance of desire.

He wanted to possess her. All of her. Not just her body, but her mind, and her soul. It was crazy, dangerous and crazy, but he wanted it—wanted *her*—more than anything he ever could have imagined....

Helen tugged the hem of his T-shirt from his jeans. He groaned at the sensuous feel of her warm hands sliding up his bare skin. Her fingers skimmed the muscles of his back and shoulders, testing his strength. When she pushed the shirt up his chest, he obliged her and broke the kiss to yank it over his head.

She leaned forward and kissed the hollow beneath his shoulder, her fingers tangling in the hair on his chest. "Mmm. You're so beautiful."

Her touch set him on fire. He stood there, eyes closed, head flung back, fighting for control as she slid her hands down his belly and across the rugged denim of his jeans to cup his male hardness. She outlined the shape of him with her fingers, and he grabbed her hands, feeling himself about to explode.

"No," he rasped. "Not yet."

Helen smiled, a woman's secret smile that sent heat blazing through him. God, what was happening to him? She'd barely touched him, but he was already as randy as a teenage virgin. And her smile—it was like warm, sweet honey trickling through his body.

Deliberately, she leaned forward and kissed him again—a slow, sensuous kiss, a kiss that was a promise of things to come. Her tongue slid between his lips to explore the depths of his mouth, and Patrick held his breath, letting her take control, loving the strength he could feel in her.

She pulled him toward the couch, pushing him down onto the brightly woven cushions. Patrick flung his arm around her waist and brought her down onto his lap, balancing her against his chest. She sighed against his mouth as he slid his hands beneath her blouse, seeking her satin skin.

She was so soft. So beautiful. Her skin was smooth and delicate, but warm and alive. He pulled open the buttons of her blouse, wanting to feel her bare skin against his chest, needing to have no more barriers between them.

Beneath the blouse, she was wearing a wispy scrap of coffee-colored lace, and he discarded that, as well, flinging it onto the floor.

Half naked, Helen was the most beautiful woman he'd ever seen. Her perfection almost took his breath away, making his heart pound even faster, his head swim with longing and desire. He ran his hands up her sides, cupping her breasts gently, almost reverently. Her nipples hardened instantly, and her head fell back with a little moan as he plucked at them with his fingers.

She was so passionate. So responsive. And for now—for tonight—she was his. Only his. Her breasts fit his hands as though they were made for him. Her soft lips, the faint scent of lavender that rose from her skin, the feel of her rounded bottom against his thighs, were everything he ever could have dreamed of.

Patrick leaned forward and took her nipple into his mouth, loving the taste and feel of her. She gasped, her fingers tightening on his shoulders. Need hit him like a fist, but he fought it down. He wanted her so badly, he knew he'd explode the minute he was inside her. Before he took her, he wanted to give her pleasure, to brand her with the force of her own passion.

He eased his hand downward and cupped her. Even through her skirt, he could feel the moist heat. He slid his fingers into her clothes, finding her slick, womanly folds. Helen was ready for him, burning with heat. He groaned, unable to resist sliding a finger inside her, and she cried out, jerking her hips forward, pushing against his hand.

"Now, Patrick," she gasped on a ragged breath. "I can't wait any longer. I want you now."

Desire slammed into him, too hot and urgent to be denied any longer. He tore away the remainder of her clothes, while she jerked open the button fly of his jeans. Just in time, he remembered the protection in his wallet. Then, putting his hands on her waist, he lifted her, and she straddled him.

She looked straight into his eyes as she took his length inside her. He sank into her with a hoarse groan, burying himself in her tight, warm depths. She leaned forward to kiss him, her breasts brushing against his chest.

The kiss was his undoing. He thrust upward, and she gasped, moving against him as they found an urgent rhythm. Within seconds, she stiffened against him, tightening her legs around his waist and crying out as her body shuddered with release. He surged into her one final time, and in that instant of perfect connection, he poured himself into her at last.

Sleep eluded Helen as she lay with her head on Patrick's shoulder, staring up at the colorful mural Moira had painted on the sloping ceiling of the spare bedroom.

After everything that had happened in the past few days, she knew she should be exhausted. She definitely needed to catch a few hours' sleep before they got up and headed downtown. Downtown—to a coffee shop at Pike and First. Her mother's neighborhood.

Tension jolted down Helen's spine. What if they ran into her mother? The thought of Patrick meeting Lana made her stomach churn. But she wouldn't worry about that now. She already had enough to worry about.

For now, she had to concentrate on getting to sleep.

Helen angled a glance at Patrick's peaceful face. He lay sprawled on his back, the blankets bunched around his hips. Long black lashes swept against his cheeks. His chest rose and fell steadily, and his strong arm was wrapped around her shoulders, holding her tightly against him. His skin smelled like clean soap and kisses, and she felt a fresh spurt of desire as she breathed in his scent.

Their lovemaking this evening had been even more explosive than last night. Every time Patrick touched her, the longing and need inside her seemed to twist deeper and hotter. After they'd made love downstairs, he'd carried her up here in his arms, and they'd made love again—slowly, gently, this time.

His touch made her feel as though she was the most precious person in the world. With his arms around her, she felt so protected, so safe. Deep inside, her heart whispered that she belonged here, with him.

But for how long? Helen winced at the thought. The case was drawing to a close. When it was over, Patrick would probably go back to flitting from woman to woman. He'd said his reputation was exaggerated, but she knew he'd never lack willing bedmates, women who wouldn't ask more of him than he wanted to give.

Taking a deep breath, she pushed the image of Patrick surrounded by other women out of her mind. She wouldn't think about the future, she told herself for the hundredth time that day. She'd think only about the present. Being here with Patrick made her happy, happier than she'd ever been. She was finally following her instincts and her emotions—and there was no reason she shouldn't.

Was there?

Helen squeezed her eyes shut as she heard the faint, taunting echo. *She's just like her mother.*

"No," she whispered. "Go away."

Thankfully, the voice faded. Helen swallowed and turned toward Patrick, seeking his warmth, his strength. He murmured something sleepy, his strong arm tightening around her as he pulled her closer.

She curled against him, feeling her eyelids grow heavy and the world darken around her. At last, in the protected circle of his arms, she slipped into a heavy, dreamless sleep.

Hand in hand, Patrick and Helen hurried through the downpour toward the coffee shop Candy had suggested as a meeting place.

The Pike Place Market had closed hours before, but even after midnight, the area was far from deserted. Lights and raunchy music spilled out of strip joints and beer parlors. Tattooed men and hard-faced women hurried by, collars turned up against the rain. In the square outside the market, a few derelicts huddled together on a bench, newspapers spread across their legs for shelter.

Being there made Helen's neck tighten with tension. The neighborhood reminded her too much of her childhood, of her mother. She hated coming back here, hated having to confront the memories that haunted her.

She cast a sideways glance at Patrick. Having him beside her, his warm hand holding hers, made it a little easier. When she looked at him, she could almost pretend that she hadn't grown up here—that they were just an ordinary couple, out for a night on the town.

Almost.

They paused outside the coffee shop, and Patrick squeezed her hand. "You ready?"

"I think so. Let's go in."

Patrick pushed open the door, and they walked inside. The rich smell of coffee and the hiss of an espresso machine dominated the small interior. The room was crowded with people on their way home from the bars, and the windows were steamy. After the chilly rain outside, it was close and warm.

Helen found a tiny table in a corner and sat, while Patrick went up to the counter to order coffees. He threaded his way back through the crowd carrying two tall glass mugs of café latté, the milky foam on top threatening to spill over the sides.

He slid one of the mugs in front of her. "Thought we could both use something other than straight coffee after drinking two pots of Moira's brew this afternoon."

Helen squeezed his hand and smiled at him. In his jeans and leather jacket, with his black hair spilling over his forehead, he looked hard and rugged and more than a little dangerous. But underneath his tough exterior, he was so thoughtful—so sweet.

Her heart gave a little pang. Suddenly she wished they really were just an ordinary couple. Wished they could sit here drinking their coffee and holding hands, enjoying the simple pleasure of each other's company. Wished they could forget about the case, forget about Candy Turner....

Patrick's voice dragged her back to reality. "Think this might be her?"

Helen jerked her head up. The woman walking through the door was about her own age. She was petite, with long blond hair tied back in a ponytail that swung halfway down her back. Her clothes were plain—an oversize yellow sweatshirt and tight jeans—and her face was scrubbed clean, like a child's. A leather backpack was slung over one shoulder.

"I'm not sure," Helen said doubtfully as the woman hesitated just inside the door. "She doesn't look like I thought she would."

"I'm not sure, either, but I might as well ask." Patrick slid his hand out of her grasp and stood. "I'll be back in a moment."

Helen bit her lip. She knew this was why they were here—to meet Candy Turner—but she couldn't help half hoping that this woman wasn't her. Not yet. She wanted Patrick to herself for just a few more minutes. Wanted to hold his hand and smile into his eyes, to hang on to the illusion that they were a real couple, like any of the other couples sitting nearby.

She watched as Patrick threaded his way through the crowded room and halted by the blond woman. As he spoke, her expression of uncertainty faded. Helen couldn't hear what they were saying, but after a moment they walked back across the room together.

It looked as if it was Candy Turner after all.

Helen pushed away a faint twinge of regret. What was her problem, anyway? She should be thrilled that Candy had arrived. After all, Candy might have invaluable information, information that would help them solve the case. And solving the case was what she wanted more than anything...wasn't it?

It was, she told herself firmly. It definitely was.

A second later Patrick and Candy reached the table. This close, Helen saw the white lines of worry that radiated from Candy's mouth, saw the bluish circles of exhaustion and grief under her eyes.

Compassion filtered through her. "Ms. Turner," she said gently. "I'm Helen Stewart."

Candy nodded. Patrick pulled out a chair for her, and she sank onto it with an audible sigh. "I'm sorry." Her voice was high and sweet. "I just got off work, and it's real good to be off my feet."

"Thank you for agreeing to speak to us on such short notice." Helen paused. "I'm very sorry about Jamie Lee."

Candy's green eyes filled with tears. "I—I'm still havin' a hard time believing she's gone. She was…real special."

"Can you tell us a little about her?" Patrick asked as he sat down. "What was she like as a person?"

Candy swallowed rapidly. "She was…a happy person. Always smiling and laughing. She looked on the bright side of things, you know? And she loved kids. She was so good to Courtney. Every time she visited, she'd always take Courtney to the Pacific Science Center or the Woodland Park Zoo for a treat."

"Courtney is your daughter?" Helen guessed.

Candy smiled through her tears. "Yeah." She fumbled with the buckle on her backpack and pulled out her wallet. She flipped it open to display a studio photo of a little girl with blond hair and a wide, gap-toothed smile. "I had this taken a couple months ago on her birthday."

"How old is she?" Helen asked.

Candy rubbed her thumb gently over the protective plastic that covered Courtney's face. "She's six."

"What a pretty little girl," Patrick said.

The husky sincerity in his voice made Helen's stomach flutter oddly. Suddenly she wondered. Patrick had told her he'd wanted to have children with his wife. Did he still want children of his own?

An image of him, cradling a baby against his bare chest, flitted across her mind, and her heart flipped over. If everything was different—if they had a child—what would he look like? Would he have Patrick's black hair, his beautiful silver eyes? Or—

Patrick interrupted her thoughts. "Don't you think, Helen?"

She snapped her head up. Patrick was looking straight at her, his gaze oddly intense. She blushed. Had her thoughts shown so clearly on her face?

She cleared her throat. "Yes," she said, her voice coming out low and strangely breathless. "She's…beautiful."

She saw a flash of heat in Patrick's eyes—heat and something else—before the sound of Candy's voice snapped her gaze back across the table.

"Thanks." Candy lifted her chin. "I want to make a good life for her. A better life than what I had when I was a kid."

"Can you tell us a little about your childhood?" Patrick asked. "And Jamie Lee's?"

Candy bit her lip, her teeth digging into the tender flesh. Her fingers tightened on the picture as if it was a talisman to ward off evil. "W-why do you want to know about that?"

"The more we know about Jamie Lee, the more likely we are to catch the man who killed her."

Candy nodded slowly, her face white. "Okay." She sucked in a deep, shuddering breath. "I'll tell you what I can."

"Where did you grow up?" Patrick asked.

Candy hesitated for only a moment. "In the Cascades. Right out in the mountains. Our dad was a logger."

"Is he still living?"

"No. He died when I was ten and Jamie Lee was six. He was a faller, and one day…."

Within minutes, the sad story of Candy and Jamie Lee Turner tumbled out.

After their father died in a logging accident, their mother had married again to survive. But the man she married was a drinker, a violent and bitter man who treated her more like a punching bag than a wife. For sexual fulfillment, he turned to her two young daughters.

As teenagers, Candy and her younger sister fled to Seattle, desperate to escape their stepfather, desperate to survive any way they could.

The rest was a story Helen had heard more times than she could count.

"But then I got pregnant with Courtney," Candy concluded

"Best thing ever happened to me. My whole life changed. Bein' a dancer might not sound like much, but it pays the bills. And it's a whole lot better than standin' out on some street corner."

"What about Jamie Lee?" Patrick asked.

"She got beat up pretty bad a few times down here, so she went up to Evergreen. Thought it wouldn't be so dangerous working up there." She blinked rapidly and cleared her throat. "I tried to get her out of the life, but she kept sayin' no."

"Why do you think that was?" Helen asked.

"Jamie Lee...she always figured things were gonna turn around for her. She was always lookin' for the silver lining in the cloud." Candy paused. "She had some plan to get rich, and as soon as it worked, she swore she'd quit."

"Do you know what this plan was?"

"Not really. Just that she and some cop cooked it up."

Helen's heart began to thump. "A cop. Do you know his name?"

"She never said. But he was a vice cop. Busted her for soliciting. That's how they met."

A vice cop. Marty used to work vice. Excitement coursed through Helen's body, and she slid a glance at Patrick. He met her gaze, his silver eyes flaring with the same excitement.

They were getting closer.

"So, this cop offered Jamie Lee some kind of deal?" Patrick asked.

"I guess." Candy dragged her hand across her eyes. "The...the cop put a video camera in her room. I remember her laughing about it, sayin' it was hidden in the ceiling."

"A video camera?" Patrick squeezed his hands into fists. "Did Jamie Lee say anything about blackmail?"

"I didn't ask. I didn't want to know." Tears welled up in Candy's eyes, flooding onto her pale cheeks. She wiped them away with the heel of her palm, her hands trembling. "Oh, God. If it was blackmail, that must've been why she was killed."

"Candy, I know this is very difficult for you," Helen said. "But we have to ask you one more question. Somebody told us you might know the names of Jamie Lee's regular customers. If one of them was the target of blackmail, he may have killed her."

"She never told me their names." More tears trembled on her lashes. "I'm sorry."

"Did she tell you anything else about them?" Patrick asked. "What they did for a living? Where they lived? Anything at all?"

"No. Nothing."

"Are you absolutely sure?"

Candy started to shake her head, and then she froze. "Wait a minute. She did tell me one thing. One of her regulars got kinda rough every now and again. One time he threatened to carve his initial in her cheek. To mark her as his."

Helen caught her breath. "Do you remember what the initial was?"

Candy chewed on her lip. "I think…I think it was the letter C."

"Carmel," Helen whispered. An image of Edward Carmel wrapping his huge hands around Jamie Lee's slender throat shot through her mind. She squeezed her hands into fists, digging her nails into her palms. "Carmel."

"Hell. It was him all along." Patrick's eyes darkened to the color of cold steel. "Marty taped him with Jamie Lee, and the girl threatened him with exposure. He knew his career would be over if the truth came out. A cop—a lieutenant—with a hooker!"

"He must have strangled Jamie Lee, not knowing that Marty also knew the truth. But then Marty blackmailed him over the murder. Carmel paid Marty off, but then he thought better of it and killed him."

Candy's eyes widened. "You know who did it?"

"Yeah," Patrick said, his voice thick with disgust and hate. "A cop. That's who did it. A damn cop. He strangled your sister, he shot my partner, and then he killed the only other person who could identify him."

"But you're going to get him?"

"Damn right." Patrick's jaw clenched. "Damn right."

The betrayal and anger on his face pierced Helen's heart. Patrick had spent his whole life standing up for justice; that was why he'd become a cop. Carmel's actions perverted the very idea of justice. Instead of using his position to protect and serve, he had used it to kill. It was the ultimate betrayal of everything Patrick stood for.

Helen reached across and curved her hand around Patrick's cheek. "I know," she said quietly. "We'll get him."

Under her palm, she felt the quivers of rage racing through him, but he gentled at her touch. He took a deep breath, his hands slowly uncurling.

Helen turned back to Candy. "If you give me your home phone number, I'll let you know what happens."

"Th-thank you. After what he did to my sister...." She gulped, and her voice thickened. "I want to know for sure that he won't get away with it." She dug a pen and a matchbook out of her backpack, scrawled a number across the inside of the cover, and pushed it across to Helen.

Patrick shoved back his chair and stood. "Don't worry, Candy. He's not going to get away with anything."

Candy stood, as well, her face white, her lips trembling. "Good luck, okay? I hope you get him. For my little sister."

Helen touched her hand. "We will."

"Yeah," Patrick said harshly. "We will."

Chapter 14

Patrick was silent as they left the coffee shop and strode out into the night and the rain. Helen could feel the anger emanating from him as they hurried up Pike Street toward her car. Even his footsteps sounded angry as they echoed against the pavement.

Helen glanced at his face as they rounded the corner onto Second. "You want to go back up to Evergreen tonight, don't you?"

"Yeah." His jaw hardened. "I want to confront that bastard Carmel right away."

"Of course. I know how you feel."

Patrick stopped abruptly and swung around to face her. A bar sign buzzed overhead, and in its faint neon glow she saw that his eyes were blazing. "Helen, I worked with the man for over a year. I figured he was involved with this somehow, but I never thought he was a killer. Never. Do you know how it feels to be wrong about something like that?"

His words cut to her heart. "Don't blame yourself. How could you have known?"

"Carmel must have been out there on the old highway Monday

night. I must have seen him. Maybe even shot at him. So why can't I remember? Why?''

"You can't help it. Didn't your doctor tell you memory loss is common with concussion?''

He gave a bitter laugh. "Yeah. But if I hadn't screwed up to begin with, I wouldn't have been concussed.''

"What do you mean?''

"Carmel must have shot me, knocked me out, and got my gun away from me. *He used my own gun to kill Marty*. If I'd been on guard, if I'd been more careful, it never would have happened.''

"It wasn't your fault.'' She squeezed his hand tight. "You couldn't have expected your boss to shoot you.''

He shook off her hand. "I'm a cop. I should have known. I should have seen him for what he was. And I should have done something to stop him. Something. *Anything*. Just like—'' He broke off, his jaw tight.

Helen caught her breath. "Just like what?''

"Nothing,'' he said, but his voice was hoarse. "Just forget it.''

She stared at him, at the pain in his eyes and the tension in his jaw, at the cords standing out on the side of his neck, and she took a deep breath. "It's not nothing,'' she said slowly. "Is it?''

He looked away, into the darkness and the rain.

"Please,'' she said. "Tell me. *Just like what?*''

It took a long time before he spoke, and when he finally did, his voice was hoarse with pain and anger. "Just like Jessica.''

Jessica?

Helen's mind spun. Wasn't Jessica his ex-wife?

Suddenly she knew they weren't just talking about the case anymore. They were talking about something else altogether. Something far deeper, far more painful. Maybe even something that could explain the scars on his heart....

"Patrick,'' she said carefully, "what should you have stopped Jessica from doing?''

His eyes were as bleak and cold and empty as the rain. "I should have stopped her from killing our baby.''

"*What?*'' The word came out as a horrified gasp, and she felt tears of shock and disbelief start to her eyes. She raised both hands to her mouth. "Oh, God, what happened?"

"She had an abortion. An *abortion*." His voice was thick, and the words spilled out as though he'd been holding them inside for so long, he couldn't stop them anymore. "She got rid of our baby as if he was nothing more than so much garbage. I never even knew she was pregnant—she didn't bother to tell me. I only found out about the abortion because it showed up on our medical bill."

"But…but why?" Helen could hardly contain her horror. "Why would she do such a thing?"

"She said she didn't want to have a baby. Not with a man like me. A man who couldn't live up to her expectations. A man who didn't have money or power or social position—and never would. A *troublemaker*. She said having my baby would ruin her life, and that I'd end up ruining the baby's life, too…." His voice trailed off in the rain.

Helen's throat tightened with grief for him, grief and anger at the woman who could be so callous, so cruel. "But, Patrick, it wasn't your fault." She looked into his shadowed eyes. "You know that, don't you?"

"Do I?" His voice was hoarse. "At first, I blamed her. Blamed her completely. Even when I found out she'd had a baby with her new husband—that lawyer—I still told myself it was her fault. But now, with everything else that's happened, I can't help thinking. What if there's something I could have done? What if I'd tried harder, done something different? Would our baby be alive?"

The anguish in his voice cut her to the core. "Oh, Patrick, you're not being fair to yourself."

"Fair?" He swore, long and fluently. "And it was hardly fair to our baby, hardly fair he didn't even get a chance to live."

She reached for him again, her heart aching for his grief. "Don't torture yourself with it. You can't change what's already happened."

He stepped back, out of her reach. "I know," he said, his voice low and raw. "But I can make damn sure it doesn't happen again.

I can make sure no more innocent people die because of my mistakes.''

"You mean Carmel.''

He clenched his fists. "I won't let him kill again.''

"He won't. We'll see to it.''

"'We'?'' he asked roughly.

"Yes.'' She squared her shoulders. "Do you think I'd leave you now? No way. I'm not going to run out on you. Not like—'' She broke off and lifted her chin. "We're going to deal with this. *Together.*''

He lifted his head and looked straight into her eyes, and she gasped.

He held her gaze. He didn't speak, but deep in his eyes she saw a flash of emotion. Something fierce and wild and strong. Something almost like....

Helen's heart hammered. "Patrick?'' she whispered.

Slowly, he reached out through the rain and cupped his hand around her jaw. With exquisite gentleness, he stroked his thumb over her wet cheek.

Shivers of pleasure danced down her spine, and a tiny sigh escaped her lips. She leaned closer to him, inexorably drawn by the force of his gaze.

When he spoke, his voice was the texture of gravel—deep, rough, raw. "Helen, I—''

A few feet away the door to the bar burst open. A couple staggered out, and the woman crashed straight into Patrick, knocking him backward.

Patrick caught the woman as she stumbled and nearly fell. Her companion managed to stay on his feet—barely. He leered at Helen through bloodshot eyes.

"Hey there, honey,'' he said with a blast of alcohol fumes.

She shot him a look of pure disgust. He was exactly the kind of man she'd grown up with, complete with half-unbuttoned shirt, leather jacket, and greasy hair.

"Get lost, pal,'' she said rudely.

His face closed with anger, in a look she'd seen a hundred other times on a hundred other drunks. Her chest tightened with a fist of remembered fear. Hastily, she took a step backward, darting a glance over her shoulder at Patrick.

He was trying to steady the drunken woman, who clung to him, giggling. Her cheap blouse was already soaked from the rain, and her breasts were pressed against his arm. As Helen watched with distaste, the woman tilted back her head. In the faint neon glow of the bar sign, Helen caught a glimpse of her face.

It was her mother.

Horror rocketed through Helen's body. She stood frozen, her feet rooted to the ground. Oh, God, she'd worried about running into her mother, but in her worst nightmares, she'd never imagined this.…

As if from a great distance, she watched as the greasy drunk staggered up to Lana and Patrick. He swore at Patrick, grabbed Lana's arm, and pulled her away. "C'mon," he slurred, putting his hand on the back of her skintight skirt. "Let's get outta here."

"Okay, babe." Lana wound her arms around his neck. "Whaddever you say."

Helen opened her mouth. She tried to say something—anything—but all that came out was a strangled sound.

It was enough.

Lana looked up, her eyes bleary with alcohol. Slowly, they focused on Helen. "Baby?" Her forehead wrinkled. "That you?"

"Yeah, Mom." Her stomach lurched. "It's me."

Beside her, she felt Patrick stiffen in shock. Felt her deepest unspoken dreams shatter into a million pieces. He would never want her now. Never love her. Not now that he knew the truth about her mother, knew the truth about what she herself could become.

Lana stumbled over to Helen. She smelled of cheap perfume and whiskey and sex—just like always. "Baby, you gotta len' me some money."

Helen swallowed hard. "Mom," she said, her voice strangled with emotion, "you know I can't give you money for drinking. If you need food or clothes, I'll take you shopping, but—"

"Iss not for drinkin'." Lana jerked her head at the man who

swayed on his feet just behind her. "Me an' Bill, we're gonna go have somethin' to eat. Isn' that right, Bill?"

"Bob. M'name's Bob." His gaze slid to Helen, and he licked his lips. "Whass your name, honey?"

Patrick clenched his fists and started forward.

"Don't," Helen said, almost choking on humiliation and misery. "Please."

He looked down at her, his eyes glinting. "You sure?"

"Yes," she whispered. Looking at him, she felt her heart begin to crack. Tears burned in the back of her eyes, and she jerked her gaze away.

She forced herself to reach out and touch Lana's arm. "Come on, you've had too much to drink. I'll take you home."

"No." Lana jerked her arm away. "Iss too early to go home."

"Please, Mom—"

"I don' wanna go home." Lana looked at Bob, her red mouth curving in a seductive smile. "Not alone."

Tears blurred Helen's eyes. "You could come home with me, stay in my apartment."

Lana ignored her. "C'mon, jus' give me the money." Her voice rose. "You're my daughter. M'own flesh and blood."

Anguish tore through Helen's chest. They were flesh and blood. Family. Lana's blood ran through her veins. Lana's eyes looked out at her from the mirror.

Somehow she knew that if she could save Lana—just this once—she could save herself.

"I know we're family." Tears trembled on her eyelashes and spilled down her cheeks, hot against the icy chill of the rain. "That's why I want to help you."

"Then gimme the money!"

"I can't give you money." Pain clawed at her, and she stretched out her hand. "But come with me. Please."

Lana stumbled backward, her face twisted with anger. "You don' care 'bout me. All you ever cared 'bout was gettin' away from your ol' Ma."

"No." Helen choked. "No, that's not true."

Her stomach churned with guilt at the lie. She'd always wanted to get away from Lana. From the drinking. From the endless parade of men. From the shame of having a mother who didn't even know who'd fathered her child.

She squeezed her eyes shut. That was the real reason she'd always worked so hard, why she'd fought to get ahead in her career. She'd wanted to put as much distance between herself and her mother as possible.

Sure, she paid her mother's rent and bought her groceries. But she and Lana both knew why. It was blood money. Practically a bribe. A way to keep Lana happy—and out of her life.

"Iss true." Lana's drunken voice dragged her back to the present. "You never cared 'bout me, an' you still don't."

Helen forced her eyes open. "Mom, I—"

"But that's jus' too damn bad. 'Cause you're my li'l girl." Lana leaned forward, so close that Helen could see the cracked lipstick in the corners of her mouth, smell her hot, boozy breath. "An' that ain't never gonna change. Never."

More tears spilled onto Helen's cheeks. Choking back a sob, she tried one more time. "Please—"

Lana spun on her heel. She lurched over to Bob and wrapped her arms around his waist. "C'mon. Less go."

Together, they staggered off into the night.

Patrick started after them, but Helen grabbed his jacket. "No. Let them go."

"Are you sure?"

She nodded, not trusting herself to speak. Patrick slid his arm around her shoulders, but she twisted away from him, wrapped in utter humiliation and shame.

He dropped his arm back to his side. "I could take care of the guy she's with, and you could drive her home."

"She wouldn't go," Helen said hoarsely. "You heard her."

"But—"

"No buts. I've been through this with her before. Over and over again." She took a trembling breath. Patrick had already seen the worst, so there was no point in hiding the truth any longer. "She's been like this for as long as I remember."

"Does your father—"

"My mother doesn't even know who he was." Shame burned in her mouth.

Patrick reached for her again, but she pushed him away. She didn't want to look at him. Didn't want to see the pity and disgust in his eyes. He was being kind, but she knew what he was really thinking. It was the same thing Joe had thought, the same thing everyone had always thought.

Like mother, like daughter.

A sob rose in her throat. It didn't matter that her blouse was Armani, and her mother's was dime store. It didn't matter that her hair was naturally blond, and her mother's was bleached. It didn't matter that she drove a BMW, and her mother drove nothing at all. Because no matter how far she ran—how different she seemed—she would always be her mother's daughter.

It was a legacy she could never escape.

Gritting her teeth, she forced back her tears. Her throat felt raw and her eyes stung and burned. But she wouldn't cry any more, wouldn't add to her humiliation by breaking down.

"Come on." She squared her shoulders. "Let's get out of here."

Patrick cast a look over his shoulder. "Helen—"

She turned on her heel and walked away. A moment later she heard his footsteps behind her, felt his presence as he caught up with her. But he said nothing, and she allowed the wordless misery to take her as they walked back through the silent, desolate streets.

Patrick took the keys from Helen's hand when they reached her car. She gave them up without a word and slid into the passenger seat, ignoring his helping hand. For a moment he just stood there, and then he closed her door and walked around to the driver's side.

The interior of the car was chilly and damp. Patrick started the engine and turned on the heater full-blast. He glanced over at Helen. Her face was set and proud, her hands curled into fists in her lap. He thought he saw the faint sheen of tears in her eyes, but it was too dark to be sure.

He raised his hand to her cheek, but she flinched away from his touch. Slowly he dropped his hand. "You're upset. Let me take you back to Moira's."

She didn't even look at him. "No."

"We have to go back there anyway to pick up our bags. I could make you some tea, and—"

"No." She uncurled her fingers and squeezed them tight again. "Forget the bags. I want to go back to Evergreen. Now."

"Are you sure?"

With a jerky movement, she slammed her palm down on the dashboard. "Of course I'm sure! For God's sake, Patrick, my whole career is riding on this. Don't you think I want to see Carmel caught as soon as possible?"

"I know you do. And I understand."

"Do you?" She twisted around in her seat to look at him, and this time he saw the glitter in her eyes. "Do you really have any idea of what my career means to me?"

His mind spun back to the words she'd said to him a few days before. "You told me...that it's all you have. That it's your whole life."

"That's right. And now that you've met my mother, you know why."

"Your mother?" He chose his words carefully. "Helen, what does she have to do with your career?"

She gave a bitter laugh. "Everything, Monaghan. Everything."

He shook his head. "I'm not following you."

"I don't expect you to. Not with a family like yours. A family where everyone loves each other, where you have sisters and brothers around you, where your parents are people to be proud of...."

"But you never had any of that," he said slowly.

"No." Her voice was hoarse. "I just had me. Me...and Mom. And she was always drunk. Just like tonight. Drunk, and sleeping with different men. And I swore—'' She broke off with a stran-gled sound.

He reached for her hand, wanting to comfort her, wanting to ease the misery he heard in the cracking of her voice. ''What did you swear?'' he asked gently.

She yanked her hand out of his grasp, and he saw that her face was tight. Tight and hard with determination and pain. ''I swore I'd never be like her. Never lose control. I swore I'd grow up and have a great career, a great apartment, a perfect life. All the things I never had when I was a kid. Do you understand that, Monaghan?''

And suddenly...suddenly, he did understand. He understood why Helen's career was so important to her. Why her apartment was so perfectly elegant, why she loved opera and antiques and designer suits. She must have fought long and hard for those things. Fought to get away from her past, to create a life for herself that was as different from her mother's as day to night.

And he'd destroyed it all.

Guilt sliced through him like a cold, steel blade. No wonder Helen wouldn't turn to him for comfort. No wonder she cringed away from his touch. Seeing her mother must have reminded her how much she'd lost—and he was the one responsible.

He had ruined her career. Ruined her life. Ruined everything she'd worked for, everything she'd fought for. And there was no one to blame but himself.

This time—this time, it really was his fault.

The old guilt and anger settled in his chest, and he tightened his jaw. There had been a moment, right before Helen's mother had appeared—a single, crystal moment—when he'd actually thought, actually hoped....

But there was no point in thinking about it, thinking about his crazy dreams. Not anymore.

The only thing he should be thinking about now was getting to Evergreen and seeing that Carmel paid for what he'd done.

Maybe then Helen could get back her career. Maybe then she could put together the shattered shards of her perfect life, the life he'd smashed into a million pieces.

Patrick looked at Helen's set profile. "We'll go back to Evergreen," he said, his voice humming with intensity. "Tonight. We'll head out to Carmel's place and confront him with what we know. He'll probably confess on the spot."

Her only response was a tiny nod.

His heart pounding, Patrick rammed the car into gear and peeled away from the curb. He roared up to Olive and headed onto the freeway, racing north toward Evergreen.

By the end of the night, he'd know the truth about the murders. And this time, he wouldn't fail.

This time, he wouldn't let Helen down.

Patrick covered the seventy miles between Seattle and Evergreen in well under an hour, but the drive seemed to take a century. A century of silence. A century of watching Helen suffer and knowing there was nothing he could do. Nothing—except get to Evergreen as fast as possible.

In the rainy darkness, he almost missed the exit. At the last moment he saw the sign and wrenched the wheel to the right. The car screeched down the off-ramp. He slammed on the brakes, coming to a halt just beside the stop sign where the ramp ended in an intersection. Glancing over, he saw that Helen was gripping the dashboard so tight her fingers were white.

He wanted to grab her hands and apologize, to kiss away the fear in her eyes, but he tightened his hands on the steering wheel instead. "Hell," he said roughly. "I'm sorry."

She took a ragged breath and spoke her first words since they'd left Seattle. "It's okay. I didn't see the exit, either." She glanced around. "Does Carmel live out here somewhere?"

"He lives in Fairview, that new subdivision by the golf

course." Patrick forced himself to step on the gas and get moving before he gave in to the temptation to touch her.

"Then what are we doing all the way out here? Isn't this the old highway?"

"That's right. Before we go see Carmel, I want to go to the place where Marty was shot and see if I remember anything new. It could give us an advantage when we talk to Carmel."

She glanced over at him. "Okay."

Patrick swallowed hard. Even in the darkness, the force of her gaze made the blood sing to his head. He could feel her eyes on his face, feel it like a physical touch. Almost instantly, he was hard and aching with need.

With difficulty, he kept his hands on the steering wheel. What the hell was wrong with him, anyway? Wasn't it enough that he'd already destroyed her life?

If he was going to fix the mess he'd made, he had to keep his mind on the case and his body under control. He couldn't get distracted—not by anything. He had to concentrate on trying to remember what had happened out here that night.

Remembering would give him an edge. And he needed every advantage he could get.

Frowning, Patrick peered ahead. This stretch of the old highway ran through forest and farmland, and the county had never gotten around to installing streetlights. The few houses were set back from the road, hidden by giant cedars and Douglas firs.

At night, in the rain, the road was pitch-black, almost eerie in its utter stillness and silence.

The thin beam of the headlights provided the only light, picking out ramshackle barns, barbed-wire fences, and muddy driveways. The single lane of blacktop, slick with rain, stretched like a satin ribbon into the night.

Patrick shoved his hand through his hair. The rain. The darkness. The sense of isolation. Just like it had been on Monday night. Only then...then, he'd been in the passenger seat, instead of driving. And he'd been with Marty, rather than Helen.

He couldn't remember any more.

Patrick gripped the steering wheel even tighter. An old barn loomed out of the darkness on the left. He knew he'd seen it before, but he couldn't remember when.

His gut twisted with a sick feeling. Instinctively, he knew. They were getting close. Close to the place where it had happened.

He tried to force his mind back, to remember more, but the elusive images danced away. Questions swirled through his mind. Where had it happened? And what had happened, exactly?

Why the hell couldn't he remember?

The darkness that surrounded them pressed ever closer. In the passenger seat, Helen seemed to feel it, too. She wrapped her arms around herself, her shoulders tense. He wanted to comfort her, wanted to—

Grimly, he forced his mind back to the case.

The rain beat down harder than ever, slashing across the windshield in waves. Patrick slowed the car and peered ahead through the sheets of rain. Suddenly he thought he saw a flash of movement up ahead. Was something blocking the road? His head throbbed with a burst of bright, sharp pain.

Pieces of memory slid across his mind in a kaleidoscope of confusing images. Monday night. Darkness. Rain. Marty driving too fast. A large dark shape, blocking the road. A...brown car. With a man standing beside it. A man he knew.

But it couldn't be!

Patrick slammed on the brakes. The car skidded to a halt, tires squealing. He heard Helen gasp, but he didn't—couldn't—stop. Not now.

He shoved open the door and lunged out into the rain. The road. The road was familiar. Memory thudded through him, growing clearer, stronger.

The other car was just ahead, parked sideways across the yellow line, blocking the road. Marty slammed on the brakes and screeched to a halt. He wrenched open the door and climbed out.

"Get the hell out of the road!" he shouted. "This wasn't the arrangement!"

Patrick climbed out of the car. The rain slashed against his face, and he cursed the endless downpour. Dammit, he was sick of the rain. And even more sick of Marty. Just what the hell was going on here, anyway?

"Do it now!" The shout came from the other man, the man whose car was blocking the road.

Scowling, Patrick turned to Marty. "What's he talking ab—"

Marty swung around to face him, his bloated face twisted with hate. Too late, Patrick saw the pistol in his hand.

Marty raised the gun and fired.

Patrick flung himself out of the way. The bullet creased his shoulder. Pain ripped through him, hot searing pain. As Marty's gun cracked a second time, he dove for cover, reaching under his jacket for his own gun.

His hand closed over the grip of his pistol just as something exploded against his head.

Blackness took him.

Standing alone in the road, Patrick flung back his head. "Noo-oo!"

His own partner had shot him. His own partner had tried to kill him.

There'd been no love lost between him and Marty, but knowing that Marty had actually tried to kill him filled him with a terrible rage and sadness.

Crack! The sound of Marty's gun echoed in his ears. *Crack!*

"Patrick?" Helen's arms went around him, holding him close as he shuddered with the memory. "Are you all right?"

He couldn't help himself. He wrapped his arms around her and pressed his face against her hair, breathing in her scent, taking comfort in the feel of her. "I remember," he said, his voice a harsh rasp. "I remember everything."

"It's okay." She stroked her hands up and down his back. "You're safe now. We'll get him. Carmel—"

Abruptly he jerked away from her. He didn't deserve her comfort. He didn't deserve her touch. Not after the way he'd failed her—again.

"Patrick?" The concern in her voice pierced his heart. "What is it?"

Dragging in a breath, he forced himself to speak. "It wasn't Carmel who tried to kill me."

In the beam of the headlights, he saw the shock on her face. "It wasn't? Then who was it?"

"It was Marty."

Helen gasped. "Marty? He tried to kill you? Why?"

"There was another car here, blocking the road. Marty stopped our car, and we got out. The other man shouted to 'Do it.' And Marty shot me."

Her hand flew to her mouth, her stiff fingers covering her lips. "Then he shot you on purpose. It was all planned—he lured you out here to kill you."

"That's right. Marty lied to me. There never was any informant. That was just an excuse to get me out here."

"But...but I don't understand. If Marty meant to kill you, then who killed Marty? What happened?"

"I dove forward when Marty fired. I must have hit my head on the door. Head wounds bleed a lot, even superficial ones. The killer probably thought I was dead, that Marty's bullet had found its mark. He picked up my gun and used it to shoot Marty. Marty wouldn't have expected it, not from his partner in crime."

"And the gunshot residue on your hands?"

"The killer probably wiped his fingerprints off my gun, wrapped my finger around the trigger, and fired an extra shot."

Helen's hands trembled as she raised them to her face. "So if you had died, it would have looked like you and Marty shot each other."

"It would've been perfect," Patrick said grimly. "The killer would have gotten away with it for sure. He must have gotten some kind of shock when he found out I was still alive."

Helen shuddered. "And to think that I sat there with him in that little interrogation room while he tried to find out how much you remembered. And he was the killer all along."

"No."

Helen looked up sharply. Her face was stark white, her eyes filled with fear and confusion. "What do you mean? I was there, remember? Carmel sat there threatening you, taunting you about your memory."

"It wasn't Carmel," he rasped.

"What?"

"Carmel wasn't out here on the road that night."

"I don't understand." Her voice was faint. "We—we were so sure."

"We were wrong." He gritted his teeth, anger and guilt burning through him. "*I* was wrong."

"But if it wasn't Carmel, then...who was it?"

"It was your boss. The esteemed Evergreen County Prosecutor." Patrick took a deep breath. "Franklin Anthony Chambers."

Chapter 15

Patrick's words hung in the air like a living thing. The only sounds were the rain slashing against the pavement and the distant purr of the engine.

"Franklin," Helen said. Her lips felt stiff, frozen. "It was him all along."

"Yeah. He was the one they were blackmailing, not Carmel. He killed Jamie Lee. And Marty. And he tried to kill me, too."

Helen raised her hands to her temples. The darkness, the chill rain, the pounding in her skull—all seemed surreal. She wasn't really here on this deserted highway. Patrick's own partner hadn't tried to shoot him. Her boss hadn't committed murder, here on this very spot, only a few days before.

Only that was exactly what had happened.

Helen's mind spun with a sickening whirl. "Franklin. I...I had no idea it was him." She swallowed rapidly and looked up at Patrick. In the beam of the headlights, she saw his jaw tighten, his eyes glitter with anger.

"Neither did I." He gave a harsh laugh. "If I hadn't remembered, I would have charged off to Carmel's to try and make him confess to a murder he didn't commit." He swiped his arm over his forehead with a jerky, angry movement, brushing away his tumbled wet hair. "I must be the biggest idiot in the world."

She stared at him. "You're not blaming yourself, are you? For not knowing?"

A muscle twitched in his jaw. "I could have put your life in danger. And jeopardized your career even further. Breaking into the house of a police lieutenant—an *innocent* police lieutenant—would've made things even worse for you."

"But I wanted to come. I didn't want you to go alone." She reached for him, wanting to comfort him, wanting to ease the pain she saw in the set of his jaw, in the darkness of his eyes. Her fingertips tingled as she touched his rough cheek.

Patrick jerked away from her as though he'd been burned.

Pain tore through her body. So he didn't want her to touch him, not even in comfort. How she must disgust him, now that he knew the truth about her, about her mother. No wonder he'd wanted to take her back to Moira's. He'd probably wanted to leave her there, to get rid of her as soon as he possibly could.

The thought made her want to curl into a little ball of shame and misery, to hide in the darkness forever.

But she couldn't. Whether he liked it or not, Patrick needed her. Until this case was over, they were partners.

And it wasn't over. Not yet.

She struggled to sound calm. "There's so many things I don't understand. Why would Marty want to kill you?"

Patrick clenched his fists. "Chambers must have bribed him to do it."

"But why?" She rubbed her temples, trying to ease the pain that pounded in her skull. None of it made any sense.

"I don't have any more answers than you do." Patrick's voice was bitter and harsh.

She stared blindly into the rain, trying to fit it all together. "So Franklin was the one who tried to kill me."

"Yeah. Must've been."

"But...but why?"

"That's what we're going to find out." He turned on his heel and marched toward the car.

He was angry. Helen could tell by the set of his shoulders, by the stiff way he walked—so unlike his usual carefree saunter.

The chill inside her intensified. No wonder Patrick was angry. Back in Seattle, he'd blamed himself for not knowing the truth. But she was really the one to blame. After all, she'd worked for Franklin. She knew him well. And she hadn't ever suspected he might be involved.

Helen squeezed her eyes shut. Looking back, she saw so many little clues. The way Franklin had looked at the police station on Monday night—rumpled and damp, like a man who'd been standing out in the rain. Which he had, Helen thought with a shudder. He'd stood out in the rain and shot Marty Fletcher.

But there was more. Franklin had repeatedly emphasized the vital necessity of winning the case against Patrick. He'd even tried to bribe her with a job offer, an offer that was only good if she won the case. She'd thought it was just his obsession with being reelected, but in truth, he'd been trying to cover his tracks.

And then there was the fact that he'd assigned her to Patrick's case, even though he knew she and Patrick had been lovers. It was a classic conflict of interest, but he'd given her the case anyway. Helen's lips twisted. Franklin must have assumed that Patrick was the one who'd ended their relationship. He'd probably thought her anger, compounded by her vocal dislike of ladies' men in general, would blind her to any hints of Patrick's innocence. And even if she did decide he was innocent, all Franklin had to do was tell everyone about their affair—just like he'd done—and her credibility would be shot.

So many hints. So many clues. And she hadn't seen the truth. She'd even handed Franklin back the only piece of evidence against him—the money he'd used to pay off Marty.

Guilt and misery washed through her. Why hadn't she seen it? Why hadn't she realized? She lifted icy hands to her cheeks. They were wet, soaking wet, and she wasn't even sure if it was from the rain or from her tears.

Abruptly, she forced her eyes open. She couldn't just stand

here, crying in the rain. Couldn't let herself fall apart. Patrick still needed her—there was still so much work to be done.

Taking a deep breath, she squared her shoulders and hurried after him.

He halted by the car and swung around to face her. "Where does Chambers live?"

"Where does he—" She squeezed her hands into fists, digging her nails into her palms. It was another clue. Another detail she'd overlooked.

"Helen?" Patrick said.

She lifted her head and looked into his face. His eyes were hard, his jaw tight. In his face, there was nothing left of the tender lover, nothing at all. The man in front of her was a hard, angry cop. A stranger.

She gulped and pointed northeast. "He lives right...right over there."

He turned and looked. "Franklin lives on a farm?"

"No, on the other side of that farm, just down Snohomish Road. He...he and Olivia built a home out here last year." Helen bit down on her lip until she tasted blood. "I went to a Christmas party there last year."

Patrick stalked around to the driver's side. "Let's go."

Racked by guilt, Helen sat silently as Patrick gunned the engine and roared down the old highway. He squealed around the corner onto Snohomish. The back tires skidded on the slick pavement, and the car fishtailed wildly.

Helen gripped the dashboard with fingers that were numb with cold and fear.

Patrick's deep voice penetrated the haze of misery that surrounded her. "How far up is the house?"

She swallowed hard and leaned forward, searching the night with her gaze. "Not very far. Maybe up around that next bend."

He slowed the car and shut off the headlights. They crawled down the road, tires crunching against gravel. "Who else lives with Chambers? Wife? Kids?"

She struggled to remember. "Olivia—his wife—is in Hawaii

this week. Both kids go to college back east. So he should be alone.''

They rounded the bend and inched their way past a stand of Douglas firs. Through a gap in the trees, Helen could just make out the faint gleam of a security light. ''I think this is it.''

''Are you sure?''

''Pretty sure.''

Patrick shut off the engine. The silence was thick—thick and charged with tension, like the hot, electric air that comes before a thunderstorm. With every second that passed, Helen felt the taut wire of anxiety inside her stretch tighter and tighter.

''What now?'' she rasped.

''Now we're going to get some answers.'' The hard determination in his tone sent shivers down her spine. ''Have you got a tape recorder?''

She nodded and opened her purse to pull out the mini voice-activated recorder she'd brought for the interview with Candy.

''Put it in your pocket. We're going to need it.'' He reached under his jacket and pulled his gun from his shoulder holster. As she watched in horrified fascination, he slid the clip out of the grip, checked it, and smacked it back inside with his palm. He shoved the gun back in his shoulder holster. ''Okay. Let's go.''

''Patrick, wait.'' She fought to think clearly. ''You can't bring your gun. A coerced confession won't stand up in court.''

He wrenched around in his seat and looked at her, his eyes burning. ''The last thing we should be worrying about is the chain of evidence. Chambers is a murderer. A cold-blooded killer. We know that, but we have no credibility. If we don't get a confession, we won't even have to worry about court, because nobody will believe us. And Chambers will walk.''

She gulped. ''Right.''

''Besides.'' His voice roughened. ''He's already killed three people. I need to bring the gun to protect you—if you still want to come.''

''Of course I do!''

''You trust me to protect you? After everything that's already happened?''

She looked straight into his eyes. "With my life." Her heart banged against her ribs. "I trust you with my life."

"You shouldn't," he said hoarsely.

"But I do."

Her words seemed to hang in the air. Patrick's face shifted, changed, and something flared deep in his eyes. For a moment she almost thought he was going to reach out to her, and her heart leaped with a wild hope, but then he turned away.

Pain speared through her chest. Ruthlessly, she suppressed it. What had she expected, anyway? Except for the case, it was over between them. All over. And the sooner she got used to it, the better.

"Okay," he said. "We're going in. Stay behind me, and when I tell you to get down, you get down. Got it?"

She forced herself to nod.

Patrick slid out of the car. He closed the door behind him so gently that it made no noise other than a soft click. Helen climbed out of the passenger seat and followed him as he slipped up the driveway like a shadow.

Ahead in the darkness, the house loomed. It was a huge bulk of cedar and glass, its asymmetrical roofline soaring toward the sky. A security light shone from the wraparound deck toward the driveway. Skirting the pool of light, Patrick headed for the front door.

Biting her lip, Helen stayed right behind him. He paused in front of the door and motioned for her to stay back. Drawing his pistol with one hand, he put his other on the door handle. Helen caught her breath, stifling an instinctive gasp of fear.

Slowly, he turned the ornately carved door handle. To her amazement, the door wasn't locked. It opened silently, and Patrick slid inside. After a moment he reappeared and beckoned her into the foyer. She tiptoed inside, her footsteps sounding all too loud against the fieldstone floor. Patrick eased the door shut behind her.

Putting his arm around her shoulders, he leaned down to speak directly into her ear. "Where's the master bedroom?"

His warm breath brushed against her neck, sending shivers of heat down her spine. She turned to speak back into his ear, and the rough silk of his hair brushed her cheek. If she turned her head just a little farther, their lips would meet.

She dragged her mind away from that thought. "The master bedroom is upstairs," she whispered. "I think."

As he straightened, she thought she felt the faintest whisper of his lips across her hair. She was imagining it—she had to be— but she closed her eyes and savored the sensation.

The warmth of his body vanished as he stepped back, and she reluctantly opened her eyes. Patrick tipped his head toward the living room. It looked as though he wanted to check the down-stairs rooms first.

Together, they circled the ground floor. Living room, dining room, study, kitchen. All were empty and silent.

Finally, they reached the foyer once again. Helen glanced at Patrick. He held his finger to his lips and motioned toward the curving staircase with the gun.

They were going up.

Patrick slipped up the staircase, his feet making no noise on the hardwood steps. Helen felt as though each of her own foot-steps echoed throughout the silent house. Surely Franklin would hear her breathing, hear the wild thump of her heart. Surely he must know they were coming....

They reached the upstairs hall, a gallery that ran the length of the living room. A railing of smoothed driftwood lined the gal-lery. Helen glanced down at the darkened living room below. The furniture cast weird shadows on the wall, shadows that all looked like Franklin, crouched and waiting to spring.

She jerked her gaze away before her imagination spun out of control, and looked to the other side of the gallery. A series of doors opened to the left. Her neck muscles tightened. These must be the bedrooms.

She held her breath as Patrick pushed open the first door. As she'd expected, it was a bedroom. It was furnished with a single bed, covered with a ruffled eyelet bedspread, and a matching set of white-lacquered furniture with gilt trim.

Patrick shot her a questioning look.

"Daughter," she mouthed silently.

Together, they retreated into the hall. The next door was open, and led to a bathroom. Beside the bathroom was a bedroom that clearly belonged to Franklin's son.

There was only one door left.

Helen bit down on her lip as Patrick stopped in front of the door. The metallic taste of blood filled her mouth, mingling with the bitterness of fear. What was behind that door? Was Franklin waiting for them? Maybe even armed? Oh, God, she didn't think she could stand it if Patrick got hurt.

Her heart hammered as he reached out and turned the handle. The door gave a faint squeal as he slowly eased it open.

The room was empty.

"Dammit," Patrick muttered.

He walked into the room and flipped on the light. Helen pushed in behind him. It was the master bedroom, but Franklin was no-where to be seen. The king-size bed was made, the covers smooth and unrumpled; nobody had slept in it tonight.

Her head spun with mingled relief and disappointment. "He's not here."

"No, he's not." Patrick shoved his gun back into his holster and swung around. "Any idea where he might have gone?"

"I don't know. Maybe the office."

"You still have keys?"

Behind them, an all-too-familiar voice spoke. "No, but I do. Although I don't think you're going to need them now."

Helen whirled around.

Franklin stood in the doorway, a gun in his manicured hand. He wore an immaculately tailored suit with a crisp white shirt and a subdued tie in his usual Windsor knot. He looked freshly groomed, as though he'd just shaved and brushed his hair, and his politician's smile stretched wider than ever. Just looking at that smile made Helen feel sick with fear.

"Helen," he said. "And Monaghan. At last. I've been waiting for you for quite some time."

Patrick reached under his jacket for his gun, his hand moving so fast it was little more than a blur.

"No, Monaghan, no," Franklin said in his cultured, precise voice. He pointed his pistol at Helen, and she stifled a cry. "You don't want Helen to die, do you?"

Patrick froze, a muscle ticking in his jaw. "If you shoot her, I'll kill you before you can escape."

Franklin gave a little chuckle, a sound that sent chills down Helen's spine. "But that won't change the fact that she'll be dead. Tell me. Are you willing to let her die?"

Patrick's fists clenched, and the muscled cords of his neck stood out with rage. "Let her go, Chambers," he said, his voice so tight with fury that Helen barely recognized it. "This has nothing to do with her. It's between you and me."

"Oh, no. That wouldn't do at all. I'm afraid I can't let either of you go."

A tiny sound of anguish escaped Helen's lips. Franklin was insane—insane enough to kill them both. She could face the thought of her own death, but not Patrick's. Never Patrick's.

She looked across the room and into Patrick's eyes. "Shoot him," she said, her voice shaking. "Shoot him, and you can get away."

Patrick's face was rigid. "I can't. He'll kill you, Helen."

"It doesn't matter," she said frantically. "He's going to do it anyw—"

"This is all very touching," Franklin interrupted. "But we don't have time for this now. Helen, I want you to walk over to Monaghan, very slowly, very carefully."

"What for?" she asked, fighting to keep the tremor of fear out of her voice.

"Do you want your lover to die?"

She flinched. "How did you—"

"How did I know you were lovers?" Franklin smiled again, and this time she saw the light of madness in his eyes. "I saw you. Through the window at Monaghan's apartment. Just like last year, when I saw you leave together from the ball. Not that I needed to. I always knew you were a whore."

Patrick jerked forward, fists clenched, eyes blazing. "Shut up, Chambers. Don't you talk to her like that."

Franklin raised the gun. "Stop right there, Monaghan. I'll kill you. You know I will. And then I'll kill her. Slowly. Very slowly. After I have her." He licked his lips. "I've wanted her for a very long time."

Patrick stopped moving, but his face was a mask of pure, cold rage.

Franklin jerked his head at Helen. "Walk."

She walked. Her legs felt like rubber, and with every step she took, she felt Franklin's eyes boring into her back, felt the heat of his gun as he pointed it at Patrick's head.

She halted in front of Patrick. Close enough to feel the warmth of his body. Close enough to touch. Her hands trembled, but she forced herself to keep them at her sides. She didn't want to do anything that might provoke Franklin into shooting Patrick.

"Good girl," Franklin said. "Now, reach under his jacket and take out his gun. Very slowly, unless you want me to kill him. When you've got it, put it down on the floor and kick it to me."

Helen gulped and slid her hand under Patrick's leather jacket. Beneath her palm, she felt muscle and the rasp of hair, felt the rapid pounding of his heartbeat. Fighting back tears, she lifted her eyes to his. He looked back down at her, his mouth twisted in an attempt at a reassuring smile. Her eyes blurred as she closed her fingers around his pistol and pulled it out of the holster.

"That's it," Franklin said. "Now put it down and kick it over here."

She obeyed. The gun clattered across the wooden floor.

Franklin pulled a handkerchief out of his pocket. He shook it out and leaned down to wrap it around the grip. Picking up the pistol, he stuck it into the pocket of his suit.

"Excellent," he said. "Now we can get down to business."

"You won't get away with this." Patrick's voice was dangerously quiet. "Too many people know the truth."

"Do they? I don't think so. I've killed three people, and nobody suspects a thing. Except you two, of course."

Helen's mind spun wildly. "How did you know we'd found out?"

"I didn't know for sure. If you hadn't shown up tonight, I would have gone to you."

"You were just going to kill us regardless?"

Franklin's eyebrows arched. "But of course! Monaghan should have died with Marty Fletcher on Monday night. Once I realized he was alive, it was only a matter of time. If he'd been arrested, he would have died in jail before he ever came to trial. A suicide." A smile curled his lips. "Can't you see the headlines? 'Former Cop Kills Self In Remorse.'"

Helen shuddered. Franklin was evil. Pure evil. He'd kill anyone who got in his way.

She tried to calm the frantic beating of her heart. She had to keep Franklin talking. At least if he was talking, he wasn't shooting. And as long as they were alive, there was still some chance of escape. Still some chance that she might save Patrick's life— and her own.

"And me?" She plastered a smile on her face. "But of course, you tried to kill me, too."

"You're referring to the incident outside Tammy Weston's condominium?" Franklin shook his head. "I admit, I acted on the spur of the moment. I had a date with Tammy, and when I arrived to pick her up, I saw you coming out of her building. It would have been an excellent opportunity if it wasn't for Monaghan's interference."

Helen felt Patrick tense beside her, but when he spoke, his voice was cool and even. "Why did you kill Tammy?"

Her heart leaped. Obviously he'd caught on to her plan to keep Franklin talking.

"Isn't it obvious?" Franklin said. "I saw Helen coming out of her building. When I asked Tammy if she'd talked, she denied it, but I knew she was lying. She had to die. And when Helen told me the next morning that she'd shaken Tammy's statement, I knew my decision had been the right one."

"What about Marty?" Helen asked. Knowing Patrick was

working with her made her voice stronger, more confident. "You'd paid him off already, so why kill him?"

Franklin chuckled. "Do you really think I'd let Marty just walk away with my money? No, I wanted it back. The merry widow wasn't very forthcoming when I went and saw her with Carmel—and she had her hulk of a brother hanging around—but it was only a matter of time before he left and I could...retrieve my property." He smiled. "Of course, you solved that little problem for me, Helen."

"Okay, that explains Marty. But why did you want to kill me?" Patrick asked coolly, as though there was nothing strange about discussing his own death.

"I had to eliminate you to be sure I was safe. Marty was too stupid to keep his secret for long. Would you believe he actually made several notations of my initials in Jamie Lee's case files?"

"So that's why you stole the files," Helen said. "You broke into my office and trashed it, hoping I wouldn't notice the missing files. And you just walked into the police station and took Carmel's copies off his desk. Nobody would have questioned your being there."

"That's right. It was so easy." Franklin's gaze swung to Patrick. "But you had to die. Sooner or later, you would have guessed the truth."

"How did you convince Marty to do it?" Patrick asked.

Franklin laughed. "That was the easy part. I told him you'd found out about the payoff and threatened to turn us both in. Marty bought it. He agreed you had to die."

"But you double-crossed him," Helen said.

"It would have been perfect. Marty shot Monaghan. I used Monaghan's gun to shoot Marty. Nobody would have found out, if Marty hadn't been so stupid." Franklin's voice thickened with disgust. "He missed his shot, and Monaghan didn't die the way he was supposed to."

Patrick snorted. "*Marty* was stupid? When you didn't even notice that my corpse was actually alive?"

Franklin jerked up his gun, and Helen gasped. Her eyes flew

to Patrick's face. What was he doing? Was he trying to get himself shot?

Patrick looked straight into her eyes. Infinitesimally, he tilted his head to the right, to the other side of the bed. His message was clear. He was going to make a move. And when he did, she was supposed to dive behind the bed.

He was crazy. Crazy…and a hero. Helen's throat tightened with fear. She didn't want him to be a hero. No matter what happened to her, she wanted Patrick to make it out of here alive.

Desperately, she glanced at Franklin. His face was red with rage, his knuckles white as he gripped the gun.

"Shut up, Monaghan," he snarled. "Remember, I'm the one with the gun. Just who looks stupid now?"

"Helen!" Patrick shouted. "Now!"

"No! Don't—"

It was too late.

Patrick launched himself at Franklin. Helen screamed a warning as Franklin leveled the gun. Patrick surged forward, slamming into Franklin just as he pulled the trigger.

The shot echoed through the room. Both men fell to the ground, rolling over and over, grappling for the gun. Bright streaks of blood stained the polished floor.

"Patrick! Noo-oo!" Helen screamed.

Frantically, she spun around, searching for a weapon. Something…anything. There was a heavy brass lamp on the table on the other side of the bed, and she lunged across the bed to grab it. She yanked it out of the wall just as a second shot rang out.

Her heart in her throat, she whirled around, just in time to see Franklin jerk violently backward. A terrible sound escaped his throat—a gurgling, desperate scream—and then he slumped to the floor.

Patrick lay on his back a few feet away, the gun in his hand. His head was tilted at a funny angle, his eyes shut, his face ashen. Red smears spread out from beneath his body, and blood bubbled out of his chest.

Oh, God, he couldn't be….

Fierce wild anguish splintered through her body. The lamp fell from her hands, crashing to the floor. She charged across the room, tears streaming down her face.

"Patrick," she gasped as she knelt beside him. "Oh, Patrick, no, please...."

He didn't move, didn't speak, and grief exploded through her. She put her arms around him, cradled his head against her chest. A keening sound filled the room. Through her haze of anguish, she realized it was the sound of her own moans.

Rocking back and forth, she smoothed Patrick's hair off his forehead, her tears dripping onto his face.

He was dead. Dead. The man she loved was dead.

Loved.

The truth exploded through her like a bomb, leaving shards of shrapnel in her heart. She loved him. Had fallen in love with him last year when he'd spun and laughed on the beach in the storm, so full of life and love and vitality. She'd loved him all along, all that year when she'd tried so hard to forget him.

And now he was dead. He had given up his life to save her...and she'd never even told him she loved him.

Guilt and grief burst through her. "I'm so sorry I never told you." She managed to choke out the words through her tears. "I love you, Patrick Monaghan. I love you."

She slid her hand over his face, tracing his sculpted lips, the hard line of his jaw. Her fingers slipped under his jaw to smooth down his neck, when she felt a flutter beneath her fingertips.

A flutter—like a pulse.

She dug her fingers under his jaw, seeking, finding the faint rapid beat of his pulse.

Tears of joy spilled down her cheeks. He was alive. Thank God, he was alive.

At least for now.

Chapter 16

Dark.

Darkness pressing in on him like a living thing. A roar in his ears, a crash like the impact of a tidal wave. Pain—hot, excruciating pain.

Blackness fading to light. Drifting weightless on a cloud. Faces hovering over him, familiar faces.

"Mom?" Patrick croaked.

Why was she crying? Her lips moved, but he couldn't hear what she was saying. His father was behind her—no, it was Adam. And his mother had turned into Deirdre, her face shiny with tears.

Behind them, her hair golden in the light, stood Helen. She looked like an angel. He couldn't see her wings, but he felt the soft touch of her fingertips against his face. He wanted to reach for her, but it was too hard, it hurt too much.

Faces blurred, blended. Who was there? The bright lights overhead confused him.

He tried to move, but pain stabbed at his chest. A thin woman dressed all in white charged at him, a needle in her hand.

The pain receded.

He closed his eyes and drifted into the darkness once again.

"He should be waking up anytime now."

The nasal voice jolted him. It was unfamiliar—it didn't belong to the darkness. Neither did the acrid smell of bleach or the feel of rough cotton beneath his hands.

Patrick slowly opened his eyes.

Fluorescent lights buzzed overhead. Their brightness made him wince. He looked down and saw that he was lying in a high bed surrounded by a metal rail. A green sheet was folded neatly across his chest, and a huge plastic IV needle jutted out of the back of his hand.

Hospital. He was in the hospital.

Patrick turned his head as the door clicked shut behind a departing figure. His mother was sitting in a chair beside the bed, her face buried in her hands.

"Mom?" he whispered hoarsely.

She lifted her head, and her face twisted with emotion. She leaped out of the chair and lunged over to the bed. Gripping the metal rail with her lined hands, she looked down at him with hope and desperation in her eyes. "Patrick? Can you hear me?"

"What—" He tried to swallow, but his throat was dry and tasted like metal. His heart thudded as he struggled to remember. "What happened?"

She reached out and smoothed back his hair, her eyes filled with tears. "Hush now, son. You've been shot, but you're going to be all right."

Shot. Patrick squeezed his eyes shut as he remembered the roar of Chambers's gun, remembered fighting desperately for the weapon. Remembered wrenching it away and firing, the thunder echoing in his ears as he fell into the darkness....

His heart almost stopped, and he forced himself to open his eyes, to look into his mother's face. "Helen? Is she all right?"

"Yes." Her mouth softened. "Yes. She's perfectly safe."

"Thank God," he whispered.

"And thanks to you, Patrick. You saved her life. Both your lives."

Pain washed through him—a pain that had nothing to do with the dull thudding ache in his chest, with the prick of the needle in his hand. Maybe in the end he had saved their lives. But he didn't deserve any praise for it. Not after the way he'd screwed up everything else.

Not after the way he'd failed Helen—again.

He had sworn he would protect her. She'd trusted him with her life, but he'd failed her. Failed her in so many ways. Failed her by not being more careful. By letting Chambers sneak up on them. By losing control of his gun.

And Helen had almost died for his sins.

Patrick's throat tightened. At least she was alive. But he had to know more, had to know what had happened after the darkness had taken him. "Chambers—is he in jail?"

His mother shook her head. "No. Patrick...he's dead." Sudden tears spilled onto her cheeks, and she smiled through them. "Oh, son, you were so brave. Helen told us how you tackled him, how you fought him for the gun even though you'd been shot."

He barely registered her words. "Helen—she's not in trouble?"

"Oh, no. She had a tape recorder running the whole time Franklin Chambers was threatening you, and she handed the tape over to the police. They heard his confession loud and clear, and both your names have been cleared. You've been reinstated at the police department—your job will be waiting as soon as you've healed up. And the attorney general has offered Helen an important job down in Olympia."

Patrick's head swam with relief. So Helen's career wasn't ruined after all—if anything, it was better than ever.

But she'd be leaving town to take the new job. A thread of pain twisted through the relief, but he pushed it away. It was better if she left. Better if he didn't have to see her, wasn't constantly reminded of the way he'd almost destroyed her life.

His mother was still talking. "But you know, Helen told the

attorney general she couldn't make any decisions until you were better. She said—''

Behind her, the door opened, and Adam slid inside, carrying two steaming foam cups. "Mom," he said in a hushed voice, "I brought you some coffee."

"Adam," Patrick said.

Adam's head jerked up and he dropped both cups. They crashed to the ground, splashing coffee over the wall and floor, but he didn't even seem to notice. A huge smile spread over his face.

"Patrick!" He crossed the room in one long stride and leaned over to give Patrick a fierce hug. "You're finally awake."

"How long have I been out?"

"It's been two days since you were shot," Adam said, straightening. "With all the Demerol they've been giving you, you've been out of it most of the time. We've all been taking turns sitting with you." He spun around and headed for the door. "I have to get Helen. She's down in the cafeteria."

"No!" Patrick barked.

Adam paused with his hand on the doorknob. Slowly he turned around. "No? What do you mean?"

Patrick closed his eyes. Doing this hurt. Hurt like hell. But there was no other way.

"I don't want to see her," he rasped.

"Do you mean not until later?" his mother asked.

Pain tore through him, but he forced himself to say the words. "No. Not now. Not later." The lie burned like acid in his mouth. "I don't want to see her at all."

"Why the hell not?" Adam asked, his voice taut and angry. "She's spent the last two days at the hospital, just waiting for you to wake up."

Patrick dug his hands into the rough cotton blankets, clenching his fingers so tight he thought they might explode. There was no way to explain. No way to make them understand the weight of his own failure, the knowledge that he'd let Helen down again. That his mistakes had almost meant her death...over and over again.

The truth was, he wasn't good enough for her. Had never been good enough—and never would be. Jessica had known the truth about him all along.

And somewhere deep inside himself, he'd known it, too.

Pain and anger and grief twisted through him, and he squeezed his eyes shut. Helen deserved a different kind of man, he told himself grimly. A *better* man. The last thing she needed was a beat-up cop who'd let her down one too many times.

She had her career back—the thing that was more important to her than anything else in the world. She might have hung around the hospital out of some kind of misguided gratitude, but he wouldn't let her screw up her life by sticking around any longer.

He'd messed up her life badly enough already.

And it was better to just end things between them now, before anyone got hurt.

"So what am I supposed to tell her?" Adam demanded, the harsh sound of his voice cutting into Patrick's thoughts.

He opened his eyes and looked straight at his brother. "Tell her...tell her to take the job in Olympia."

Adam spun on his heel. He stalked out of the room, slamming the door behind him. Patrick closed his eyes against the intrusion of the bright lights, of his mother's unhappy gaze.

He'd done the right thing. He was sure of it.

But the pain of the gunshot wound was nothing compared to the pain in his heart at knowing he had to let Helen go.

Helen slumped in the uncomfortable plastic chair, staring at the wall in front of her. Someone had painted the walls yellow—no doubt trying to make the cafeteria a little more cheerful than the rest of the hospital—but the paint had faded and cracked, leaving it the sickly color of jaundice.

In the past two days she'd spent seemingly endless hours sitting at this ugly table in this ugly room, praying for news of Patrick. After the first morning, she hadn't even bothered going home to try to sleep. There was no point. She knew she'd just toss and turn in her cold, empty bed, thinking of Patrick lying wounded in the hospital.

Wounded...after saving her life.

For the hundredth time that day, Helen felt hot tears start to her eyes. Swallowing hard, she forced them back. She couldn't break down now. She had to be strong. For Patrick. When he woke up, he would need her to be strong....

Curling her fingers around her mug of coffee, she lifted it to her lips and took a sip. It was lukewarm and bitter, but she forced herself to swallow a mouthful. After three days straight with no sleep, the coffee was the only thing keeping her alert.

She took another sip and grimaced. Setting the mug down on the table, she pushed back her chair. It was time to go check on Patrick, and—

The cafeteria door swung open and Adam walked into the room. He headed straight toward her, his jaw tight, his expression grim.

Helen sprang to her feet, her hands suddenly icy cold. "What's happened?" she demanded as Adam reached the table. "Patrick isn't—"

"He's fine."

"Thank God." She sank back down in her chair. "For a moment, I thought...I thought the worst."

"You don't have to worry about that anymore." Adam pulled out a chair and sat heavily. "He's awake."

She gasped, elation shooting through her. "Awake?" She stumbled to her feet once again. "Why didn't you tell me? I'll go up right away."

Adam's hand clamped around her wrist like a band of iron. "No."

"The doctors won't let me.... But surely—"

"It's not the doctors." Adam looked at her, his green eyes softening. "Helen, I don't know how to tell you this."

A cold feeling of foreboding curled through her. "Tell me— tell me what?"

He tugged her back to the table and pushed out her chair. "Sit down. Please."

Helen sat slowly. "What is it, Adam?"

He cleared his throat, and then he leaned across and took her hand. "Patrick says he doesn't want to see you."

"What?" Helen whispered. Nausea flooded through her, lodging deep in her stomach. "You mean, not right now?"

Adam's fingers tightened on hers. "No. He says he doesn't want to see you at all." He paused and looked down at their hands. "He wouldn't explain it to me. He just insisted he wouldn't see you."

A sudden wave of tears rose in her throat, blurred her eyes, and she struggled to keep them back. "Did he say anything else? Anything at all?"

Adam raised his head to look into her eyes, and she saw pity in his expression, pity and anger. He cleared his throat. "He said to take the job in Olympia."

Her hands flew to her mouth. "No." She choked, her throat so tight she could barely speak. "No."

"I'm so sorry, Helen. Patrick isn't himself. It's not too surprising. He's been pumped full of drugs for days, and—"

She stood abruptly, almost knocking over her chair. "It's not the drugs. It's me. He doesn't want me." The truth of her own words sliced through her with an agonizing pain. A sob welled up in her chest, a sob so huge she thought it would tear her apart.

Adam got up, his face a mask of sympathy. He stretched out his hand, reaching for her.

Helen turned and fled.

Patrick lay on his back in the darkness, staring at the shadowy ceiling overhead. Somewhere out in the hall, he could hear the soft squeak of a nurse's shoes and the rattle of a cart, and low voices hummed in the room next door.

But here in his room, everything was quiet. Too quiet. Other than the labored rasp of his own breathing, there was nothing but a bleak, empty silence.

A silence that was slowly driving him out of his mind.

Visiting hours had ended hours ago, and the nurses had shooed out the crowd of friends and family and fellow police officers who'd stopped by to say hello. But even when they'd been there—even when his room had been filled with talk and laughter and the warmth of old friends—he'd felt the emptiness. The silence of the one voice he wanted to hear.

Helen's voice.

Patrick squeezed his eyes shut. He could hear her voice in his mind, hear the low husky notes of it as she said his name. Hear the sound of her aching moans as he'd made love to her for the last time.

And he could see her, too. Even in the empty darkness, even with his eyes closed tight. Oh, yes, he could see her and smell her and feel the satin of her skin against his hands....

He'd tried to put her out of his mind all night, tried to concentrate on the weight of the blankets against his legs, on the pull of the needle in his hand and the scent of the roses Deirdre had arranged by his bed. But nothing had worked.

Nothing.

Whatever he did, he couldn't get Helen out of his mind.

Restlessly, he opened his eyes and stared up at the ceiling again. But the pattern of cracks in the plaster somehow reminded him of Helen's smile, and the alabaster color, shadowed with moonlight, made him think of the way her skin had looked when he'd made love to her on the beach that very first night....

The memory made his groin tighten painfully, and he let out a groan of frustration and anger. Dammit, why was she haunting him like this? He'd done the right thing by sending her away. He was sure of it. So why couldn't he just forget her?

He couldn't count the number of women he'd broken up with over the past three years; the women he'd sent away after a day, or a week, or a month. And he'd never had any trouble forgetting any of them.

So why was Helen so different? What was this hold she had on him? And not just on his body, but on his mind? And on his—

Patrick caught his breath. On his...

Heart.

The realization crashed through him like a bolt of thunder. The hold Helen had on him wasn't just on his mind. Or his body. It was on his heart. *His heart.*

Because he was in love with her. Wildly, crazily, desperately in love.

He loved her for her courage. For her strength. For that stubborn determination that kept her fighting even when things were at their worst. He loved her for her beauty, for her smile, for…so many things.

And if he was honest with himself—brutally honest—he had to admit he'd been in love with her all along.

Patrick's heart began to thump as the memories raced through his mind. Memories of the first time he'd seen her, striding up the courthouse steps with her briefcase in her hand. Memories of the funny tingles that had slid through his body as he'd watched her, of the joy that had burst through him when he'd danced with her at the ball that magic night.

He'd started falling in love with her the very first time he'd seen her. And when he'd made love to her on the beach that night, made love to her with his heart and his mind and his soul, he'd fallen completely, utterly, in love.

That was why he hadn't been able to forget her, even after the way she'd left him that night. That was why he'd never really been able to let her go.…

He'd told himself he didn't care about her. Told himself that all he wanted was a casual affair. And when he couldn't lie to himself about that anymore, he'd told himself he wasn't good enough for her.

But it was a lie. All a lie. He'd only told himself those things because he'd been angry. Angry and in pain. Because of Jessica. Because of the child he'd lost. And because he'd been afraid of getting hurt all over again.

Oh, God, he was a fool.

Because even if he did get hurt—even if Helen told him she could never love him, never want him—it didn't change the one essential fact. *He loved her.*

And it didn't change what he had to do.

Shoving the bedcovers down to his waist, Patrick pushed himself upright. Pain knifed through his chest, but he gritted his teeth and swung his legs over the side of the bed. Yanking the IV needle out of his hand, he shoved himself to his feet.

Four days ago, on the rain-swept beach, he'd told Helen that she had to fight for what she wanted. And that was exactly what he had to do.

He loved Helen. Loved her. Needed her. Wanted her.

And this time...this time, he would fight.

Helen sat on a giant, ragged piece of driftwood with her hands clasped around her knees, staring out at the water as the tears ran down her cheeks.

The tide was on its way out, pulling kelp and driftwood with it. A wet expanse of fresh, unmarked sand stretched out before her in the starlight, empty and cold and dark.

Like her life.

Helen's throat tightened. Of course, her life wasn't really empty, she told herself bleakly. She still had her career. Her name was not only cleared, but the papers were calling her and Patrick heroes. In the past two days, she'd had job offers from half the counties in the state. Even the state attorney general had called. She'd heard about the case, and she'd wanted to congratulate Helen and to personally offer her a job.

Two weeks ago she would have been thrilled. It was another step up in her career. A sure thing.

But now, the job meant less than nothing to her.

Her career just didn't seem so important after all.

Helen stared sightlessly out at the dark, heaving ocean. Somehow, all the trauma of the past few days had brought things clear in her mind.

All those years when she'd fought to get ahead, she hadn't really been striving toward something in the future—she'd been running away from her past. The truth was, she'd used her career as a way to escape her childhood. And as a way to avoid getting close to anyone.

For as long as she could remember, she'd always been afraid. Afraid that she really was like her mother, the way everyone had always thought. Afraid that if she let anyone get too close, they would see who she really was. See her—and reject her.

She'd put herself in a rigid box, where everything went according to plan. An organized life where she progressed from job to job according to what was best for her career. No messy emotions or entanglements. No real risks. Just logic.

And then Patrick had come blazing into her life, shattering everything she'd ever believed in, blowing her tidy, organized life to bits. But the days she'd spent with him, the days of danger and uncertainty and risk, the nights of hot, sweet passion, had been the best of her entire life.

And now that they were over, she didn't know how she was ever going to go back....

A fresh wave of tears welled up in her throat, and this time, she didn't try to stop them. There was no point. It was late—so late it was almost morning—and she was alone on a windswept beach in the middle of nowhere.

There was nobody here to see her cry.

As the tears dripped down her cheeks, a gust of wind blew her hair around her face. She lifted her hands to push it away, and as she did, she saw a flash of movement out of the corner of her eye.

Her breath snagged in her throat, and she jerked her head around. In the shadowy distance, she saw a figure walking across the sand. Against the star-capped waves, she could just make out the dark shape. It was a man, and he was tall, tall and familiar and—

"Patrick," she whispered. Her heart began to thump, and she stumbled to her feet. "You came!"

Almost as if he could hear her voice, he lifted his head and looked straight at her across the expanse of darkness. She couldn't see his face—or hear his voice above the noise of the wind and the waves—but she saw him spread his arms wide in a silent invitation.

Her heart leaped crazily. Kicking off her shoes, she began to run. Elation and joy and hope coursed through her as she raced barefoot across the cold wet sand, the wind tangling her hair around her face.

Patrick strode toward her along the edge of the surf, still holding his arms open wide. As she neared him, she saw his face in the starlight, and it was filled with a raw, aching emotion that made her heart almost burst. With a little cry, she flew over the last few yards of sand between them and flung herself into his waiting embrace.

"Ah, Helen," he said against her hair as he wrapped his arms around her. "Helen, I've been such a fool."

"No—"

"Yes," he said firmly. "I have. Because I love you. I've loved you from the first time I saw you. I love you so much that I couldn't stand the thought of spending even one more minute away from you...."

She tilted back her head and looked into his eyes, her happiness almost too much to bear. "Oh, Patrick," she whispered, "I love you, too."

And then he kissed her—kissed her with all the passion and love and possession she felt in her own heart. She kissed him back, and he tightened his arms around her waist and lifted her off her feet. He twirled her around and around and around, until she was dizzy and laughing, and they collapsed together onto the beach.

He didn't let go of her even then, but kept his arm tight around her waist, holding her close as they lay in the sand.

Helen pushed herself up on her elbow and looked into Patrick's eyes. "I'm so glad you found me."

He looked at her, his face dappled with starlight, the wind ruffling his hair, and he gave her a slow, beautiful smile. "So am I."

"How did you know I'd be here?"

He reached up and cupped her cheek, stroking his thumb across her lips. "Just a lucky guess." His eyes crinkled. "This seems to be where I always find you."

"I didn't think you'd come," she said softly. "Not this time."

His expression turned serious, and he looked straight into her eyes. "Helen, I'm sorry. I—"

She put her fingers across his mouth. "No. Don't apologize. You have nothing to be sorry for. Not with me. Never with me."

"Yeah, I do," he said bluntly. "I acted like a jerk by refusing to see you today. I was scared—scared of the way I felt—"

"But so was I. I was scared of letting myself feel anything, and you made me feel so much. I was scared of letting my emotions run out of control. Scared of being like...being like my mother."

He put his arms around her and held her tight. "You're nothing like her. Nothing at all."

"I know that now." She put her head against his shoulder. "And I'm sorry. Sorry for the way I treated you last year, for running away."

"You weren't the only one who was running away." He stroked her hair with his rough hand. "I never should have told Adam I didn't want to see you. I was a fool, a coward, and I can't tell you how sorry I am."

She shook her head. "A coward? How can you call yourself a coward after the way you saved my life? After you got shot and ev—" She broke off with a gasp and pushed herself upright, scattering wet sand across them both. "Patrick! Shouldn't you be in the hospital?"

He lay back against the sand and grinned. "Probably. But somehow this seemed a little more important than lying around in some hospital bed."

"But are you sure you're all right?" She ran her hands over his chest, feeling the lump of bandages beneath his unfamiliar wool jacket. "You've probably burst your stitches and—"

"I know." He grabbed her by the wrists and dragged her back down into the sand. "But isn't it worth it?"

"I—"

He put his hand around the back of her neck and held her against him as he kissed her, long and deep. When he finally lifted his mouth away from hers, she was breathless and her heart was pounding, and even the starlight seemed to dance with joy.

He looked down at her, and his sculpted mouth curved upward. "Well?" he said, his voice husky. "Is it worth it?"

"Yes," she said as she wrapped her arms around his neck. "Oh, yes."

He gave a low laugh. "Good."

They lay there without speaking for what seemed like forever. Lay in each other's arms, in a world of perfect bliss. The soothing roar of the ocean, the smell of salt in the air, the soft wind that whipped across their skin—Helen couldn't even imagine a more perfect night.

Only it wasn't really night any longer. All around them, the starlit darkness was fading into dawn. On the horizon she could just see the first pale light streaking across the clear blue sky.

Helen took Patrick's hand and pointed toward the dawn. "Look," she said softly. "Isn't it perfect?"

"Perfect." He kissed her neck, his unshaven cheek rasping faintly against her skin. "Our first sunrise together."

She turned her head and smiled at him. "The first of many."

"The first of many," he said, his silver eyes filled with the dawn's reflected light. "And then many more after that."

She caught her breath. "Patrick...."

He tightened his arms around her. "I love you, Helen Stewart. I love you and I want to marry you more than anything else in the world."

Tears of joy sprang to her eyes. "And I love you, Patrick Monaghan. I want to marry you and have your children and—"

"Ah, sweetheart." He buried his face in her hair, his breath warm and sweet against her skin. "You couldn't say anything that would make me happier. But you don't have to say that for me. I know how much your career means to you."

"It is important to me," she said slowly. "But it's not the only important thing. Not anymore. Patrick, I *want* to have your children. I want to have a family. Here in Evergreen. With you."

"Here?" He pulled back just a little and looked into her eyes. "What about that job in Olympia? The one the attorney general offered you? Don't turn it down for me—I'll move there with you. Gladly."

She shook her head. "I want to stay here, where our children can grow up surrounded by family." She smiled suddenly. "And do you know, I've been asked to run as the new Evergreen County Prosecutor?"

An answering smile spread across his face. "You have?"

"Yes, and I think I'm going to do it. If I win the election, I'm sure I can run a good clean office where justice is more important than politics. Running is a gamble, but I think it's worth the risk." She looked into his eyes. "You taught me that, Patrick. You taught me that nobody can live their whole life in control of everything. Sometimes...sometimes you have to risk something—even everything—to get what you really want."

He curled his callused hand around her cheek. "But once you've got it," he said, his voice and his eyes filled with love, "you know you're the luckiest person alive."

"Yes," she whispered against his mouth. "Oh, yes."

* * * * *

MEN at WORK

All work and no play?
Not these men!

October 1998
SOUND OF SUMMER by Annette Broadrick

Secret agent Adam Conroy's seductive gaze could hypnotize a woman's heart. But it was Selena Stanford's body that needed saving—when she stumbled into the middle of an espionage ring and forced Adam out of hiding....

November 1998
GLASS HOUSES by Anne Stuart

Billionaire Michael Dubrovnik never lost a negotiation—until Laura de Kelsey Winston changed the boardroom rules. He might acquire her business...but a kiss would cost him his heart....

December 1998
FIT TO BE TIED by Joan Johnston

Matthew Benson had a way with words and women—but he refused to be tied down. Could Jennifer Smith get him to retract his scathing review of her art by trying another tactic: tying him *up*?

Available at your favorite retail outlet!

MEN AT WORK™

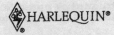 

Take 2 bestselling love stories FREE

Plus get a FREE surprise gift!

Special Limited-Time Offer

Mail to Silhouette Reader Service™

3010 Walden Avenue
P.O. Box 1867
Buffalo, N.Y. 14240-1867

YES! Please send me 2 free Silhouette Intimate Moments® novels and my free surprise gift. Then send me 6 brand-new novels every month, which I will receive months before they appear in bookstores. Bill me at the low price of $3.57 each plus 25¢ delivery and applicable sales tax, if any.* That's the complete price, and a saving of over 10% off the cover prices—quite a bargain! I understand that accepting the books and gift places me under no obligation ever to buy any books. I can always return a shipment and cancel at any time. Even if I never buy another book from Silhouette, the 2 free books and the surprise gift are mine to keep forever.

245 SEN CH7Y

Name	(PLEASE PRINT)	
Address	Apt. No.	
City	State	Zip

This offer is limited to one order per household and not valid to present Silhouette Intimate Moments® subscribers. *Terms and prices are subject to change without notice.
Sales tax applicable in N.Y.

UIM-98

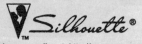

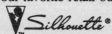

COMING NEXT MONTH